Finding Grace

NATIONAL BOOK AWARDS FOR *FINDING GRACE*

The Silver Award is bestowed on books that expertly deliver complex characters, intricate worlds, and thought-provoking themes. The ease with which the story is told is a reflection of the author's talent in exercising fluent, powerful, and appropriate language.

The Southern California Book Festival's panel of judges recognizes books based on:
- General excellence and the author's passion for telling a good story.
- The potential of the work to reach a wider audience.

Winning Category: Spiritual/Religious

The Pinnacle Book Achievement Award honors special recognition for an outstanding contribution by an author, or book, to the industry or society at large. Experienced editors and judges select books based on content, quality, writing, style, presentation, and cover design.

Winning Category: Inspirational

Authors and publishers from around the world submit their work to the **Firebird Book Awards**. Two judges from a select panel of 17 judges read each book in its entirety and independently score each entry. All judges are committed to a set of standardized criteria that evaluates the quality of the writing as well as production aspects. Only entries with the highest of scores are awarded the coveted Firebird.

Winning Category: Southern Fiction
Second Place Category: New Fiction

The Maincrest Media Book Award winners are considered superior in their category. Judging criteria is based on the following:
- Plot
- Characters
- Theme
- Style
- Appeal to target audience

Winning Category: Literary Fiction

PRAISE FOR *FINDING GRACE*

In *Finding Grace*, author Gary Lee Miller draws on personal tragedy to craft the story of Judith Lee, who is drawn into a journey back home and the real world. Every mile of her wonderful road trip is filled with unforgettable characters who bring tears of both laughter and sadness. *Finding Grace* reminded me of Horton Foote's *The Trip To Bountiful*, and I highly recommend it.

—**Brian Helgeland,** Academy Award-winning
screenplay writer of *L.A. Confidential*

The thing about *Finding Grace* is that it is without question the thing that makes Gary Lee Miller so special. He seems to find grace everywhere and in everyone, and it somehow reflects back on everyone he meets. *Finding Grace* is just the latest collection in written form of how he sees the world.

—**Barry Courter,** *Chattanooga Times Free Press*
reporter/columnist

Life lessons are delivered in many ways, and Gary Lee Miller, in his book *Finding Grace*, takes the reader on a journey of self-discovery through the eyes of his relatable, and often unpredictable, characters. An easy and insightful read, *Finding Grace* will leave you thinking about your own journey and the grace we can give to ourselves and others."

—**Steve Anderson,** *Wall Street Journal* and *USA Today*
best-selling author of *The Bezos Letters*

FINDING GRACE

a novel

In a world that sometimes seems out of control,
we are each on our own journey in hope of finding grace.

GARY LEE MILLER

with ADÉLE BOOYSEN

NEW YORK

LONDON • NASHVILLE • MELBOURNE • VANCOUVER

FINDING GRACE

In a world that sometimes seems out of control, we are each on our own journey in hope of finding grace.

Publisher's Note: This novel is a work of fiction. Names, characters, places, and incidents are either products of the author's imagination or used fictitiously. All characters are fictional, and any similarity to people living or dead is purely coincidental.

Published in New York, New York, by Morgan James Publishing. Morgan James is a trademark of Morgan James, LLC. www.MorganJamesPublishing.com

Proudly distributed by Ingram Publisher Services.

Morgan James BOGO™

A **FREE** ebook edition is available for you or a friend with the purchase of this print book.

CLEARLY SIGN YOUR NAME ABOVE

Instructions to claim your free ebook edition:
1. Visit MorganJamesBOGO.com
2. Sign your name CLEARLY in the space above
3. Complete the form and submit a photo of this entire page
4. You or your friend can download the ebook to your preferred device

ISBN 9781631956591 paperback
ISBN 9781631956607 ebook
Library of Congress Control Number: 2021939536

Cover Design by:
Megan Dillon
megan@creativeninjadesigns.com

Interior Design by:
Chris Treccani
www.3dogcreative.net

Morgan James PUBLISHING **Builds** *with...* **Habitat for Humanity** Peninsula and Greater Williamsburg

Morgan James is a proud partner of Habitat for Humanity Peninsula and Greater Williamsburg. Partners in building since 2006.

Get involved today! Visit MorganJamesPublishing.com/giving-back

PG | PARENTAL GUIDANCE SUGGESTED
SOME MATERIAL MAY NOT BE SUITABLE FOR CHILDREN
MILD LANGUAGE

DEDICATION

In memory of my late wife,
Dr. Sharee Sanders Miller.

I will love her until the day I die.
And then I will love her forever . . .

TABLE OF CONTENTS

1995

Dispatcher: "Nine-one-one. What's your emergency?"

Caller: "I need help! Mommy and Daddy won't wake up!"

Dispatcher: "What's your name?"

Caller: "_____." (Redacted for privacy)

Dispatcher: "I'm Kathy. How old are you, _____?"

Caller: "Ten."

Dispatcher: "Who's at home with you, honey?"

Caller: "Just Mommy and Daddy." (Crying)

Dispatcher: "I'm sending help now. I want you to stay on the phone, okay?"

Caller: "Okay."

Dispatcher: "Where are your mommy and daddy?"

Caller: "They're on the sofa."

Dispatcher: "Are they breathing?"

Caller: "I don't know. I don't think so."

Dispatcher: "_____ honey, I need you to put your ear by your mommy's mouth to hear if she's breathing. Can you do that for me?"

Caller: ". . . I don't hear anything. She feels cold."

Dispatcher: "How about your daddy?"

Caller: ". . . I don't hear anything with him, either. Mommy! Daddy! Wake up!
. . . They're not moving! What's wrong with them?"

Dispatcher: "An ambulance is on its way. They'll be there in just a minute or two, okay?"

Caller: "Don't leave me!"

Dispatcher: "I won't leave you, honey. I'll stay with you till the ambulance is there, okay?"

Caller: "What if Mommy and Daddy won't wake up?"

PART 1

JUDITH'S JOURNEY

ROAD KILL

CA
BARSTOW

AZ FLAGSTAFF

Grand Canyon
National Park →

ALBUQUERQUE
NM

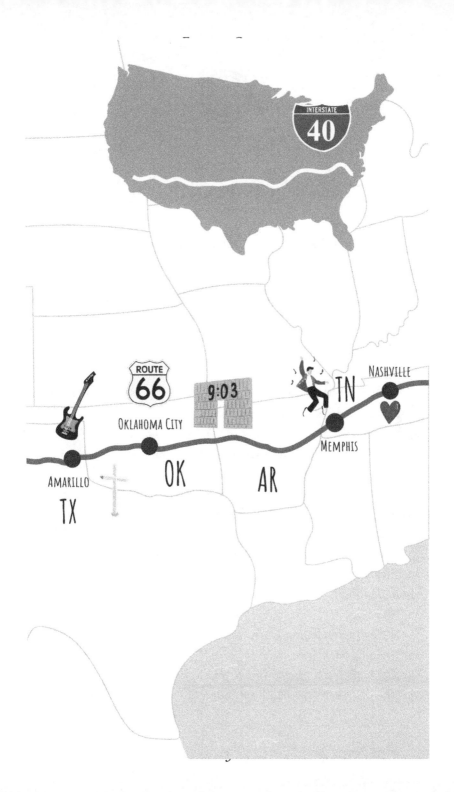

CHAPTER 1

The Great Escape

Sara | Present day

S ara tiptoed to the front door, her heart racing. A floorboard creaked under her petite frame.

Please, please, please don't let him wake up.

She froze and listened. There were deep, drawn-out snores coming from the La-Z-Boy. Wyatt was still passed out.

Just three steps and she would be out. Free. Well, almost. She still needed to make it to Flagstaff. *Then* she would be free.

Wyatt won't dare come to Flag. Dad would shoot him if he did.

She held her breath as she turned the doorknob and stepped into the thick September air. She only breathed again once the door closed without a sound.

My phone!

She had intended to search for her phone before she left, but there was no going back now.

Sara had all she needed in her little backpack purse and her wallet with the debit card she had been hiding. She had opened the account in secret and had put a few dollars in whenever she could skim off some cash without Wyatt noticing. Just a dollar or two at a time. After more than a year, the balance in the account was $109.27—hopefully enough to get out of Dodge.

There was also some makeup in the purse. And not a single thing that would remind her of the poor choice she made to move to Barstow. Nothing that would remind her of Wyatt.

If only she could leave the bruises and memories on the nightstand along with the note.

"Do NOT contact me ever. Go to rehab. You need help."

She walked the three miles to the bus station, looking over her shoulder every time she heard the sputter of a pickup, ducking behind a dumpster or a shrub a time or two. But Wyatt was probably still snoring away right where she left him.

If things went as they always did, it would be hours before he would wake up and yell her name, demanding some coffee.

Only this time, the house would be quiet.

A car slowed down, and the driver rolled down the passenger window. "Hey there, gorgeous. Wanna go for a ride?"

Sara kept quiet, kept walking.

I ain't for sale, jerkwad, she wanted to yell. But the words were stuck in her chest.

The tires squealed as the car sped up.

Sara did not stop, not even to buy a bottle of water, afraid she might miss the bus, afraid it would leave her without enough money for a ticket out of Hell. She sped up once she turned the corner onto East Main Street. She could almost taste freedom.

Ninety minutes after closing the front door, Sara rushed up to the ticket window at the Barstow Station.

"When's the first bus to Flag?"

"Flag?"

"Flagstaff."

"Well, you just missed the five fifty-five. The next one's at eight."

"I'll take that."

"Round trip?"

"One way."

"How many passengers?"

"One."

"Got luggage to check?"

"Nope."

"That'll be $87."

Sara slipped the card into the machine, took the ticket from the clerk, and looked for a safe spot to hide for two hours. She headed to the McDonalds across the street and ordered a coffee, positioning herself near the window where she watched for Wyatt's black truck. Just in case.

———

When Sara went to the restroom, the reflection in the mirror scared her. Wyatt was careful to make sure bruises were not visible. But the disheveled look and circles under her eyes screamed abuse.

She pulled out her makeup and did what she could to look presentable.

The sound of the door opening made Sara flinch.

"You okay?" a lady asked. Just another early-morning patron.

"Couldn't be better."

Sara headed back into the restaurant, seeing a limousine pull out from the station.

Probably lost, she thought. *Strange for this hour.*

———

At a quarter to eight, after having scanned the area one more time for a black truck, Sara made a beeline for the only bus on the lot.

Other passengers were dropping off their luggage, but Sara headed straight for the door.

"Ticket," the driver demanded. She held it out to be scanned then stepped onto the bus, looking for a safe spot.

There were several single seats—all next to men—and just one spot with two open seats.

If I sat in the open row, a guy would come sit next to me. Shoot!

Sara's heart pounded.

I'd better get off the bus and go home before Wyatt wakes up and finds I'm gone.

She stepped back off.

"'Scuse me," she said and pushed past a lady dressed like she was ready to fly first-class.

But the woman did not seem to hear her. She looked ticked and a bit out of place with her Gucci tote draped over her shoulder.

Must be fake.

Sara stepped away, her heart beating out of her chest.

What the heck am I doin'? Get back on the bus. Go sit by that lady.

Sara rushed back up the steps, seeing the woman settle into the open row.

"Mind if I sit here, ma'am?" she asked.

"Sure."

"My name's Sara."

But the lady did not answer. She was staring at stuff on her phone.

Whatever.

CHAPTER 2

Worlds Apart

Sara and Judith | Barstow, CA to Flagstaff, AZ

Judith Lee would not be caught dead on a bus. Nor was she the type who would sit staring out a window at the heat haze dancing on the barren soil of the Mojave Desert.

But on this September Sunday, she found herself doing just that on a supposedly luxury tour coach emblazoned, Scenic City Bus Line.

Luxurious would be the last word Judith would use to describe the bus, though. *Slow* and *inefficient* would be more like it.

She would have to endure six days of this. It might as well be six months.

"Oh, Mimi," Judith muttered, shaking her head.

Barstow, CA to Needles, CA

"You sayin' somethin', ma'am?"

The twenty-some-year-old neighbor jumped at the chance to strike up a conversation. Judith had avoided talking to her for the past hour.

"I was just thinking out loud," Judith said, only briefly looking up, then turning her attention back to the reports on her phone, annoyed by the fact the tray table wasn't spacious enough for her to be working on her laptop.

"I used to do that all the time," Sara said with a tentative smile. "If you don't mind me askin', is this your first bus trip?"

Oh. My. Gosh. What's with the question—first from the guy at the ticket counter, then the driver, now my neighbor? Is it that obvious?

"You can call me Judith," she responded, her tone nowhere as irritated as that of her internal dialogue. "And why do people keep asking me that?"

"Askin' you what?"

"If it's my first bus trip."

Sara gave a sympathetic smile. "Weeeeell . . ." she said as she looked Judith up and down. "This is only like the third trip I've ever taken on a bus, but I've *never* met anyone on *any* of those trips who was dressed quite like you are."

Judith gave a curious smile. "Uh . . . thanks?"

"So, I've been dying to ask," Sara continued, "is that Gucci tote for real? If it's not, you sure got yourself a mighty good fake."

To Judith, it seemed that the words just spewed out from Sara's pretty face.

"I worked in a little boutique in Barstow," Sara said, "so I know my stuff. And this outfit of yours? It's legit. Like what them rich ladies would come buy before a fancy date or an interview."

Does she ever come up for air?

"You're definitely not goin' on a date—not on *this* bus. So, it must be for an interview. Are you headin' to Flag for an interview?"

Judith was not ready to share personal information with a stranger, so she turned the conversation around. Her sixth-grade language arts teacher taught her this valuable skill.

"People love talking about themselves," Mrs. Miller once told her. "The quicker you can ask them a question, the quicker they'll forget they even asked you one."

Judith slowed the pace of the conversation. "Where are you heading, Sara?"

"Home." Sara barely missed a beat. And as quickly as her words had poured out, they stopped. She stared at the road before them as if doing so would make it shorter. She fidgeted and bit her lip.

Judith turned her attention back to the spreadsheet on her phone. She tried to focus on the tiny rows and columns, but her attention drifted to the girl beside her and to the promise she had made to her grandmother.

Darn it!

"Tell me about the people you meet on the bus, the things you see," her grandmother had said.

Mimi made her promise she would take the bus—*this* bus, the one that would stop over in several towns along the way. It had been Mimi's dream to travel this way to visit Judith, but now, that was no longer possible.

"Where's home, Sara?" Judith enquired politely, clearing a lump in her throat.

That one little question unleashed a fount of information.

It's like she's trying to free words that had been locked up, like her words needed somewhere to go.

Judith listened to every word. For Mimi's sake.

———◆———

Home was Flagstaff—or "Flag," as Sara called it. "But I've been away for a mighty long time. I left after graduation, havin' been promised the sun, the moon, and the stars," she told Judith, tears close to the surface. "Wyatt bought me all a girl could want. Like, fancy stuff—though not as fancy as what *you're* wearin', if you don't mind me sayin'. If I knew I'd be payin' with my freedom, my dignity, my sanity, I'da never've gotten in that truck of his."

She got quiet for a while.

"We met at a Toby Keith concert on an autumn evenin' a few years back. We sang our hearts out and danced till our boots were thick with dust. Wyatt swept me off my feet and lassoed my heart like only a cowboy could."

She took a deep breath, then carried on. "I didn't care that he was twice my age, figured he'd take care of me. He promised I could go to college in Vegas. That we'd get married. Have kids."

Sara got quiet again.

"It's true what they say—whoever *they* are. Love is blind. And hindsight's twenty-twenty."

Sara stared at some tumbleweed, then carried on.

"College turned out to be the school of hard knocks if you know what I mean. And the promise that he'd take care of me? That was a load of bull—I mean, hogwash. I was the one taking care of *him*. He made me sign over every damn paycheck to him, and then he got mad that I made more than him. He'd sit there all day watchin' TV and drinkin' beer, and when I walked in, I had to cook for him and clean and do stuff I'd never thought I'd have to do."

She shook her head.

"I worked hard, lemme tell you that. At home *and* at the store. Wouldn't just sit there at the boutique hopin' a customer would buy a thing or two. No, ma'am. Someone would walk in there thinkin' they might could buy a new shirt and walk outta there with a whole wardrobe of fancy new clothes," she said with a brief smile and a nod.

"Now I know what you're thinkin'. You're thinkin', 'Girlfriend, why did you not just keep your paycheck, pack your things, and head home?' "

"Why didn't you?" Judith asked.

"Weeeeell, to tell you the truth, I was too scared and too damn proud. Scared he'd hurt me if I left. Scared that I wouldn't know how to make it on my own. Plus, Wyatt made sure I couldn't call my folks or talk to any friends. He took away my phone the first time I complained. Told me he could take away much more if he found out I was talkin' to others."

She bit her lip, talking under her breath. "He'd be crazy mad if he knew I'm on the bus home tellin' you all these things."

Taking another deep breath, Sara continued, "One time, he thought I was too friendly to the cashier at Walmart, said I was flirtin' with the guy. So, he whipped me that night—the first of many times. I shoulda walked out that day. Shoulda gotten on the bus right then. Shoulda borrowed a phone so I could call my folks and tell 'em they were right. Why I didn't do it, I dunno. But they were right, yes, ma'am. As right as the first drop of rain on a spring day, as my daddy would say."

Sara grew quiet, then continued, "That's the first thing I'll tell 'em when they open the door tonight. 'Daddy, you were right . . . Wyatt's a sorry excuse of a man.' "

A glimmer of light appeared in Sara's eyes. "Tonight," she said, "I'll be home. And for the first time in three years, I'll be safe."

Her countenance lifted as splashes of irrigated farmland appeared in the distance ahead of them.

"They don' know I'm comin'."

"Will they be home?"

"Heck yeah—it's Sunday night football. Ain't a chance under God's blue sky they won't be home watchin' them Cardinals and havin' pizza."

National Old Trails Highway

At the sign for Laughlin, the driver slowed down to exit the interstate. He slowed the bus even more, then turned onto a bumpy road.

"Just taking a slight detour here, folks," the driver announced. "This here isn't on the typical route, but we had a request to go down the National Trails Highway before our pit stop this morning. This stretch of road is part of the original coast-to-coast highway from Maryland to California."

A little boy two rows ahead of Judith pointed out the window. Judith's gaze followed to where he was pointing. An almost holy silence had descended on the bus, on strangers momentarily united by desert rocks that someone had arranged along a road leading nowhere, memorials to the US Coast Guard, Navy, Marine Corps, for prisoners of war, and those who went missing in action.

Some names were spelled out with rocks, with the Stars and Stripes waving in the wind atop a beam emblazoned, "Never forget."

Judith became aware that she could hear her own breathing.

After a while, the driver broke the silence. "Welcome to the town of Needles, folks. You might want to read up more about the town on our app. If you have not yet downloaded it, go ahead and do it. Details are in your seatback pockets."

Might as well, Judith figured. *After all, this will my world for the next six days—God, help me.*

The app was basic but listed some trivia based on where the bus was—population, history, other tidbits.

For Needles, it listed trivia for movie and literature buffs.

> **Did you know?**
> The town of Needles appears in *The Grapes of Wrath* as the Joad family enters California from Arizona.

Well, now I know.

The road followed along the Colorado River. It felt good to see some green after the miles of desert landscape. Soon, they crossed the California-Arizona Bridge.

A notification popped up on the app, stating, "Arizona is home to twenty-two national parks and monuments—including the Grand Canyon—and thirty-five state parks. The eight-hundred-mile Arizona Trail is popular for biking, hiking, and horseback riding. Arizona is also home to three of the nation's top ten best spas, including one in Sedona, an hour south of Flagstaff."

Now we're talking. I wonder if there would be time for me to rent a car and head to one of the famous spas.

But Judith remembered Grace's request that she stay at the type of hotels and eat at the type of restaurants her grandma would. Visiting a spa was not on the list of things her grandmother wanted her to do along the way.

Still, she googled Sedona, and what she found enticed Judith. She created a list on her phone of places to visit and added Sedona.

Dr. Sanders would be proud of me for planning something rejuvenating. Self-care.

Her therapist had been encouraging her for months to find ways in which she could "do something that would be good for her soul."

Just across the state border, they pulled in at Love's Travel Stop.

"We'll be stopping to drop off and pick up some passengers," the driver announced. "We'd prefer that you use the facilities at these stops rather than the restroom on the bus. Thank you, and please be back on the bus in twenty minutes. Tweeeeenty minutes!"

Judith stepped off the bus, relieved for a bit of a reprieve. Her thoughts drifted back to something Sara had said about her parents trying to convince her not to run off with Wyatt.

I am lucky to have grandparents who have always supported my choices, no matter how hard. No matter my mistakes, they were always forgiving, always understanding. And they encouraged me to follow my dreams.

"That mind of yours will get you far, Judy," Granddaddy used to say. "But don't let those feet of yours go running where your mind can't catch up."

Not that Judith was much of an athlete. Back in school, she couldn't run if her life depended on it. It was only recently—thanks to her doctor insisting she had to work out to counter the amount of stress her work caused—that she discovered the joy of spin classes and running.

From as far back as she could remember, though, it was her mind—or her *smarts*, as Mimi called it—that drove her and what set her apart.

Judith swallowed at the lump in her throat when she thought about Mimi again and about their conversations two days before.

She was surprised when her grandma called just as she was looking at her calendar for the next week, something she did religiously on a Friday afternoon. She would review the goals of the week and plan for the week ahead before joining her staff for their late afternoon weekly social gathering.

Downtown Los Angeles, CA

"Hi, Mimi. Are you okay?" were the first words out of Judith's mouth when she answered the call. Her grandmother *never* called her during the workday.

"Hi, sweetie pie. Oh, Judy, I'm so sorry to bother you. Do you have a moment?"

"Of course."

"Oh, gracious goodness it's good to hear your voice," Grace said. Her voice gave away that she was tired, but she tried hard to pretend otherwise. "I'm doing as good as an old woman my age can expect, I guess—"

"Did you get your test results?"

"Yes, we got the results. Rachel wanted to call you, but I made her wait and let *me* tell you first . . ." Judith could hear Grace take a deep breath. "Dr. Samples says I got the leukemia."

There was a pause before either of them spoke again.

"How bad is it, Mimi?" Judith whispered.

"Well, Rachel wrote down some of the stuff the doctor told us. Besides all them other tests, they did a bone marrow biopsy. The doctor said a normal blast count is five or less. When you get above ten, you're in full-blown leukemia," Grace continued as Judith jotted down the details.

The numbers Grace shared did not quite make sense to Judith yet, but it was clear that her grandma was in bad shape. She started making plans in her head for how soon she could fly to go see her grandmother and to meet with the doctor in person to talk about treatment options.

"My blast count? It was over four hundred." Judith heard Grace say.

"Oh, Mimi . . . What did Dr. Samples suggest for treatment?"

"I'm too old for a bone marrow transplant, honey, and my blast count is too high even if we shaved off a few years," Grace said, trying to make light of the situation. "There's no chemotherapy that will help me."

Judith felt her chest tighten. "There's got to be something we can still do." She did her best to try to hide the desperation that accompanied the reality of the news. "I'll come talk to the doctor."

"They gave me two units of blood and a bag of platelets before Rachel brought me home," Grace continued. "Dr. Samples said I'll need to get lab work done on Mondays and Thursdays, and I'll begin needing more and more blood and platelets to keep me going until that stops helping."

"No, we'll figure this out, Mimi," Judith insisted as tears ran down her cheeks.

"If Virgil were still alive, he'd take care of me and I wouldn't need to bother you none," Grace said with a sigh.

Judith would have none of it. "You're never a bother, Mimi. There's nothing under the sun I wouldn't do for you."

She needed to take care of some things at the office before she could head home and plan for her time away. "Mimi, is it okay if I call you back as soon as I'm home? Maybe in an hour?"

"I'll be right here, honey. You know Jimmy Fallon only comes on at ten thirty. So, you take your time," Grace replied with a smile in her voice. "I love you, Judy."

"I love you too, Mimi. Talk to you in a bit. We'll figure things out, okay?"

No sooner had Judith hung up than she called her assistant.

"Cara, please tell the team I'm sorry, but I cannot join them this evening. Something's come up. And tell Tony and Tiffany that I won't be able to join the two of them for the celebratory dinner at Spago tonight either. Tell them to enjoy the evening on me. But I'd like them and you in my office tomorrow morning at nine. I need to add some responsibilities to their management roles for the next few weeks."

Cara knew better than to ask any questions. While they all worked long hours Monday through Friday, Judith placed great emphasis on her employees spending uninterrupted quality time on the weekends with their families. However, based on the mountain of work that awaited her on Mondays, Cara knew that her boss spent her weekends working.

For Judith to schedule a Saturday meeting, this had to be serious.

Judith turned back to her calendar, but instead of the business tasks she was about to map out, she crossed off two weeks and wrote in all caps: MIMI.

She buzzed Cara to let her driver know she will be heading home soon.

———◆———

On the commute home, Judith called Rachel, Grace's home health-care nurse. Officially, Rachel's role was focused on Grace's health, but Judith added to that, asking that she provide whatever else Grace might need.

Over the last two years, Judith noticed that Grace and Rachel developed a special friendship.

Bel-Air, Los Angeles

Judith's address afforded her a beautiful view of greater Los Angeles. On a clear evening, she would relax with a glass of wine fit for a connoisseur—2015 Scarecrow Cabernet Sauvignon was her most recent favorite—and take in the lights of the city to the south and the Getty to the west.

Oh, did she love the Getty. When she first moved to L.A., Judith used to walk the grounds for hours every weekend, getting lost in the exhibits.

That is where she learned to appreciate great art, where she fell in love with the work of Anselm Kiefer, Ai Weiwei, and Makoto Fujimura.

She had one Fujimura piece that filled almost the entire back wall of her open-plan living space. A wall of windows allowed light to dance off the pulverized minerals of the Nihonga-style painting. Every time she looked at the piece, she saw something new.

———◆———

Judith exchanged her fancy pumps and business suit for something more comfortable. She still looked chic, though. Always did.

Pouring a glass of her favorite red, Judith savored a few sips before she settled on the sofa.

The tranquility of the scene was a stark contrast to the storm within.

She took some time to prepare herself emotionally. "Call Mimi," she instructed Alexa and took a long sip of the wine.

"Calling Mimi," Alexa replied.

Judith knew the sound of her grandmother's phone well. In her imagination, she could hear the peculiar ring of the pink princess phone. And she could see Mimi walking as fast as she could to get to the phone sitting on the end table, next to the photo of her grandparents.

"Judy honey, you called at the perfect time," Mimi answered just like she usually did, no matter the time of day.

"Hi, Mimi. I just spoke with Rachel."

"Isn't she a dear?"

Judith was not about to make small talk. "This was quite a surprise you sprung on us," she said.

"I'll have to admit, honey," Grace responded with spunk in her voice, "even though I knew something was going on, this kinda caught me by surprise too."

"Rachel told me about your prognosis." Judith swallowed hard to get rid of the lump in her throat. "Five or six weeks?"

"The good Lord's got a plan for us, Judy. You know I've always trusted him. Still do."

At that moment, Judith was more ticked at God than trusting him, but there was no sense telling Mimi that. Not now, at least.

"I've started making arrangements to be away from the office for the next month or two. I'll fly in the day after tomorrow, Sunday, to be there with you."

"Honey, that's what I wanted to talk to you about," Grace responded. "You remember when Granddaddy took me down to Chattanooga to see Rock City and visit Ruby Falls and the Tennessee Aquarium? We even spent the night in one of them Pullman cars at the Chattanooga Choo-Choo."

"I remember, Mimi." Judith was confused why Grace felt it necessary to reminisce at this very moment about a trip she and Virgil had taken thirty years ago. Still, she humored her grandmother. "That photo on your end table of you and Granddaddy is from that trip, right?"

"Sure is, sweetheart. You know that was the farthest I've ever been from Nashville, don't you? I've always been such an old homebody."

"I know, Mimi. And *you* know how many times I've tried to convince you and Granddaddy to come visit me in Los Angeles."

"I'm going to tell you about something you don't know, Judy."

Mimi paused. "Ever since Virgil passed, my dream has been to get on the bus and visit you."

"Mimi, I'd have sent for you, had I only known."

"You know you'd never get me on a plane, sweet child. But the bus? *That* has been my dream. I've imagined all the people I would meet and places I would see," Grace shared with a hint of mischief in her voice. "Did you know the I-40 runs all the way from Nashville to Barstow, California?"

"I do."

"Well, there's a bus service that stops over in some of the major cities so you can see places along the way."

"Can't say I knew that," Judith responded, puzzled by Grace's "confession."

"Well, *that* has been my dream, honey—to take that bus."

Is this some joke?

She listened to Grace continuing to lay out her dream.

"I should have done it before now, but now I've run out of time."

"I'm so sorry, Mimi. I wish I had known."

"Well, I've been thinkin' about it since our call this afternoon. You said there's nothing under the sun you wouldn't do for me. I know that's true, but Judy, you know I'd never ask you for a favor."

"That is true."

Pausing briefly, Grace gathered herself. "Well, that is about to change, sweetie pie," she said. "I'm sorry, but not too sorry to ask. I want you to catch that bus in Barstow to come home to Nashville."

"You want me to *what*? Are you serious?" Judith blurted out, coming across stronger than she intended.

"I've never been more serious in my life. I want you to take the trip I've dreamed of. But I want you to do it in reverse, of course. I want you to call me every night to tell me about the sights you saw that day. I want you to stay in the motels I would've stayed in, eat at the restaurants I would have eaten in, and then tell me about it all. But most important, I want you to tell me about the people you meet. I want to hear their stories. Stories they would've shared with me if I were on that bus."

Silence.

Judith's mind was racing, thinking about what an ineffective use of time this would be. *Flying would get me there in a handful of hours, but Mimi wants me to go by road—on a bus?*

"So," Grace asked hesitantly, "are you in?"

"Do I have a choice?"

"Not really. Unless you want me to come back and haunt you."

Grace laughed.

Judith did not.

Needles, CA to Seligman, AZ

Once Judith got back on the bus, Sara was already seated. "I just realized you never answered my question. You headin' to Flag?"

"I'm actually going all the way to Nashville to visit my grandma."

She handed Sara a bottle of juice and a bag of jellybeans. "I got us a little something. No sense being on a road trip and not enjoying some snacks, right?"

It had been years since Judith had eaten jellybeans, but she figured Sara might enjoy them. She got herself some Perrier and a bag of organic almonds.

Sara had fun combining different flavors of jellybeans. "Here's a fun one," her neighbor giggled as she put cinnamon, caramel corn, and marshmallow ones together. "It tastes just like Christmas."

Sara offered some to Judith, but she passed.

———◆———

"This year will be the first Christmas in three years I'll be back home," Sara said out of the blue. "The first year, I begged Wyatt to let me come home, but he told me I ain't goin' nowhere, and if I tried, I'd regret it." She shrugged. "So, I stayed."

Her nervous energy seems to have calmed down some, the reality of her being out of Wyatt's clutches probably setting in.

Sara talked about Wyatt controlling her every move, monitoring her every call. He started drinking more and when he did, Sara could neither say nor do anything right.

"Last night, I done had it. He came home drunk and when I didn't give in to his unwanted advances, he went crazy." Sara grew still again, tenderly rubbing her arm.

"I'm so sorry," Judith whispered, noticing the edge of a bruise sticking out from under Sara's sleeve. After many miles of silence, she added, "You did the right thing."

Sara lay her head back, a tear escaping every so often. Though Judith was thankful for some silence, her heart broke for what her neighbor had been going through.

Several miles later, Sara turned her attention back to the bag of jellybeans. "How 'bout this combo," she said, sitting up straight. "Two banana ones and one buttered popcorn make banana bread. Wanna try?"

Judith declined politely.

———◆———

"Well, folks," the driver interrupted Judith's dreaming of her grandmother's homemade banana bread, "we'll be pulling in at Seligman for lunch pretty soon. We'll be there for forty-five minutes."

Are we seriously going to stop every two hours all the way to Nashville?

It looked like the bus had pulled into an old cowboy movie set complete with Old West storefronts.

You couldn't miss the sign outside: "You kill it, we grill it."

The bus app sent another notification:

Did you know?
When the Roadkill Café first opened,
patrons could grill their own steaks.

Outside the grill and OK Saloon,
you'll see the old Arizona Territorial Jail,
the former home to notorious outlaws.

In 1866, some Navajo inmates escaped from
the jail by digging a tunnel to the saloon.

While Judith could think of nothing nastier than what the café supposedly dished up for paying patrons—whether you grill it yourself or not. She knew, though, that Mimi would get a huge kick out of this place.

"Fooooorty-five minutes, folks!" the driver reminded them. The air brakes hissed, and the bus door flung open, letting in hot air.

"Surely the health department wouldn't let someone serve *actual* roadkill," Judith objected—only half-jokingly—as she and Sara disembarked.

"Well, you just never know out here." another passenger mused as he passed them. You couldn't miss the handsome guy in his jeans, cowboy boots, and Western-style shirt. "Rumor has it that you can't go wrong with the splatter platter."

Sara laughed, her countenance lifting even more the closer she got to home. "I might just do that, thanks."

"Johnny's the name," the man said with a polite nod of his head. "Enjoy lunch, ladies."

Judith noticed that Johnny was missing his left hand.

I wonder what his story is.

They browsed a bit first. Judith picked up a Route 66 fridge magnet for her grandmother.

Mimi would like this, she thought when she saw it. True, she might object to me spending any money on her. But then again, she would probably like to add it to her small collection of fridge magnets.

That *a bus trip* would be her grandmother's dying wish? It still infuriated Judith.

Judith and Sara sat down for lunch. "Eating is more fun when you know it was hit on the run," the menu read. It listed items such as bad-brake steak, swirl of a squirrel, and highway hash.

Judith stuck to "Perrier with lemon and a salad *with no meat whatsoever* thank you very much."

For the heck of it, she dared Sara to try one of the signature dishes. "If you do, lunch is on me."

"Deal," Sara said, relieved that she did not have to make up some excuse for not eating much. If her calculations were right, she had just enough money left on her card for a cab ride home once she got to Flagstaff.

Now, she was free to try the dish Johnny had recommended.

Seligman, AZ to Flagstaff, AZ

Judith couldn't remember the last time she took an afternoon nap, but after lunch, the desert heat, and the monotonous hum of the engine, she fell asleep soon after boarding again.

At Williams, they passed the turnoff to the southern gate to the Grand Canyon.

"Ever been to the Big Ditch?" Sara asked when she saw Judith waking. When she saw the confused look on Judith's face, she giggled. "The Gran' Canyon," she clarified.

"Nope," Judith said and wondered if she should add that to her list of places to visit. She could only imagine Dr. Sanders's look of surprise if she told her about *another* thing she was considering doing.

"Well, you better get your gran'ma one of 'em fridge magnets then. What's her name, by the way? She's lucky to have someone like you."

"Grace," Judith said. "She's not doing too well, though," she continued hesitantly.

"I love that name. Amazing Grace. That's my favorite church song," Sara continued like she did not even hear what else Judith had said about Grace.

Her knee bounced up and down with nervous energy as she stared out the window.

"I'm home," she whispered to herself.

"Welcome to Flagstaff, Arizona, folks, the City of Seven Wonders," the driver announced. "Thank you for traveling with Scenic City Bus Line. For those of you continuing with us tomorrow, we'll be departing at eight o'clock. Please check your surroundings for all personal items before you disembark."

The bus pulled into the bus station, and the passengers poured out into the early afternoon heat. Sara giggled again as she saw Judith's reaction to the heat reflecting off the tarmac.

"Don't you worry, Miss Judith, it's dry heat. You'll be fine. Where you stayin' tonight?"

When Judith told her the name of the hotel, Sara did a double-take.

"You sure? That doesn't strike me as the kind of place you'd like."

"It's what my grandma wanted."

"Well, then maybe we can catch an Uber together, if you don't mind. Your hotel is *literally* on the way to my parents' place. I'll take a cab home from there."

"Works for me," Judith said, "but how do you get an Uber?"

"You've never taken an Uber?"

"I've never had to," Judith defended with a smile.

"Just download the app, then take it from there. Easy as pie."

After setting up an account, Judith insisted on punching in Sara's home address and simply adding her motel as a stop along the way.

"It's simpler that way. Let's just get you home," she said, delighted to notice the option to choose a luxury car for just a few bucks extra.

———◆———

"What the heck?" Sara blurted out when a shiny Mercedes Benz pulled up.

"Let's just say it's so your day can end on a better note than it began," Judith said and winked.

When they pulled up at the motel, the driver double-checked. "*This* is where you're staying, ma'am?"

"I'm afraid it is. Wish me luck."

Sara reached out for a hug. It took Judith by surprise, but she hugged Sara back and smiled.

"I'll be prayin' for your gran'ma. She'll be okay, Miss Judith, don't you worry."

"And *you'll* be fine too, Sara. I'm proud of you for standing up for yourself. You take care, now. And I'll be praying for your conversation with your parents."

Saying those words felt foreign to Judith, yet she meant them.

The "Unfussy Budget Hotel"

Judith cringed when she rolled her Gucci bag into the hotel room. "Can I please see a different room?" she asked as politely as she could.

She changed rooms twice, by which time the clerk offered a snarky, "Why don't you try the Marriott up the road?"

"Oh, don't tempt me!" Judith retorted before slamming the door.

"Judith Lee, you can do this," she said out loud. "This is exactly the type of place Mimi would have chosen, right on Route 66. Deep breaths."

The smell . . . What the heck?

Judith set up her travel-sized diffuser and added water and some lavender oil.

"You've lived to tell about things much worse than a cringy, old hotel room," she continued her pep talk. "Let's see if some essential oil can do the trick."

As if it would protect her from something unseen, Judith placed a towel on the bed before sitting down to change into comfortable walking shoes. She wanted to walk around Flagstaff a bit, taking note of things to share with Mimi.

On her walk, Judith paused at a small coffee shop to work for a while. On a typical Sunday afternoon, she would indulge in scanning reports, analyzing trends, and strategizing how she could solve problems and create systems that increase efficiency. She would anticipate complications and devise algorithms to avoid inefficiencies and overcome obstacles.

Place a problem before Judith, and she would figure a way around it. If not around it, she would go over, under, or through it if necessary. It is what she thrived on.

The immediate obstacle before her was the bus trip. Try as she may, there was no way around completing this journey. It was what Grace wanted.

The bigger challenge was to find a cure for Mimi's leukemia. There *had* to be something they could do, regardless of her blast count.

Judith had asked Cara to research the latest breakthroughs in leukemia treatment and send her what she found.

None of what showed up in her inbox looked promising, though.

Nashville, TN

Rachel and a small group of friends walked out of Tootsies in downtown Nashville laughing. "Oh, my! I needed this. This was the perfect way to end the weekend. You were right," Rachel said as she turned to Kate, her best friend, "Kylie Morgan? Good grief, she's good."

"I told you, she's the next Carrie Underwood," Kate reminded her. Rachel quickly replied, "I think she'll be the first Kylie Morgan. Wow!".

Rachel's friends had been after her for months trying to get her to go out, giving her a hard time for the hours she had been putting in taking care of one client in particular.

"I can't tell you anything about her—you know, HIPAA," Rachel had told them when they grilled her for having missed their get-togethers for far too long. "I care about my clients. All of them. But this one lady has become a friend. If you knew her, you'd understand."

"Yes, you have a heart of gold. We get it, Mother Teresa," Kate joked.

The nickname Rachel's friends gave her was well-earned. In addition to her job-related duties, Rachel also did volunteer work for various non-profit organizations, most of which provided food, shelter, or services for the homeless. During the holidays she and her friends were often organizing outreach to homeless women.

Working hard came naturally for Rachel. During her high school and college years, she was consistently an honor student. But her grades never came as easy to her as to others. She had to study multiple times longer than her friends to make her grades. While this was challenging for her, it instilled a discipline and work ethic that served her well in the real world.

Ignoring Kate's "Mother Teresa" crack, Rachel paid particular attention to a new face in the group, a guy named Rob. Kate had told Rachel about him in the past, insisting that the two of them would hit it off. "He volunteers at a homeless shelter just like you do, and he goes on trips with Habitat for Humanity *all* the time," Kate had told Rachel.

Rachel thought Rob seemed nice, but she did not imagine he would call her. Despite the delectable nachos, the music, and the great company, Rachel was not as present as she was known to be. Her mind kept drifting to Miss Grace whose health had taken a turn for the worse.

She was glad Miss Grace's granddaughter, Judith, was on her way home to say goodbye. Not that Miss Judith saw it that way. She was bent on finding a doctor who would do more to help.

Rachel knew better, though she would not tell Miss Judith that. In the five years of being a registered nurse and doing home health care, she had learned to see when enough is enough, when a patient is ready to be done fighting.

She did not like it. Not one bit. She *always* hoped the patient would pull through. That Miss Grace would somehow take a turn for the better.

But hope is not a strategy. Which is why Rachel was determined to do all she could to support her, to do what she could to help Miss Grace regain strength.

Even if it was only just till Miss Judith was here.

Sunday Night Call

"Judy honey, you called at the perfect time," Grace answered when Judith called. She sounded tired, but she insisted on hearing about the first leg of Judith's trip.

Judith told her all about Sara's escape and her quest to start over.

"Oh, I'll bet her mama and daddy are over the moon to have her home tonight. Can you even imagine? We all need a second chance sometime in life, right? That poor child. God bless her. I'm so glad you got to sit next to her. See? I told you you'd meet wonderful people."

Judith loved her grandmother's positive outlook on life. She told her about their lunch, making Grace laugh out loud. "Oh, honey, you should've tried the squirrel dish. I'll bet it tastes like chicken."

And she told her about towns along the way. There was Ash Fork, smaller than one city block, and signs for places like Catfish Paradise, Santa Clause, and Nothing.

Grace laughed with delight. "Thanks for indulging me, sweetie pie. It means the world to me."

"I'll let you go so you can watch Jimmy Fallon."

"Honey, it's Sunday. He's only on weeknights, remember?"

"Of course. How could I forget? Well, I'll let you go to bed then so you can get some proper rest before your doctor's visit tomorrow. I love you, Mimi. I'm one day closer to seeing you."

"One day closer. Now, *that* will make me sleep well. G'night, Judy."

Before Judith crawled into bed, she added twice as much lavender oil as she normally would to try and mask the smells.

She found herself praying for the first time in years—for Mimi, for Sara, and for grace to endure this journey.

SARA'S SONG

"*Red Eyes and Your Lies*"

A hundred times it happened and a hundred times I knew,
The love we had was dying and I think you knew it too.
Well, if hard times make me stronger, I got muscles by the ton.
It broke my heart, then made me mad that this hasn't been more fun.
I've thought long about the day I'd leave you dead, stone cold.
I knew that you would never think that I could ever be so bold.

Red eyes, your lies, and a tailwind at my back.
I'm leaving you forever, I'm on a different track.

Red eyes, your lies, and a tailwind at my back.
You never told me single lies, you told them by the pack.
If every lie you told me was a bullet for my gun
then I could hunt forever, and you'd be on the run.
So, listen up now darling, if you can stay awake,
this old gal is giving what she's always had to take.

I put up with your drinking and running 'round at night.
You'd come home feeling lovey-dovey and we'd end up in a fight.
You'd say, "Oh please forgive me darling, I know that I was wrong.
My drinking days are over now. I won't take a single sip."

I'd know that you were lying 'cause I'd see you move your lips.

Red eyes, your lies, and a tailwind at my back.
I'm leaving you forever, I'm on a different track.

Why do women always think that they can change a man?
I know hope springs eternal, I guess that's just God's plan.
But now I know that what we've got's not what he had in mind,
so back off now old bucko, I'm just starting to unwind.
Good luck you drunken redneck, you lazy, lying bum,
I'm leaving you forever for a new life yet to come.

Clear eyes, blue skies, and a tailwind at my back.
I should have done this years ago. I'm on a different track.

CHAPTER 3

A Five-Foot Surprise

Gary

"I just got off the phone with Shirley. She and her friend Sherry can get tickets to Sunday's 5th Dimension concert," David said when he called. He was clearly excited.

"I'll bet it would be cool to see the 5th Dimension live. Good for them," Gary replied. "How'd your test go?"

"The test was fine. Point is, we could go to the concert too. Their boyfriends don't want to go."

"Are you kidding me?"

"No kidding. Shirley asked if we could join them."

Gary rolled his eyes. "David, you know I don't do blind dates, pal."

"It's not a date. They both have boyfriends. Plus, we'll go Dutch. How about we do it as a favor for Shirley?"

"You've convinced me," Gary replied with a huge smile. "So, what's the plan?"

"Let's pick them up at five at their dorm, have an early dinner, then head to the show at Memorial Auditorium. Does that sound good? I can pick you up just before five."

"That'll work."

———◆———

Stagmaier Hall, where both girls boarded, was on the campus of the University of Tennessee at Chattanooga. The guys joined fellow male students as they waited in the lobby.

Gary shifted away from a guy holding a bunch of flowers, lest their non-dates got the wrong impression.

Sherry arrived first.

Gary may have stared. His jaw may have dropped. His heart may have raced. He was not sure. All he was sure of was that he had never seen a girl as beautiful as Sherry. She wore a purple mini dress and stacked heels, giving additional height to her five-foot stature. Her long, dark hair was pulled back, revealing dangling earrings.

And then she smiled. Time stopped and the sun shone even brighter.

Next time, I'm bringing flowers.

———◆———

Over dinner at the Western Sizzlin steakhouse, their conversation was as easy as breathing.

While Gary had agreed to the evening only to see the 5th Dimension live, he now wished they did not have to go to the concert. He would much rather linger and learn more about this girl who had swept his feet out from under him, more than her zodiac sign—she was Gemini, he a Cancer—more than her taste in music and what classes she was taking.

34

During the concert's opening act, a comedian joked about dating and how awkward first dates could be. "You know what's one of the best icebreakers to use?" he asked the crowd. "Just ask, 'What's your sign?' "

Gary and Sherry burst out laughing. Looks from folks around them seemed to say, "It wasn't *that* funny." But they knew better. There was mutual chemistry and magnetism neither had experienced before.

And that was the beginning.

It was March 5, 1972.

CHAPTER 4

Carrying Memories

Gary and Judith | Flagstaff, AZ to Albuquerque, NM

Judith's prayers were not working. "Grace to endure the journey? What was I thinking?" she muttered as she rolled over again.

She knew the darkness and relative silence outside had to mean it was around three. She heard an ambulance pass by, the lights cutting through the poor excuse for curtains.

The mattress had seen better days, the sheets could be no more than two hundred thread count, and God only knows what the carpet had seen. The shag predated Judith's birth. And there was that musty smell.

"I will *not* be staying in another budget hotel. I don't care if you come back to haunt me, Mimi," Judith seethed.

God, help me.

She filled up the diffuser with water and lavender oil again.

Third time's a charm, right? Maybe I can get another hour or three of sleep.

But when another siren passed by, Judith had had it. She got up.

While she would typically be on her Echelon bike before sunrise and join a live class streaming from the East Coast, she would not be working out this morning. A gym was not on the short list of amenities the hotel offered. And there was no chance she would risk going for a run in a strange city.

Judith needed something to get her going, so she turned her hope to the coffee pot on the corner of the bathroom counter. "Now serving hot coffee in every room," a quaint, coffee-stained sign read.

She filled the machine with water—its tank took exactly one paper cup worth—placed the cup in place, ripped open the single bag of coffee grounds, hit the ON button, and got into the shower. She cringed. "You can do this, Judith Lee."

By the time she got out of the shower, the coffee was tepid. Judith took one sip and threw out the rest.

This is going to be a long day.

For the next couple of hours, Judith lost herself in her work before packing her things back into her bag and heading out the door. The Arizona dust was thick, even at the early hour. Judith pulled out her phone to order an Uber.

She did not think she would ever use the app again, but here she was doing just that, booking her second Uber ride.

"Judith Lee?" the driver asked as he pulled up just minutes later. She nodded. "I'm Tom," he said as he placed her bag in the trunk of the Lexus.

"How has your time in Flagstaff been?" Tom asked as she pulled onto Highway 66.

"Uneventful."

"I guess that's good," he said with a smile. "I've got to admit, I have never picked up guests on this side of town. There's a first for everything, right?"

"Right."

"Heading to Local Juicery, correct?"

"Yep."

"They have some of the best and healthiest breakfasts this side of Flagstaff."

"That's what I read." Judith was as cordial as she could be, considering her lack of sleep. "I'll be heading to the bus station in about an hour. How does it work? Do I have to book another trip, or—"

"I'd be glad to wait till you're done," Tom offered. "Then I'll drive you to the station. I might step into the Local and read the paper."

"Thank you," Judith said, staring out the window. "Goodness! This wind . . . and all the dust."

"Well, it's not called Dusty Arizona for no reason," Tom agreed, smiling. He pulled into a spot right in front of the red-brick building. "Here we are—and rock star parking at that. It's your lucky day."

———◆———

Maybe my prayers are being answered after all, Judith thought as she walked into what seemed like health-food heaven.

After the best avocado toast and bulletproof coffee, Judith got two bottles of cold-pressed juice to go, feeling like she was leaving a much-needed oasis and heading to what just as well may have been a camel ride through the desert.

They made the short drive to the bus station, and after Tom pulled Judith's bag from the trunk, she handed him a generous tip. His eyes widened.

"Thank you," he said. "I hope you have a great trip. May the firsts you experience all be as good as your visit to the Local."

Judith gave a polite nod. Whether it was the coffee or the to-die-for avocado toast that did the trick, she headed toward the bus with a little less reluctance than the morning before.

She looked out for the bus driver. Instead of the mellow driver from the day before, a chatty fellow was standing by the luggage hold. He was also shorter and older than the guy from the day before. The man's face lit up as he saw Judith rolling her suitcase in his direction. "Good morning. First trip by bus?"

Judith rolled her eyes, ignoring the question. The semblance of a good mood from a moment ago was gone.

"Ticket, please."

Judith held out her ticket and the man nodded.

"So, technically this is *not* your first bus trip," he answered his own question, trying to lighten the mood. "Let's see, you would've been on Barry's bus yesterday, right?"

"If Barry was who drove from Barstow to Flagstaff, yes."

"Well, I have the pleasure of being your driver today. I'm Harold, but you can call me Harry if you'd like. Happy-go-lucky Harry, it is."

Harold chuckled at his own joviality.

"Nice to meet you, Harold."

"Well, we got good weather today, so you should enjoy the scenery on our way to Albuquerque. We're full up. Hop on board!"

The cool, clean air on the bus was a welcome reprieve from the Arizona heat and the wind. Nevertheless, Judith was irritable. She was not sure what she was most annoyed at. The fact that she had hardly slept? That she kept being interrogated about whether this was her first bus trip? That the bus was full? That she might have a talkative neighbor again?

Probably the reality that I'm on a freakin' bus trip across the country. If it weren't for that, none of the rest would be true.

There was only one empty seat near the back of the bus. As Judith made her way toward it, she noticed the handsome cowboy-looking man from the day before.

Early forties, I'll bet. Jake? James? John?

The man looked up and gave Judith a big grin, adding a nod as she passed. Caught off guard by him catching her looking, Judith scowled and looked away before passing.

Flagstaff, AZ to Winslow, AZ

"Excuse me," Judith said as she got to the only open seat. "May I join you, please?"

She seemed to have startled the man who appeared to be in his mid-sixties.

"Oh, sorry. My mind was a million miles away. Yes, of course," he said as he stood so Judith could take the window seat. He was holding a small cedar chest. "Please have a seat, young lady."

Judith stepped into the spot and placed her tote under the seat in front of her.

"My name is Gary."

"And I am Judith," she responded with a smile. "I'm sure glad that I didn't miss the bus."

Gary returned her smile, "Now, that would have ruined your whole day, wouldn't it?"

"Most definitely."

As they pulled out of Flagstaff and headed toward Albuquerque, New Mexico, she and Gary chatted about this, that, and the other—just like she would have with her granddaddy.

"Do you know much about New Mexico's history?" Gary wanted to know.

"Can't say that I do."

"Well, I find history fascinating."

"So, what can you teach me about this part of the world?"

"Would you like the CliffsNotes version, or in depth?"

"High-level CliffsNotes."

"Let's see . . . Around the time the Americas was first colonized, the territory that is now the state of New Mexico was part of Spain's ever-expanding colony called New Spain. The colonies fought back against Spain, and after a decade-long war, they gained independence and established the Mexican Empire. That was 1821—if I remember correctly. After independence, they established a new monarchy."

"So, New Mexico used to have a king?"

"Well, they had an emperor, and it wasn't just for New Mexico. It was for the whole Mexican Empire. But the empire lasted only two years before the people revolted. Eventually, it became a republic, and what we now know as Mexico emerged. That's a seriously short version of a looooong history."

"So, if I'm following, you're telling me *New* Mexico predated Mexico?"

"By about two hundred and fifty years, yes."

"How did New Mexico end up as part of the United States?"

"What we have today is a result of a peace treaty that ended the Mexican-American War in 1848. Before Mexico conceded and signed the treaty, Colorado, Utah, Nevada, California, Texas, Arizona, and New Mexico were all either partially or wholly part of Mexico."

"That was in 1848? I don't remember New Mexico being listed as part of the Union or the Confederacy during the Civil War in 1861, but if memory serves me right, much of the New Mexico population sided with the Union."

"You have a good head on your shoulders, missy."

Gary's kindheartedness and his Southern accent reminded Judith of her grandfather, Virgil.

"I've had good teachers," she said and winked. "So, when did New Mexico become a state?"

"That only happened years later. Lincoln had tried to convince them to join the Union, but the Apache and Navajo people resisted."

"So, what happened?"

"Well, things changed in . . ." Gary squinted as he worked at retrieving dates and details from his memory bank. "Things changed in 1866 when Geronimo was captured."

"I know that name."

"Yes, he was a prominent leader and medicine man within the greater Apache Nation. He played a strategic role in their resistance against colonizing forces, both American and Mexican."

"So, how'd Geronimo getting captured lead to New Mexico becoming a state?"

"Well, he was held as a prisoner of war until the day he died, almost twenty years later. His people were essentially annihilated once they lost their leader—and *that* after the Apache and the Navajo, had successfully resisted colonial efforts since the late 1500s, first by Spain, then Mexico, and then America."

"How sad," Judith told Gary. "And how *wrong*."

"Don't even get me started."

Judith shook her head. "So, statehood? When did that happen?"

"Well, with Geronimo out of the picture and the power of Native American groups seriously curtailed, lots of people from outside the region started settling there. The straw that broke the camel's back was probably when the railway was extended to Santa Fe in the late 1800s. It led to a boom in ranching. With that, the balance of power shifted dramatically."

"Okay, I can see where this is going," Judith groaned.

"Yes, it became inevitable. In 1912, under President Taft, New Mexico became the forty-seventh state. Speaking of Taft," Gary piped up, changing the subject, "did you know he's the only person in history who served both as a US President and eight years later as Chief Justice?"

"As in the chief judge of the Supreme Court?" Judith clarified.

"Precisely."

"I did not," Judith admitted. "Do you know this much about *all* fifty states and *all* the presidents?"

Gary laughed. "Not off the top of my head, no. I recently read a fascinating book about the history of this region." He was quiet for a moment, then continued, "It was a special place for Sherry and me."

"How did you two meet?"

"We met on a non-date."

Judith shook her head. "A non-date? Not a blind date?"

"I don't do blind dates," Gary said with a smile. "Sherry and her good friend Shirley—who also happened to be a good friend of mine— wanted to go to a music concert, but their boyfriends didn't want to go. My buddy David convinced me that we should go with them as a favor, as an official non-date."

"Let me guess: She swept your feet out from under you."

"That, she did. For me, it was love at first sight. But it took her a few weeks longer to come around," Gary added, laughing.

"Are you originally from Flagstaff?" Judith wanted to know.

"No, I grew up in Cleveland, Tennessee. I couldn't find any girls who would have me there, then I met Sherry in Chattanooga," he explained as he laughed again—something he did a lot of. Right after we married, I received a job offer in Flagstaff, so we moved there, and she got her teaching position. That became home."

Gary looked down at the box on his lap. "I can't tell you how many times we made this trip from our home here in Flagstaff," he said with a little melancholy in his voice. "Sherry was an art teacher, and she *loved* the art community of Albuquerque."

Gary cleared the lump in his throat before continuing. "We even talked about moving there, but she had her tenure in Arizona, so we just visited as often as we could afford. We had a special place where we would always go to watch the sunset."

He grew quiet. Judith noticed Gary's thumb gently caressing the carving on the side of the cedar chest. "That's where she wanted to be, so that's where I'm taking her ashes now," he said, looking down at the box, "and someday I'll join her there. She was my girl."

"I'm so sorry, Gary," Judith started saying, but he stopped her.

"Don't be. We had almost forty-six years together. Hoped we'd have forty-six more. Don't know many other men as blessed as I was. She was better than I deserved. I've got two daughters and a granddaughter who live close to me. They're my reason for living now. I'm just learning how to keep on my happy face in public and find my new normal until I see my Sherry again."

Pausing for a moment, he continued, "I have a good friend who told me, 'You must live for the two of you now and get some fun stories in the bank for when you see her again. She'll want to know what you've been up to, so it better be good stuff.' "

Gary smiled. "You know, he changed my whole perspective on my grief. So, that's what I attempt to do now. Live each day, trying to find *fun stuff.*"

43

Judith reached out and touched her neighbor's arm lightly, saying, "I believe she was very lucky to have you, Gary."

He just smiled, "Thank you. Truth is, I was the lucky one."

Nashville, TN | 1958

"Gracious goodness, Virgil," Grace exclaimed, covering her mouth with both hands. "Is this really *ours*?"

One would have thought Virgil had just purchased his wife a palace. Compared to the humble farmhouse Grace had grown up in, it was. The thirty-year-old Craftsman-style home showed some wear and tear, but it was perfect for the couple.

"It even has a porch! And a swing? Virgil, did you go rob a bank?" she teased, knowing full well how hard they had been working to save up for the down payment of $2,000.

For two years, they lived on her $1-an-hour salary from her job at the garment factory so they could save Virgil's paycheck toward buying a house. They ate more egg sandwiches than they cared to admit and more bologna sandwiches than they could swing a bat at. Once in a while, they would switch out bologna for SPAM. And on the rare occasion, they would splurge and have poor man's steak.

"We did it, Grace," Virgil declared. "We bought a home—our very own home to grow old in."

With that, he scooped Grace up and carried her across the threshold.

They were an hour out from Flagstaff when Harold announced they would be taking a slight detour. "We're just swinging through Winslow here for any Eagles fans."

He turned on "Take It Easy" and invited passengers to sing along if they knew the words.

Are we on a karaoke bus? Judith wondered with some irritation, but when Gary started singing along, she felt compelled to join in.

They stopped briefly for those who wanted to take a photo with the statue on the street corner.

Play along, Judith Lee. Mimi would have taken delight in this bit of Americana.

She asked Gary if he would join her for a photo. "Bring Sherry along if you'd like," she said with a smile, and he did.

"We're finding fun stuff right here," he chuckled as one of the other passengers took their photo.

Heading back to the interstate, the road took them past the town's 9/11 Memorial Garden. You couldn't miss the rusted beams at the center of the garden.

A notification popped up on the bus app.

> **Did you know?**
> The town of Winslow holds an annual memorial service at the 9/11 Memorial Garden.
>
> The 15' and 14' beams are *actual* fragments recovered from the World Trade Center—the largest pieces given to any community in the nation.
>
> The flag is the one flown at the Pentagon on September 11, 2001.

Just beyond was a large cement monument with black letters: "UNITED WE STAND."

As the day before, the bus was shrouded in reverent silence.

Winslow, AZ to Lupton, AZ

The lack of sleep from the night before had Judith fighting to keep her eyes open. "I hope you don't mind, Gary, but I'm going to rest my eyes for just a bit," she said, only to find that Gary's eyes were already shut.

She could not sleep, though. Her mind darted between Grace's prognosis and the project her team in L.A. were working on. They had just landed the biggest contract in the company's short history and had a ninety-day window for implementation.

She was going to celebrate at Spago with Graham and Tiffany on Friday evening. Then Mimi phoned her at work and the bottom fell out of her world. Though she would have preferred to be there to keep close tabs on the project, her team knew what they were doing.

What would Dr. Sanders say about that level of trust in my team? she wondered.

It had been about a year since Judith started seeing a therapist.

For months, Judith woke up at one or two every morning. More often than not, she would lie there thinking about work, about life, about Mimi, about projects on her desktop until it was time for her early-morning Echelon bike class.

Pills were not an option. She was adamant that she would try *anything* else. Just not pills. Especially not pills.

Her doctor suggested that she talk with a therapist about the things that kept her mind racing at night. So, talk therapy it was.

Judith quickly realized that meeting with a skilled professional helped with more than just her insomnia.

After a year of weekly sessions, Judith knew what Dr. Sanders would ask.

"How do you feel about being away from the office at such a crucial time?" she would undoubtedly want to know.

Despite the five hundred miles between her seat on the bus and her therapist's office, Judith could feel the anger rise within. "I think it's ludicrous."

"How does it make you feel, though?"

"I think having to take a bus trip at such a critical time is completely inefficient."

"Does it make you feel frustrated?"

"No. All I feel is anger."

"Okay, tell me more about that."

"I am angry that Mimi is dying, and I feel guilty that I haven't been there for her. My team will be fine. They'll be *just fine,* but Mimi won't be. I'm pissed that I'm going to lose her, and that there's no cure yet for her leukemia."

Judith felt tears welling up. She took a slow, deep breath to fight the tears, then forced a big smile on her face—another of Mrs. Miller's tricks from long ago that saved her on many occasions when unexpected emotion welled up.

Petrified National Forest

"You don't want to miss this part," Gary said in his kind manner. The road was passing right through the Petrified Forest National Park.

"The area's famous for the trees that had been fossilized around the time dinosaurs roamed the area. It's the smallest of the national parks, and other than the I-40 cutting through, there's only one road that takes you through the entire park, north to south."

The bus app echoed what Gary was telling Judith.

Did you know?
Petroglyphs are images carved into rocks.
There are more than six hundred and fifty of those
scattered throughout the Petrified Forest National Park.

The carvings date back more than 2,000 years,
and they mark events such as solstices and equinoxes.
They also mark migratory routes and family symbols.

"Sherry loved the colors of this area—the richest hues of red, blue, purple, and pink. She used to say that God painted the desert out here," Gary told Judith. "We went camping out here a time or two, and the rocks are like kaleidoscopes in places. And the stars? They'd take your breath away."

Gary captivated Judith with stories of his wife's artistry and the adventures they had, pausing to point out the massive red rocks when they got to Lupton with its booming population of twenty-five. "Those rocks," he pointed out, "they contain rock paintings that I believe reflect some of the history I told you about earlier."

To drop off a passenger, they pulled into a rest area with several Native American trading posts selling lovely jewelry and local art.

Harold announced that the bus would pull out in twenty minutes. "Don't get carried away shopping, or you'll have to find a place to sleep here tonight," he chuckled. "Next stop: Albuquerque!"

Lupton, AZ to Albuquerque, NM

Judith bought a fridge magnet of a teepee for Mimi before taking her seat next to Gary. As the bus headed into New Mexico, she pulled out the cold-pressed juice and handed one to Gary, relieved that she had bought two bottles at breakfast.

"Sorry they're not that cold anymore, but these should tide us over for the next leg of the journey."

Gary pulled out a bag of Fig Newtons and offered Judith some.

"I haven't had these in ages," she laughed as she took one. "These were my granddaddy's favorite."

———◆———

"You know, Gary," Judith said as she brushed a crumb from her lap, "having learned a little about the history of this area from you, it makes me look at a trading post such as this with different eyes."

Gary listened as Judith continued, "I haven't researched this enough to voice an informed opinion. But I found a book on Audible that I'll listen to over the next few days that should help me understand more about the plight of the Native American people."

"Most people don't care about issues that don't affect them directly," Gary observed. "What is it about this that's piqued your interest?"

"To be honest, I'm not quite sure. I just know that I need to know more to begin with. We're all Americans, after all. Surely, we can't remain oblivious to the pain of others, can we?"

"We could. And we often do," Gary replied. "The real question is what it's costing our nation. We're all connected, after all."

The neighbors in the back of the bus were quiet for some time.

"I haven't even asked you where you're heading today," Gary finally said. "I didn't mean to be rude. Is Albuquerque your final stop?"

"I'm afraid not." Judith told Gary about the purpose of her journey, sharing more than she had ever done with anyone.

The app on Judith's phone buzzed when they passed Red Rocks Park and its famous Church Rock.

> **Did you know?**
> The cliffs of Red Rock Park are believed to have formed during the Age of the Dinosaurs, more than two hundred million years ago.
>
> Here, you can take a three-hour hike to visit ancient dwellings of the Navajo people.
>
> The Red Rock Balloon Festival is one of the world's largest balloon rallies with more than one hundred balloons floating through the sky. Each year, it takes place the first weekend in December.

49

Judith and Gary paused their conversation to take in the beauty of their surroundings.

When Gary took another nap, Judith slipped her headphones on and started listening to *Empire of the Summer Moon,* a story about the Comanches, considered the most powerful Native American tribe in history.

It was just about lunchtime when the bus pulled into the bus station.

"Welcome to quirky Albuquerque, folks," Harold announced, "the hot-air balloon capital of the world, and more than three hundred and ten days of sunshine. Thanks for choosing Scenic City Bus Line. Please remember to check your surroundings for any personal items. And for those of you continuing on with us, we'll see you bright and early tomorrow morning."

Once they got their luggage, it was Judith reaching out to hug her neighbor.

"Thanks for sharing your story with me, Gary," she said. "And enjoy finding the fun stuff!"

Judith was relieved to discover that the closest hotel to the bus station was a four-star hotel. She felt terribly guilty when she booked a room at the Andaluz and ordered the third ride of her life in an Uber Black.

There was no way she could be kind to her neighbors on the bus while having had no sleep, though. She would help Mimi understand the importance of her getting a good night's rest.

Once she was checked in—this time she did not have to see multiple rooms, nor did she feel the urge to put down a towel before sitting on her king-sized bed—Judith changed into walking shoes and headed back down.

The clerk at the concierge desk told her that the absolute best coffee in town was at the Little Bear Coffee Co. in Uptown, and yes, they had great WIFI, too, as well as standing desks.

Oh, not to have to sit for a while.

Pour-over coffee and a muffin would do for lunch. When the barista heard Judith was from out of town, she told her about a hole-in-the-wall Tex-Mex restaurant close to her hotel.

"Since you won't be staying," she joked, "I won't get in trouble for sharing a local best-kept secret. Just ask for the special of the day for dinner. You can't go wrong with that."

The barista was right.

———◆———

Back in her room, Judith took a long, hot shower and slid into her silk pajamas. She almost felt normal again.

As Judith closed the curtains, she noticed several hot-air balloons floating in the distance against the sunset.

———◆———

Gary stood holding the cedar box. He was taking in the spectacular sunset of reds, pinks, and grays. For this occasion, he knew both God and Sherry were smiling down on him.

Though tears were running down his face, he was smiling, thankful for the beauty of the moment and for the many memories the cedar box represented.

As the sun slipped below the horizon, he started spreading her ashes. Through his tears, Gary could not help but smile as he thought of Sherry's final photo op on the corner in Winslow with him and Judith.

"My sweet Sherry," he said quietly, "you're home. I'll join you someday, but until then, I will love you to the day I die." With his voice
breaking, he added, "Then, I will love you *forever*."

In the distance, where the sun had been glistening just minutes
before, Gary noticed a burst of flames light up the colorful patch-
work-canopy of a hot-air balloon. The balloon lifted ever so slightly as
the hot air pushed it upward.

Gary raised his arm in a wave. For a long time, he stood quietly as
the balloon drifted further away, showing off its brightly lit colors.

Barely visible, there was one last burst of color before it disappeared.

Monday Night Call

"Judy honey, you called at the perfect time. I've been *so* looking
forward to your call! How is Albuquerque?"

Smiling at Grace's excitement, Judith replied, "Hi, Mimi. It's a lovely
city. You would have loved seeing the hot-air balloons around sunset."

Judith told Grace about the colorful balloons that were floating in
the distance earlier and about her surprisingly good dinner at the little
Tex-Mex restaurant nearby.

Learning about these little details delighted Grace to no end.

"How about you, Mimi? How are you doing?"

"Oh, I'm fine as frog hair split three ways," Grace laughed. "I'm in
the good day/bad day phase, and this was a good day. But enough about
me. Please tell me about what else you saw and who you met today!"

"Before I tell you about my day, I have to tell you about a liberty I
took." Judith explained that in order to be present and enjoy the passengers she meets, she would have to stay at nicer places so she would get her
rest, rather than places that Mimi perhaps would have chosen to stay at.

"That's fine, sweetheart. I wouldn't want you to be grumpy. As long
as you don't hop on a plane next . . . Now, tell me about your day."

Judith delighted Grace with the sights she saw and the things she
learned. "There was even a sign for a town named Snowflake. In the des-

ert, Mimi!" They both laughed at the story Judith made up about what would have precipitated naming a town after a single snowflake.

"Oh, Mimi, you'd have loved my seatmate, Gary," she insisted. "We took a photo together standing on a corner in Winslow, Arizona. He reminded me a lot of Granddaddy when he was younger."

She told Grace about Gary's loss and the stories he shared with her.

"Well, bless his heart. He's got a tough row to hoe. He'll never get over losing her, but he'll learn how to live without her. We have no choice, you know."

Having had her share of sadness for the day, Judith pivoted. "Now, I've given you my update for today. I know this was a lab day. Let's go back and you tell me how you're really doing so I don't need to call Rachel tonight."

"Rachel took me to the outpatient clinic. My hemoglobin was 7.2, so they gave me one unit of blood," Grace relayed the events. "I didn't need platelets today, so that was good. A small victory from the Lord. Like I said, this was a good day."

"You know I worry about you, Mimi."

"Judy, please don't. I'm okay with what's to come. Virgil is waiting for me to join him, just like Sherry is waiting for Gary. You can't imagine how I've missed him. What a homecoming that will be."

Not ready to go down that road tonight, Judith changed the subject again. "You get some rest tonight, Mimi. You've had a busy day. I'll call you about this time tomorrow night, okay? Love you."

Softly, Grace replied, "Judy, you just be careful. I love you too sweetie pie. Good night. I'm praying for you."

GARY'S SONG

"One More Yesterday"

I remember when I met you, we had dinner, then a show,
And when the night was over, I didn't want to go.
You laughed and then you teased me, "Oh now what would people say,
we'll have lots of time together," then you sent me on my way.
Then, we didn't know, that someday I would say,
"I'd trade all of my tomorrows for just one more yesterday."

Before too long I popped the question, and you became my wife.
We didn't have two pennies as we started out our life.
But we both worked hard in hopes our dreams would all come true,
then the babies came and before too long I fell more in love with you.
I remember how the four of us would laugh and sing and play.
I'd trade all of my tomorrows for just one more yesterday.

Through the good times and the bad times,
you were my beacon in the night.
Whenever I was down, you would make all things all right.
I remember all the love notes that you'd leave me and I kept,
and I remember all the times that I watched you while you slept.
I'll never understand why God sent you my way.
I'd trade all of my tomorrows for just one more yesterday.

Finding Grace

The years have come and gone, and the kids have moved away.
I look out on the yard where all of us would play.
I remember how you told me someday soon that you must go,
then you held me while I cried, and I said it wasn't so.
I remember holding you while you gently slipped away.
I'd trade all of my tomorrows for just one more yesterday.
When my time on earth is over, to St. Peter someday I'll say,
"I've prayed all of my tomorrows will be like our yesterdays."

CHAPTER 5

One Day at a Time

Johnny

"**E**asy does it." Johnny pulled back on the reins and brought the stallion to a stop.

"Walnut's as jumpy as spit on a hot skillet," he told the stable hand as he walked the brown stallion in to unsaddle and brush him.

"Maybe he'll do better for you again tomorrow," she replied with a shrug, giving Johnny the kind of smile he was used to seeing from women since he'd reached puberty.

Shortly after, Johnny was sitting in the sun across from his therapist. The breeze from the Pacific was pleasant, what you'd expect on a late-summer day in Malibu.

It was the start of his twelfth week here, and while Johnny knew with all his heart that he was ready to face the real world again, he was more than a little anxious.

"How do you feel about next week?" Dr. Baker asked, pouring them lemon spritzers.

The sound of the ice meeting the glass used to trigger Johnny.

"Rehab's a breeze. *Leaving* rehab? Not so much. But ready, I am." He took a deep breath and smiled his winning smile. "Still, Walnut was antsy today. Can't BS a horse. He could sense I'm nervous."

"What are you most nervous about?"

"Seeing old friends. Fooling myself that I could have just one drink, that I can stop whenever I want. You know? The real world."

"You've got tools now. You know who you are and what you can and cannot do. Right?"

"Right." The ocean sounds usually calmed the storm within. But not this day. The waves were deafening.

"Anything else making you nervous?"

"That I'd screw up someone else's life again."

"Did you?"

Johnny thought a while before he answered. "She made choices of her own," he finally said. "I know that. Sometimes, though, my head and my heart are at war."

"And when that happens, what can you do?"

"Talk about it." Johnny paused for a moment, then shifted the conversation. "Speaking of talking about things, remember me telling you about Dale, the guy who hired me to work at his studio? He'll be my sponsor."

"How long's he been sober?"

"It'll be thirteen years this Christmas."

The therapist nodded slowly. "Tell me again how you two know each other."

"He was my drummer in a band back in high school." Johnny's face lit up. "We thought we were all that and a bag of chips. Opened for some bands at county fairs around southeastern New Mexico. Dale had a fake ID and was the one who got us booze. We were convinced we were better musicians when we had a few."

The winning smile disappeared as Johnny slowly shook his head. "He tanked a few years after that. Ended up in rehab courtesy of a judge. It was either that or jail. He's been sober ever since."

"Sounds like he'd be a good sponsor."

Johnny took a deep breath and slowly exhaled, taking another sip of his lemon spritzer.

"I decided to take the slow road out to Amarillo so I can ease back into the real world. I'll be taking a city-to-city bus."

"Interesting choice."

"Once I'm there," Johnny continued, "I'll get back in the swing of things in the studio. Right now, that's the thing I'm most excited about."

"Tell me more."

"I thought I was a hotshot guitarist. I cut my teeth as a studio musician back in Muscle Shoals, Alabama, and later up in Nashville. So, I've always been a working musician. This is gonna be different."

Johnny swirled the ice around his glass. "I look forward to the challenge of working on the other side of the glass wall, learning from Dale about the finer skills of running a studio, of recording and mixing. I'd still get to be surrounded by music and musicians."

"Any concerns about that?"

"Not really," Johnny lied. He had been waking up the past few nights dreaming of banging on the window of the control room, trying to get the attention of the guitarist.

"I think what I like most about it is the sense of control," he continued. "My life's been out of control for far too long. These four months here have given me a semblance of control. I know we don't use the serenity prayer here in this program, but still, I went out and had it inked on my arm the other day."

Johnny pulled up his sleeve so the therapist could see the artwork on the inside of his left forearm.

The therapist had a knowing smile on his face. "You're going to do fine Johnny, taking one day at a time."

CHAPTER 6

Second Chances

Johnny and Judith | Albuquerque, NM to Amarillo, TX

J udith was on a bike in the hotel gym before sunrise, crushing it. She was drenched. The class she streamed promised sixty minutes' worth of spinning in just twenty-eight.

Efficiency. Judith thrived on it.

By the time she headed to the bus, she had packed more into her early morning than most would do in several hours.

Spin. Shower. Quick breakfast. Work.

Having had a better night's sleep certainly helped. Mimi's prognosis had her tossing and turning some but being as tired as she was and with the room a huge step up from that of the previous night, it did not take long before Judith was fast asleep.

For the first time in years, Judith dreamed about the time she moved in with Mimi and Granddaddy.

———◆———

In the dream, Judith was off on the side, watching ten-year-old Judy struggle to make sense of the world around her. She noticed how threadbare her clothes were and how her hair had obviously been cut at home, the bangs a solid inch above her eyebrows.

Instead of cringing, Judith felt compassion toward Judy.

C'mon, Judy Lee, you can do this, she encouraged her younger self. *Don't let the other kids' taunts get you down. You are strong. And you are smart. Their money can't buy them better grades.*

When she watched Judy cry in bed—quietly so Mimi or Granddaddy would not hear—Judith wiped her tears, telling Judy how much she was loved.

She was older now, in the eighth grade, and a girl had ripped the sleeve of her dress when she walked by in the cafeteria. "*Poor* Judy," she mocked her, then simply kept walking.

You cannot change the past, but you can *change the future, Judy Lee. Just watch. Don't let anything or anyone stand in your way.*

In the next scene in her dream, she was a student at Vanderbilt. Judith watched as her younger self started transforming. She was gorgeous but did not see herself as being so. By now, she knew that she was smart, but she did not rely only on her brilliant mind. Judy worked extremely hard to stay at the top of her class.

Judith sat in the front row at graduation, watching as Judy delivered the valedictorian speech.

In the dream, though, the speech was one she would deliver five years later, standing in front of her staff. Her company had just been recognized as the fastest-growing software company on the West Coast.

In the middle of the dream, it was no longer Judy delivering the speech but Judith. Judy stood off on the side, her head tilted and her eyes squinting.

"Are you happy, Judith?" Judy asked as her older self walked by.

Judith was determined not to risk missing the bus like she almost did the day before. She rolled up her bag with plenty of time to spare, thankful for the cold water she sipped on along her walk to the bus station. The heat was even more relentless than what she had grown accustomed to in Southern California.

"Good morning, ma'am. You traveling with Scenic City Bus Line today?" It was the driver, an African American woman with a million-dollar smile.

"Sure am," Judith replied, wishing she could give a different answer. *I'd much rather be traveling the friendly skies.*

"My name's Lucille, and it is my pleasure to be your driver today. You heading all the way to Amarillo?"

"Yep," Judith said, handing the driver her suitcase.

"Well honey, I hope you brought a book 'cause today's stretch of road doesn't have a whole lot to see, that is, till we get to Amarillo."

Judith did not mind this one bit and decided to finish the book on Audible and work on some emails. Unless she had a neighbor, in which case—*thanks, Mimi*—she would be compelled to chat.

"If you don't mind me asking," Lucille started asking just as Judith was about to step onto the coach.

Judith rolled her eyes. "Yes, this *is* my first bus trip."

"Oh, honey, I could tell that a mile away. I was going to ask, is this a *real* Gucci bag?"

Judith took a deep breath. "It is. But really, it's just luggage, Lucille."

"Mm-hmm. Well, would you ever. What day is today? I'd better take note, 'cause this here is the first *real* Gucci bag I've ever seen, let alone *handled*. You go on up and find you a good seat now. I'll take real good care of your bag."

As Judith climbed on board, the driver chuckled. "Them rich folks can pay more for luggage than ordinary folks do for a whole vacation," she said under her breath.

Albuquerque, NM to Tucumcari, NM

Despite Judith being there early, the bus was almost full.

Darn it.

At the rear of the bus over on the right side, she spied two empty seats, side-by-side. Hearing the driver talk to another passenger outside, Judith made a beeline to the open spot, taking the window seat and placing her tote on the seat next to her.

No sooner had she placed her tote on the seat when a man reached over and in one swoop picked it up, handed it to her, and plopped down on the seat next to Judith. He flashed her a huge smile.

"Well, if it isn't Miss Gucci. Today must be my lucky day."

Only a handful of passengers had been riding all the way from Barstow, and none had a smile as charming as this man. Plus, there were the cowboy boots and checkered shirt with snap buttons.

If he had a hat, I'd bet he's a ranch hand from Texas.

Still, she was taken aback at his assumed familiarity.

"We met at the Roadkill Café the other day. My name's Johnny, but my friends call me Jukebox Johnny. And you are?"

"My name is Judith," she responded coldly.

"It certainly is a pleasure to meet you, Judith. You out slummin'?"

"Excuse me?"

"No need to get all bowed up, baby doll. Just lookin' at your clothes and bags and fancy stuff, it's obvious that this is your first rodeo. You look as out of place as a turd in a punchbowl."

He flashed her another smile. "And by *rodeo,* I mean bus trip, of course. Welcome to the club. It's my first commercial bus trip too."

As if slapped in the face, Judith spat back, "Is that language really necessary? And I'm not your or anyone else's *baby doll.*"

Johnny tilted his head and pulled back. "Sorry, sweetheart. That stick up your ass must make the seats on this bus trip pretty uncomfortable."

Judith stretched her neck to see if she could find a different seat, but to no avail.

"Listen, whatever your name is. If there were another seat available, I'd be moving right now."

She could not be any clearer about how she felt about Johnny's language and attitude. Judith continued, "I suggest you mind your business and leave me alone before I call the bus driver over and arrange for you to start walking to Amarillo."

She paused for effect and drove home the knife, asking, "You capiche? And *capiche* means *do you understand*, like in *did you get the message*? Moron."

Judith rolled her eyes, shook her head, and turned to face the window.

Johnny's jaw dropped. He had never had a woman give any real pushback to his charms, much less take him to the proverbial woodshed and give him a spanking.

He was quiet for a while, then tried again, this time using a much different tone. "Hey, Judith," Johnny said gingerly, "please accept my apology."

He waited until she looked at him before continuing, "When I saw this was one of the only empty seats left, I just couldn't believe my luck. I got carried away. Guess my idea of impressing a beautiful woman like you is different from yours. Again, I am sorry. Believe it or not, most of my friends think I'm a nice guy. A little irreverent at times, but overall, fun."

He paused briefly, smiled hesitantly, and asked like a scolded child, "Start over? Please?"

Judith looked away without taking the olive branch. She put her earphones in and hit play on Audible.

Johnny had swung at a hanging curveball and missed big time. He knew that much.

I must be losing my touch, he thought. *Or maybe I'm just rusty.*

The silence between Judith and Johnny stretched well beyond the outskirts of Albuquerque. Try as she might, Judith could not focus on the audiobook she had been so taken by the day before.

She was bothered by the interaction with her neighbor. If she could, she would move, but the remaining few seats had filled up before Johnny had even taken his seat.

And Mimi would be disappointed if she heard that Judith refused to extend grace to a neighbor.

Finally, Judith straightened in her seat. "I was curt with you. I am sorry. I have a lot on my mind."

"No worries," Johnny replied with a slight smile. "I didn't mean to offend." He stuck out his hand. "Can we call a truce?"

Judith accepted the offer and shook Johnny's hand. He looked her straight in the eyes and smiled with the same smile that had caught her off guard the day before.

She felt her cheeks turn red. Hoping Johnny did not notice, Judith changed the topic.

"That's some nice ink," she said, gesturing toward the line of an elaborate tattoo sticking out from under his sleeve on his truncated left arm. "It looks fresh. How long have you had it?"

Johnny rolled up the sleeve to reveal his entire forearm. While the edges were still red, the lettering was exquisite: "God, grant me the serenity to accept the things I cannot change, courage to change the things I can, and wisdom to know the difference."

With a slight grin, Johnny observed, "Yeah, you're a classy lady, alright, pretending not to notice my missing hand, but I'll get to that in a minute. I'm calling this tattoo my crib notes to life. Just got it a week ago in Malibu."

He took a deep breath in, figuring he had nothing to lose sharing his story with Judith.

"Spent the last four months out in Malibu at a rehab center drying out," he started, testing the waters for how she'd respond.

"Congratulations," Judith said warmly. "One day at a time, right?"

"You betcha. By the time I checked myself in, I had no idea how messed up I was."

"Who does? Most addicts are convinced that they can stop using or drinking if they want—they just don't *want* to, right?"

Johnny nodded slowly, letting out a sigh. "Exactly. I used to say that all the time. But that's just BS."

He tried to read Judith's body language. She seemed to have relaxed, to be listening.

"I wasn't ever knee-walking drunk," he continued. "But I always found an excuse to pour another whiskey or drink another beer. After the crash that took my hand, the excuses for drinking got more. I drank to ease the pain. To get through the day. To forget. If I didn't have an excuse, I'd make one up. 'Hey look, it's Tuesday morning. Let me drink to that!' "

"So, what made you look for help, if you don't mind me asking?"

"I don't mind. There's no shame in it for me. Regrets, yes, but no shame." He took a big sip of water.

"We were in a massive wreck the summer of last year. Ran head-on into a semi. We were heading west on I-70 and the semi was coming east." Johnny paused as if viewing the accident in his mind's eye. "It hit us at full speed. Damn near took my life. I was lucky to be alive, the docs told me but say *that* to a guy who just had his hand ripped off his arm. I didn't feel so lucky."

Judith was shocked by the events he described. "I am so sorry," she said.

"Yep. So, am I."

"A semi? Head on with a semi? How *did* you survive that?"

"Well, I almost didn't. I was out of it completely. Had a tube stuffed down my nose. My ass was airlifted to Denver General. I ended up getting the works. Ya know, soup to nuts. I got blood, platelets, and I got stitches in my liver. And God knows, I wished they could superglue my ribs. I wanted to Duct tape a pillow around my rib cage, it hurt so bad to breathe."

"I cannot imagine . . ."

"I spent the next fourteen days in the ICU at Denver General. Our driver wasn't that lucky. Dennis was killed on impact. They told me when I woke up."

"You had a driver? What kind of car were you in?"

"It wasn't a car, which is what saved my life. We were in Ethel."

The perplexed look on Judith's face said it all. Johnny laughed. "That's what we called our tour bus."

"A tour bus? Didn't you say that this was your first bus trip?"

"Well, yeah, this is my first *commercial* bus trip. Our bus was much nicer than this one here, more like a house on wheels, ya know? We were goofin' around making some silly video when we got hit."

"Who's *we*?"

"Well, I was with the Carlsbad Cowboys back then." When Johnny did not see the glimmer that usually comes from people recognizing the name, he added, "It was a band. I played lead guitar with a couple of old buddies of mine. You must not be into country rock."

"Not so much. Work keeps me busy."

"No kidding? What crazy life do you have that doesn't allow time for music?"

"We're still talking about you," Judith smiled, succeeding to turn the conversation back around. "When did you start playing the guitar?"

"I saved up working on our ranch and bought my first Gibson when I was thirteen. I spent every free moment learning chords and strumming techniques. Haven't stopped playing since."

He raised his eyebrows and gave a half-smile. "Well, till that night in Colorado. I got my ink on the first anniversary of the crash, so that's how long it's been since I've picked up any of my guitars."

"Was the crash what led you to go to rehab?" Judith asked tentatively.

"Yes and no. I was fit to be tied once I woke up and realized what was to be my new reality. Cut myself off from the band and from most of my family. It was hard on my wife," Johnny said, a somber look coming over him. "She'd gotten used to the good life, with all the glitz and glamour. After the crash, she went overboard with drinking."

Johnny grew quiet for a moment. "Drank herself to death—literally. Since losing her, my life's been as empty as a prostitute's promise."

Judith's heart ached with empathy for this man she barely knew. "I am *so* sorry," she said in a whisper.

"It hurt like hell—I can tell you that. So, I drank to drown the pain. About four months ago, I woke up one Sunday having *no* clue what happened the night before or how I got home. That's when I called a friend and told him I needed help. It was one of the hardest and most liberating calls I've made in my life."

Johnny grew quiet and stared at a tumbleweed rolling across a stretch of nothingness.

Judith broke the silence after a while.

"That seems like a brave step to take."

"I didn't feel brave one bit. Desperate, hell yeah. And that friend I called? Dale's the guy I'm now heading out to work for. He started a new music production studio, the only one in Amarillo. Said he was lookin' for a good right-hand man."

He held up his right hand. "I guess I'll fill the bill."

Judith noticed that Johnny had dimples under his eyes when he smiled.

"Have you ever lived in Texas before?" she asked.

"Haven't yet, no. But I reckon' the change in scenery will be good."

"One last question," she said, "then I'll stop grilling you. What's the story behind your name? Is it because you could play any song, just like a jukebox?"

Johnny laughed. "Good guess, Gucci, but that's not it. After I got out of the hospital, there was this pub in Nashville I used to hang out at. The regulars there all knew that first thing when I walked through that door, I'd head to the jukebox and choose my favorite song. Five songs for a dollar. I'd put in my dollar and punch in J-3 five times in a row. Eventually, the barman started calling me Jukebox Johnny, and the name stuck.

"What none of those guys knew was that J-3 was the Carlsbad Cowboys' first number one hit. It's the residuals from that song and our other hits that give me the freedom and time to try to find myself again."

———◆———

For the next almost two hundred miles, Johnny regaled Judith with stories about life as a musician, about his first band, and about a former career as a studio musician.

It had been a while since Judith had a conversation about much more than work or the arts. She could barely recall the last time she had a conversation that did not require her continuous input.

It was refreshing.

Johnny finally paused, saying, "Enough about me, though. Tell me about you."

Inwardly, Judith squirmed. She did not like talking about herself, but a promise to Mimi is a promise. "What would you like to know?"

"Here's an easy question. What instrument do you play?"

"None, unless you count Texas Instruments calculators as instruments," she said with a shrug.

"No kidding? Doesn't every kid take obligatory piano or violin lessons?"

"Not me."

"Okay, so if you could play any instrument, what would it be?"

Before Judith could answer, the bus slowed to take the exit to Tucumcari, and Lucille announced that they would be making a pitstop at Love's Travel Stop for a couple of passengers who would be getting off.

"Twenty minutes, folks," Lucille announced over the PA system. "Next stop will be Amarillo, Texas."

———◆———

Judith stepped off the bus to buy some fresh fruit and juice, thinking about Johnny's stories.

He's easy to listen to.

She was anxious about him asking her questions about herself, though.

He seems to trust me. Why not trust him? After all, I won't see him again after he gets off in Amarillo, she tried to convince herself.

She wrestled with the idea of explaining why she did not take piano lessons like every other kid in her class because, as Mimi used to say, they did not have two pennies to rub together.

Telling him that would inevitably lead to him asking about her grandparents, which would lead to questions about her parents.

Nashville | 1995

Judy was staring at the grownups around her. She had been at Mimi and Granddaddy's home since the day her parents "went to be with Jesus," as Mimi referred to the incident. Judy could not understand why her parents had to go to Jesus.

"I know it hurts, honey," Mimi comforted her. The ten-year-old's lip was quivering as she tried hard not to cry, to be strong. "Someday, you'll understand."

"Mimi, if I just got up earlier, I could have woken them up."

"It's not that simple, honey. There's nothing you could have done to help." Little did her granddaughter know how she and Virgil, too, were wrestling with how they could have missed the red flags.

After their son's back injury the year before, the doctor prescribed a new "miracle drug," oxycodone. At first, he raved about how great the pills were, how just one pill helped numb the pain for hours.

But instead of lowering the dosage, the doctor kept increasing it for refills as Grace's son insisted that it was not doing the trick any longer.

They would only later find out that he had started sharing the drugs with his wife, and that they also were going from one emergency room in Nashville to the next, faking injuries just to get their hands on more.

What exactly happened on the fateful night of their final high, no one knows. All they knew was that their ten-year-old daughter found them on the sofa, long having breathed their final breath.

The paramedics called DHS, and a representative was on the scene even before the ambulance left. Mrs. Alonge told Judy she was a social worker, though the child had no idea what that meant. She, along with two police officers, took Judy to her grandparents' home.

"You are the next of kin, I believe," Mrs. Alonge told Grace and Virgil. "Is there anyone else whom the parents had identified as godparents?"

"Not that we know of," Virgil replied, holding his wife who was having a hard time processing the news that their only son had passed away.

Their granddaughter, meanwhile, was not crying. She just bit her lip as she fought the tears.

It took just a few weeks for a judge to finalize the arrangement. "From this day forward," she said with final authority, "Virgil and Grace Lee are the legal guardians of Judith Lee of Nashville, Tennessee."

Tucumcari, NM to Amarillo, TX

Johnny was curious about Judith's story, but it did not take a shrink to see that Judith was not yet ready to trust him. So, he stuck to the question he had asked before they pulled up at the rest stop.

"So, have you thought of an answer to my question yet?" Johnny wanted to know. "If you could play any instrument, what would it be?"

"Promise you won't laugh," she said as she offered him a cup of fruit.

"Scout's honor!" Johnny responded holding three fingers in the air, then took the cup and gave a polite nod.

"Well, how could I *not* trust you after that?" Judith chuckled, continuing, "If I could wake up and magically be able to play any instrument, it would be the double bass."

"Then you'd have to drag around even more luggage," Johnny teased. "Why the bass?"

"I'm a patron of the L.A. Philharmonic, and whenever I go to watch their performances, I can't keep my eyes off the bassists."

"One in particular? Is he tall, dark, and handsome?"

Judith smiled. "It's not that. They add a rich sound to the orchestra, like adding heavy cream to a cup of good coffee. To me, their sound is what brings all the other sounds together despite them being off on the side. I've always been an outsider—just like the bassists."

"And here I thought you would choose something ordinary like the guitar or the piano . . ."

"Why be ordinary?" Judith poked back with a smile.

"Right on! Plus, *ordinary's* the last word I'd use to describe you, Miss Gucci," Johnny said and winked.

Please tell me I'm not blushing again, Judith wrestled inwardly. *Is this the eighth grade that I blush at a boy flirting with me?*

"So, what in the world led to you taking a cross-country bus?"

Judith took a deep breath in and slowly exhaled through pursed lips.

What would Mimi do? She'd tell the story and do it with delight. Here goes . . .

"I'm heading to Nashville to visit my grandmother," she said, tentatively at first, but then committing to go ahead. "I haven't seen her in two years. She has leukemia, and it's terminal. The *only* reason I'm on this bus is because she asked me to do this. She's never traveled, so she's living vicariously through me."

"No kidding?"

"Do I look like I'm kidding?" Judith retorted. "She asked that I call each night and tell her about the places we pass through and about the people I meet."

"So, you'll be telling her about *me* tonight?"

"Yep. And about Lucille and whomever else I might meet in Amarillo this afternoon."

"She must be pretty special to you."

Judith looked at Johnny, trying to judge again if she could trust him. Though she wanted to share more, she simply was not comfortable doing so on a bus where others are probably listening.

"*That* she is. She's the closest person to me in my entire world. She and my grandfather raised me. It's more than a little complicated."

Johnny quietly waited for Judith to share. He could see she was struggling as she gathered her thoughts. A mile or two passed before she spoke up again.

"My parents died from a drug overdose when I was ten, which is why Mimi and Granddaddy raised me. You might say it's the best thing that's happened to me, but that's sorta like folks telling you that you're lucky to be alive."

"Sounds about right . . ."

"Two years ago, my grandfather died, and that's the last time I was back in Tennessee to see Mimi." There was a lull in the conversation before Judith carried on. "Saying that out loud makes me sound pretty bad, doesn't it?"

"I'm sure you had good reason."

Judith thought for a moment before responding. "Work's kept me busy, and before you know a week turns into a month and soon a year or two . . . I've been trying to at least call her every Sunday evening."

"What line of work are you in?"

Judith was relieved to change the topic.

"Software."

She told Johnny about a college professor connecting her with a job in Silicon Valley. "I left the day after graduation and have been living in California ever since."

"What did you go to school for?"

"Computer science."

"Nashville State?"

"Vanderbilt." She smiled at the fact that Johnny could not hide his surprise.

"No kidding. So, you're not only pretty; you're also smart *and* rich," he said half-jokingly.

"*Au contraire.* We were dirt poor. I got a full ride based on my grades and the fact that I qualified as a low-income student."

"Look at you. Here I was figuring you were one of those silver-spoon types, but you're just the opposite. If I were wearing my hat, I'd be raising it out of respect."

Johnny popped a couple of grapes in his mouth, then continued, "So, you're still up in Silicon Valley?"

"Nope, I'm down in L.A. now. In my first two years up north, I learned how companies were started, structured, developed, and grown. I moved south and started my own company so I wouldn't have to answer to someone else again." Judith shrugged. "Oh my gosh, can you imagine if I had to go talk to someone and try and explain that I needed an indefinite period of time off to take a bus across the country to see my dying grandmother . . ."

"Well," Johnny said as he laughed and emptied the last of the fruit into his mouth, "thanks for making me excited about my new job starting tomorrow where I'll be working for someone else."

By the time they crossed the border into Texas, Judith was the one telling Johnny stories about her amazing team back in L.A., of their projects, and about some of the challenges of running her highly successful tech company.

From time to time, they would be quiet, but neither seemed uncomfortable with the silence.

"I've never told this much of my story to anyone but my therapist," Judith finally said. "She'd be proud of me for trusting you. Thanks for listening."

"Thank you for your trust, Judith. I'm honored."

Judith smiled, then turned to look out the window. Gigantic John Deere planters were kicking up red dust all around.

"Do you happen to know what crops grow in this region?" she asked Johnny. She chuckled at her sudden reluctance to google the answer or to look to see if the app had any insights to share.

"I could be mistaken, but I believe it's winter wheat they're putting in right now."

A notification popped up on the app, stating they would soon be entering Amarillo. "Welcome to the Yellow Rose of Texas."

> **Did you know?**
> Amarillo is Spanish for *yellow*, which is why the city is called the Yellow Rose of Texas.
>
> Amarillo is the largest producer of helium gas in the nation.

"Folks," Lucille announced, "for those of you who'll be spending some time in this city, if you haven't yet been to the Cadillac Ranch, it's a hoot to see. You can check our app for more info."

They pulled in at the Amarillo Bus Center minutes later. While they were waiting for their luggage, Johnny wondered if Judith might want to have an early dinner with him. "Goodbye right now just doesn't seem right. There's a Steak Ranch in town that I've heard a lot about. Care to join me? I'm buying."

The question the younger Judy asked her in her dream the night before came to mind.

Are you happy?

Judith wrestled with the reality of work emails waiting to be attended to but convinced herself that she had to eat in any case.

"Why not?" she heard herself say.

Johnny had to pick up a rental car first, so Judith opted to Uber to her hotel and drop off her bag.

While they waited for their luggage, Johnny shared his phone number with her. "That way, you can contact me if something comes up."

Lucille handed Judith her bag and apologized that the day's route had nothing of real interest, like she was personally responsible for that stretch of the I-40 being boring.

"It was far from boring, Lucille. I learned some valuable lessons today."

The older woman smiled knowingly. "Sometimes getting rid of all the other distractions helps us see what's really important, ain't that right?" she said and winked at Judith.

"Well, look at that. We have ourselves a driver *and* a philosopher," Judith joked and turned her attention to the approaching Uber.

Big Texan Steak Ranch

"Howdy, y'all!" a hostess greeted them with the thickest Texan accent Judith had ever heard. "Table for two?"

She led them to a quiet spot and placed their menus on the table. "Your server will be right with y'all."

Every word sounded like it had an extra syllable in it, and Judith had to listen closely to follow. She found it quite amusing, though.

"Can I get y'all some Coke or tea while you wait?"

"I'd *love* some tea, thanks," Judith said.

"And I'll have soda water with lime," Johnny added.

The server showed up minutes later. "Howdy, y'all. I'm Juanita. Who got the spritzer?" Johnny gestured that it's his, and with that, she slid a huge glass of iced tea over toward Judith.

"I'm sorry. I ordered tea," Judith objected.

The server laughed. "Honey, this is Texas. Here, *tea* is sweetened iced tea. Did you want hot tea?"

"My bad. It's been too long since I've enjoyed some sweet tea. I'm fine, thanks."

"Let me tell you about our menu. Our signature item's a seventy-two-ounce steak. If you can eat it in an hour, it's free. If not, it'll be $72."

Neither Judith nor Johnny was up for the challenge. "Then there's Mountain Oysters—this is *not* seafood, though," she said and winked. "And then there's the Oh My Chicken Fry, our famous chicken fried steak, my personal favorite."

Juanita listed a few more items before leaving them to decide. She had to come back twice to get the order since Johnny and Judith were deep in conversation about the project Judith's team was hitting out of the ballpark. She could not be prouder of Tony and Tiffany for the work they were doing.

Staying on target in anything IT-related was notoriously difficult. Most in the industry accepted by default that they would routinely overrun deadlines. But not Judith's company.

By the time their food came—chicken fried steak for Johnny and a pork chop for Judith—she asked him how he felt about starting his new job the next day.

"Well, all I know is that tomorrow I'll be showing up at my friend's studio and begin playing it by ear." He paused briefly, "Musician joke. Weak one, I know."

With a slight smile, Judith pressed in more, "Nice try avoiding an uncomfortable question, cowboy. I'm ninja level at that."

"*Touché.*" Johnny drank some of the spritzer, then continued. "To answer your question, I don't have a clue. I'd like to think I can find a normal life. Whatever that is."

"What would a 'normal life' look like?"

Judith watched Johnny struggle with his thoughts before he began to speak. "Since losing my wife, there have been times when I've been overwhelmed with loneliness and emptiness. It exacerbated my drinking, and for a while, I thought it helped. Until it didn't."

He took another sip of his drink and added, "Now, I'm just taking it one day at a time. But I hope one day there will be someone special again to share my life with. Guess I'm looking for someone with low expectations," he said with a smile. "How about you? What would a 'normal life' look like for you?"

"I have no idea, no point of reference. People choose to either follow their head, their heart, or their gut. I learned at a young age to do what my head tells me, but even more so, what seems right in my gut."

"Is that for business, or is that how you approach relationships? A beautiful woman like you . . ." This time, it was Johnny who blushed. Even in the dimly lit restaurant, it was clear to see his discomfort with flirting again.

Judith gave a long pause, trying to decide how much she wanted to share. "It goes for all of life, really. Though I can't say how it would work in relationships since I've never been in one."

"For real?" Johnny did not even attempt to mask his surprise.

"For real," Judith said and smiled. "I told you earlier that we were dirt poor. I was made fun of a lot in school. Eventually, I just shut myself off from everyone and kept my face buried in books. The only thing that changed once I moved to California is the object I chose to hide behind . . ."

"You're not kidding me," Johnny asked.

"Oh my gosh. I can't believe I'm letting you know just how dysfunctional my private life is."

"No relationships? None ever?"

"No relationships. It's less complicated that way . . ."

Johnny stared at her, then shook his head. "You, Judith, are a unicorn, a mythical creature!"

They paused the conversation for Juanita to hand them refills on their tea and spritzer. Emboldened by her newfound honesty, Judith continued, "Do I feel like I've missed something? You bet. But what's a poor girl to do?" She smiled jokingly at her question to Johnny's still-shocked face.

"Track with me," he began, "would you? The reason I'm shocked is that the best times of my life have been those when I was sharing life experiences with someone I loved. That's why the past year has felt pretty meaningless."

"So," Johnny continued, "a normal life for me means I'll be hoping to find someone who fills that empty space. Would that apply for you too?" He paused slightly before exclaiming with some frustration at himself, "Listen to me spilling my guts . . ."

Judith was moved by Johnny's willingness to respond to her candor with his own. "Actually, you sharing your feelings is pretty disarming," she said. "I'm used to those few men who have expressed an interest in me trying to impress me with their achievements and balance sheets. Of course, that's my world."

Judith continued, "But listening to you has given me real pause about my life."

Johnny looked at Judith, "For me, the worst mistakes I've ever made happened when I didn't trust my heart. That little nagging feeling that something is not right, you know?"

Judith smiled at Johnny, confirming, "The older I've gotten, the more I trust that feeling. My Mimi always said that feeling was a combination of part of your brain recognizing something wasn't quite right, along with the good Lord whispering in your ear."

She added, "And I've got a good gut feeling about you Johnny. You're going to be just fine. Some woman out there is going to be incredibly lucky."

Johnny looked down at his almost empty dinner plate, then slowly back up at Judith, replying, "Well it sounds like your Mimi is a really smart woman, but you're certainly more optimistic than I am Judith. I'm guessing there's not much demand for a broken, washed-up, one-handed musician coming out of rehab."

Judith reached one hand across the booth, laying her hand on top of Johnny's hand, saying, "Everybody's a little bit broken, Jukebox Johnny. Some people are just gifted at hiding the cracks in their life from everyone." She paused before adding, "I guess that's one of my gifts too."

When Juanita brought the check, Johnny asked the server about the Cadillac Ranch. "Is it far from here?"

"Y'all'd've passed the turnoff on your way here if you came in on the I-40 from out west," she drawled.

Johnny convinced Judith to go check it out with him. In another atypical move for Judith, she agreed.

Cadillac Ranch

They made the short drive to where ten Cadillacs were buried, the tail ends sticking out of the sand.

"It reminds me of Carhenge in Nebraska," Johnny said as they pulled up.

"Carhenge? That sounds like Stonehenge."

"Precisely. But it has cars instead of stones. We shot a music video there once. This one here's much more colorful."

While the site in Nebraska was a playful take on the prehistoric site in England, the one in Amarillo was an art installation showing the changes in the tail design of Cadillacs over the years.

Spray cans littered the area, and visitors were encouraged to add some graffiti.

"New beginnings," Johnny wrote, and Judith took a selfie of the two of them in front of Johnny's artwork.

He drove Judith back to her hotel just as the sun was setting, stopping briefly at a gift store so Judith could purchase a fridge magnet of a Cadillac tail sticking out of the sand with the Texas flag painted on it.

"Everything's bigger in Texas," it said.

As are the surprises.

———◆———

"Johnny, I can't tell you how much I've enjoyed visiting with you today," Judith said as they pulled up to her hotel.

A smile crept over Johnny's face as he looked at her, yet his smile gave away a tinge of sadness—the way someone feels when reading the last chapters of a great book, knowing the end is near. "The pleasure's been all mine, Judith," he replied. "It's the first time I've felt normal in a *long* time. Thanks for going on a date with *me.*"

"I . . ." Judith stammered, then laughed. "I guess you're right. Thank you for a memorable date."

"Well, here you are," Johnny said, eyeing the hotel entrance, "Would you like to invite me in for some . . . dessert?"

Johnny was charming but not pushy.

Judith returned his smile, then softly laughed before answering, "Thank you for a great day, Johnny, but no. You are a special man. And you're going to find joy and happiness again. Of that, I'm certain."

"I hope our paths cross again," he said, "and I hope you find joy and happiness too."

He reached out and hugged Judith tightly.

"It's been a fun day, Jukebox Johnny. I will certainly remember you."

Judith smiled wistfully as she closed the car door behind her. Johnny waited until she was safely in the hotel before pulling away, slowly shaking his head.

"What the hell just happened?" he wondered out loud.

Tuesday Night Call

Judith got everything ready for a quick exit from the hotel the next morning. While doing so, she could not get her and Johnny's conversations out of her head.

She took a long shower and redirected her attention to the matters in her inbox. Several hours flew by before she closed her laptop for the night, turned on her travel diffuser, and crawled into bed. Then she called Mimi.

"Judy honey, you called at the perfect time," Grace answered. "Are you in Amarillo?"

"Sure am, Mimi. This town and the road here have been full of surprises, though the road itself was uneventful."

She told Grace about Johnny, about his accident, the death of his wife, and him having spent the last three months in rehab.

"That feller had quite a story for you, didn't he?" Grace said.

Judith hesitated before answering. "I've never met anyone quite like him, Mimi," she admitted. "What type of man can go through those kinds of highs and lows and come through the other side in one piece with a positive attitude like that?"

"That's a man that the good Lord has a plan for, Judy. He's going to be just fine. Sounds like his story kinda got to you . . ."

"Oh, he was just another passenger who had an interesting story that I could share with you, Mimi," she said dismissively.

Grace looked at Judith's picture on her end table. "If you say so, sweetheart. If you say so . . ."

Judith told Grace about the Cadillac tails sticking out of the sand just outside Amarillo and about lunch at the steakhouse.

"Well, Mimi, today's meal was by far the best. It was an early dinner. I had a pork chop that made me think of how you'd cook 'em—except yours is better. No one can cook good Southern food like you can."

Grace beamed with delight at Judith's comment. "Well, when you get here, I'm going to cook you a big baked ham, baked beans, broccoli

casserole, sweet potato casserole, and fried okra. With fresh, sliced toma-
ters, of course," she declared. "And I know how you've always loved my
sweet tea, so I'll have gallons of it. Not to mention your favorite: lemon
meringue pie."

Judith savored Mimi's enthusiasm. "I've just eaten, and you've
already made me hungry again. We'll see how you're feeling when I get
there. Of course, you'll let me help you in the kitchen, won't you?"

Judith's reply was music to Grace's ears. "Judy girl," she said, "it'll be
just like old times. Nothing could make me happier—other than getting
these calls each night and listening to these stories." After a slight pause,
she continued, "Lordy, how I wish I were there with you, child."

"I wish you were here with me too, Mimi. But I'll be there in no time.
You get some rest now. I'll let you go so you can watch Jimmy Fallon."

Grace laughed heartily.

I must remember to record a conversation so I'll never forget that laughter.

"Yep, it's almost time for Jimmy. I know you need your rest so you'll
be ready to visit with whomever the good Lord has for you as a neighbor
for tomorrow. Be sure to say your prayers now, honey. Sweet dreams,
Judy. I love you."

"I will, Mimi. Sweet dreams to you too. I love you to the moon and
back."

Before going to sleep, Judith caught herself praying for the man who
seemed to have stirred the waters of her soul. Judith was not certain how
she felt about that, but just to be sure, she saved his number on her phone.

God only knows why I might need that number was the last thought
that crossed her mind before she fell asleep.

JOHNNY'S SONG

"Jukebox Johnny"

Jukebox Johnny's what they call me and J-3's my favorite tune,
as I relive my favorite memories, my head begins to swoon.
"More jokes and smokes and cold draft beer,"
I cry as my friends all gather 'round.
We laugh and drink and pass the time, till it's time to shut her down.
The bartender says, "It's time to close now Johnny, you better head on out.
I'll see you here tomorrow night." Of that, he has no doubt.

Long ago and far away I played a different tune.
I had a wife who loved me, we'd married just that June.
We had no doubt I'd be a star, I played guitar in a band.
Our first song hit number one and our time was now at hand.
"You'll be big time now," they said, and we were on our way,
but the bus crash crushed our dreams that night,
and the demons came to stay.
The doctors had to take my hand, and the whiskey took my wife,
And now my days are numbered, as I lead a different life.

Jokes and smokes and cold draft beer, night after night I'm just sitting here.
Jukebox Johnny's what they call me, and they all know my name.
To me, their smiles and faces all just look the same.

Still, now they're my friends, but they'll never know why J-3's my favorite
tune.
They'll never know of my other life or the wife I took that June.
All they'll know is what I let them know and J-3's my favorite song.
They'll never know how right life was, or how it went so wrong.

"So, gather round, my friends," I laugh. "It's time to party now!"
They don't know that Jukebox Johnny's fighting hard to hide a tear.
They just wait to hear old Johnny say,
"More jokes and smokes and cold draft beer."

CHAPTER 7

Use What You Got

Daisy

"I don't know what spell you've placed on my husband, but this ends here and now. Back! Off!"

The woman on the other end of the phone did not introduce herself. She did not need to either. Daisy knew exactly who she was and how it would end.

Once the wife got a whiff of things, it did not take long before the twenty-some-year-old had to find a new target.

For some, the giveaway was that the husband had made no sexual advances in months. Or that he had a sudden increase in libido. For others, the giveaway may have been a sudden interest in working out while he had not set foot in a gym in decades.

Once the wife got ahold of the credit card statement, well, it was truly over.

How this one knew Daisy was not sure. She feigned innocence. "Sorry, I didn't catch your name?" she said in an accent much more Southern than even her urban Alabama roots would have her sound.

"You know damn well who I am, so back the hell off, or you'll regret ever having set your sights on Dan."

With that, the wife hung up.

Daisy called her mother, trying to get sympathy. "Dan and I broke up, Mama."

"Bless your heart," her mama said, her accent as thick as Birmingham molasses. "Why don't you come home, pum'kin. It's time. You're not gettin' any younger either. Pretty soon them perky boobs of yours will start saggin' and you know, no rich man looks twice at a woman who looks like she's been ridden hard and left out to dry. Come on home, and we'll find ya a goooood Southern man with a thick wallet. How 'bout that?"

Daisy knew her mama was right. But she was not ready to move home, though. She packed her bags that very night, bought a one-way ticket, and updated her profiles on a selection of sugar daddy websites.

Baiting her hook, she posted, "This sugar baby's lookin' to find her an Okie. Anyone interested in meetin' up in Oklahoma City?"

CHAPTER 8

Chasin' Money

Daisy and Judith | Amarillo, TX to Oklahoma City, OK

T he Texas sun was still well below the eastern horizon when Judith woke up. The letters shone brightly on the bedside clock. Five twenty-nine.

"Rise and shine, sweetheart!" Judith could hear Mimi's cheery voice in her mind.

In the beginning, either Virgil or Grace would wake her up every morning, sitting down next to her for a moment. Whichever of the grandparents were there when she opened her eyes, she knew she could trust them to tell her what a beautiful day it was, and how precious she was, and how blessed they were to have her.

By the time she was a teenager, the morning chats annoyed her. She posted a "Do not enter" sign on the door, a request Virgil and Grace honored despite it paining them to do so.

"She'll come around," Virgil would tell Grace, but deep down, he too feared that Judy would slip away like her daddy did. The carpet by the side of his bed had imprints from the hours he knelt there, praying for their precious Judy.

Pray, Grace did too. And every Friday, she would tuck a note into Judy's lunch box to remind her of how precious she was to them. "Virgil, we may not have much money to our name, but we're rich in love," she'd remind him when he teased her about the notes.

"And we're rich in grace," he'd add without fail, pulling his wife closer.

Sometimes, Grace would write out a Bible verse for Judy, other times a poem or a quote, and yet other times simply a note with an "XO, Mimi" scribbled on a piece of paper and tucked in beneath the wax paper her bologna sandwich was wrapped in.

It became her Friday custom, and all week, she would be looking out for just the right thing to write.

Judy never said anything about the notes, but Grace kept tucking them into her granddaughter's lunchbox, or her bookbag, or into one of her textbooks. Judith would look for them on Fridays. She kept her favorite ones in a shoebox under her bed and her *absolute* favorite one in her journal. It was an excerpt from "Amazing Grace."

Not only was Grace's penmanship a work of art; the words of the hymn moved Judith despite her not being someone who loved hymns, per se. Judith knew the words to be true: "Through many dangers, toils, and snares I have already come; 'Tis grace has brought me safe thus far, and grace will lead me home."

As an adult, Judith would argue that while grace may have played a role, she believed that it was a whole lot of hard work that got her where she was in life. While it was true that she had a good head on her shoulders—as Mimi would often remind her as a child—Judith always studied harder than any of her classmates.

A professor of hers had contacted a Vanderbilt alumnus in Cupertino and recommended Judith for a position at his thriving tech company. There, Judith spent every waking hour working to learn all she could about succeeding in the tech industry.

It was her ability to think strategically that ultimately led to major breakthroughs.

"My willingness to work hard coupled with my ability to strategize is my magic sauce," she told Dr. Sanders recently. "It's that simple."

"What drives you to succeed, Judith?" her therapist asked in response.

Judith told her it was about making a difference in the world, but she knew the real reason was that she refused to live in poverty ever again.

Judith's staff would agree that no one could keep up with her. She could run circles around even her most ambitious staff and was constantly on to the next step in her plan.

On that morning in Amarillo, though, Judith was a little behind thanks to the time she spent with Johnny.

Thankful that no one else was in the hotel fitness center, Judith opted for a self-paced cycling workout so she could dictate responses to messages.

"Cara comma new paragraph please schedule a video call for three central with Tiffany and Tony period new paragraph I'll expect an update from each on progress toward our goal period new paragraph any update on leukemia research question mark new paragraph also please look into options for taking private double-bass lessons period."

By the time another guest entered the gym, Judith had knocked out at least forty email responses, adding several more back in the room while she got ready.

While she was having breakfast at the hotel, she ordered an Uber Black back to the bus station, thankful for the sliver of independence this newfound "luxury ride" gave her. For a moment, she was tempted to put Oklahoma City down as the destination but surprised herself by thinking whom she might miss out on getting to know if she did that.

After all, the visits with Sara, Gary, and Johnny had been enlightening.

Amarillo, TX to Erick, OK

Judith was surprised to see Lucille ready to take her bag, greeting her with that same million-dollar smile as the morning before.

"Well, good morning, Ms. Gucci!" she exclaimed, her eyes sparkling. "You look positively bubbly this morning. Had a good night's rest, I assume."

Lucille did not wait for an answer; her observations poured out like coins from a penny slot machine. "Mm-hmm. Positively bubbly *and* mighty fine, dressed to the nines. Fine shoes those are. Don't know how anyone can balance on those without breakin' somethin'."

She chuckled. "My, my. That I would have the pleasure of handling a fine piece of luggage like this *two* days in a row."

Judith pressed her lips together, trying not to smile.

Who knew my luggage and attire would end up being such a big deal?

As Judith boarded the bus, high clouds pushed in from the prairie causing the morning Amarillo sunlight to blink on and off.

Several single seats were available. Scanning the options, Judith's glance landed upon a gal wearing a tight, low-cut blouse, a noticeably short skirt, and knee-high boots.

A man seated on the opposite side of the aisle a row ahead of her had his eyes on her, practically undressing her with his gaze. The young woman did not seem to mind.

He was reaching for his bag to make a move, but Judith thwarted his plans.

"Mind if I sit here?" she asked the gal.

"Are you kidding me? Is that a *real* Gucci tote?" she blurted out in a thick Southern accent. "Yes, *please* sit with me!"

For a moment, Judith questioned her choice of seating. Still, her protective instinct made her take the seat, ignoring her enthusiastic neighbor's question about the authenticity of her tote.

"I *love* your outfit!" Daisy seemed to speak at only one volume: loud. "Someday," she continued at top volume, "that's the way I'll be dressing every day. By the way, my name's Daisy! What's yours?" she asked as she offered Judith her hand.

Amused, Judith shook Daisy's hand. "I'm Judith," she said.

"That fits you *so* well. *Such* a classy name! And *such* classy shoes you're wearing. I have a thing for purses and boots," she declared. "This here is one of my favorite pairs. Fits like a glove. Barely know you're wearing anything," she giggled. "Feel how soft this is."

Daisy raised her knees and insisted Judith feel the leather. "Soft as a lamb's ear, ain't it, Judith?"

It was not quite the words Judith would have used to describe the boots, but they looked sassy on Daisy.

"Got them for $11.95 at the Salvation Army," she half-whispered. "Wouldn't have known that unless I told ya, right?"

"Never would have known," Judith responded in a significantly lower volume and pace to try and tone down Daisy's energy. It did not work.

"Man, do I love shopping at the Salvation Army!" Daisy continued at full volume. "I can sniff out a bargain like I could the scent of a blooming magnolia tree on a hot summer day."

———◆———

They had barely pulled out of the bus station and Judith had been thoroughly educated on boots: the way they should feel, the whoosh they should make when you put them on, and the sound they should and should *not* make when you walk.

Daisy told Judith about her likes and dislikes when it came to supple calf leather, pleather, and patent leather. She preferred the last. "The shinier and the longer, the better," she declared.

She had a thing for boots, she said, especially ones with pointed tips. She had as much to say about purses—the perfect number of compartments, shoulder or cross-body, a clutch or a tote, and which color or color combination.

"Why have one purse when you could have ten, right?" she asked enthusiastically.

"Right."

Daisy's dream was to own a bright pink Prada purse. "A real one, not a fake like you can buy in the tents on the side of the road," she said. "You didn't buy yours on the side of the road, did ya?"

"Positively not."

Any other day, Judith may have been offended by Daisy's over-the-top energy and personal questions, but on this day, Judith was amused.

They were not even on the interstate yet, and she knew more about Daisy than she did about just about anyone else.

They passed a big sign on the side of the road. Happy State Bank, it said.

Are you happy, Judith? The question from her younger self in the dream two nights ago popped into her mind.

Am I happy? Content, yes. Driven, focused, proud, successful. All words I could use to describe myself, but happy? Was what I felt last night happiness?

"I was asking what you do for a living," Daisy repeated a question that had gotten lost to Judith's moment of contemplation.

"I have a software company in L.A."

Daisy's eyes widened and she leaned back. "Whaaaat?" She continued, taking her excitement to an even higher level. "I knew it'd be something exciting like that! You must be *beaucoup* rich! What the heck are you doing on a bus?" She switched to a loud whisper again. "I'll bet you have your own jet."

Judith smiled politely. Still hoping to tone down Daisy's excitement, she responded in a much quieter tone. "I'm traveling by bus as a special favor for my grandmother whom I am going to visit. How about you?"

Daisy leaned in continued in a loud whisper, "Oklahoma City's where I'm heading. With all those big energy companies headquartered there, there are oodles of millionaires. I'm going to cull one of them from the herd and have some fun." She giggled. "Who knows, we might even fall in love."

From the corner of her eye, Judith saw a giant cowboy at the side of the road, the sign for The Big Texan Steakhouse where she and Johnny had an early dinner the day before.

What happened last night? she wondered as her gaze followed a Learjet coming in low over the restaurant for a landing somewhere just beyond.

Judith had never shared the stories she shared with Johnny. She had never wanted to invite a man to her room. Except for last night. She was flattered he asked to be invited, but Judith was glad she did not succumb. Plus, she was pretty sure Mimi did not quite mean to get to know other passengers *that* well . . .

Daisy noticed the slight furrow in Judith's brow. "Don't judge me, Judith." Her words yanked Judith back to the present. "A girl's got to do what a girl's got to do to secure her future. Ain't that right?"

"So, you're just going to pick one out and that's it?"

"Pretty much."

"Will he have a say?"

Daisy blinked her eyes widely and flashed Judith a coy smile. "When I give a man this look, it's all over. I'm like a gambler with a winning hand at a poker table. I just smile and rake in all the chips!"

She pulled out her phone to show Judith one of several sugar-daddy websites she was on. "I changed my location to Oklahoma City just last night, and I already have *three* men who are interested. In less than twelve hours. How 'bout them apples?"

Judith laughed out loud. "Those poor millionaires."

"This time, though, I made it clear that I have no interest in anyone who's still married. That, I've learned, is sorta like a cluster cuss."

"Tell me more." Judith felt like she was channeling Dr. Sanders.

"Well, I've had the po-po show up at my doorstep once—ya know, the police. Some lady accused me of stealing her husband. Told them I wasn't *stealing*, just borrowing. It wasn't a crime, but she had connections, so I dropped that man like I dropped ninth grade Spanish."

"Sounds a bit scary if you ask me."

"Not really. It's like a game. No one gets hurt."

"Except for the emotional pain, right?"

"Well, yeah, that can be a bit of a twister. But the gains? Oh boy! Being a sugar baby pays, even if just in the short run." She stared out the window at a tractor kicking up dust. "I had the shiniest metallic orange Ford Mustang Coupe for a while, compliments of Frank. Once the missus found out about us and cut the purse strings, the dealership came to take back the car."

Daisy had story after story of such benefits coming to an end once the wife found out. There was a luxury apartment in Dallas, stays in the fanciest of hotels, and vacations in Cancun and St. Maarten. There were clothes, jewelry, and enough broken promises to fill up a junkyard.

"So, what if your 'hunt' doesn't work out? What other plans do you have to make a living?"

"I'm a Plan-A-all-the-way type of gal, Judith. Always have been. Always will be!"

There was no doubt in Judith's mind that Daisy would succeed in finding someone who would take care of her.

As for Judith, life had always been about working hard to succeed. Perhaps it was something she had picked up from the plaque Virgil had above the workbench in the little garage. "Work hard. Get paid," it said.

He might as well have had one next to it with, "There's no such thing as a free lunch." But that would have been too much for a simple man such as her granddaddy was.

Judith noticed something on the horizon that looked different than all the other wind turbines that dotted the landscape. "Is that a cross, Daisy?" she asked.

"Sure is. You know what they say. Everything's bigger in Texas. From my experience, though, it ain't so—if you catch my drift." She winked at Judith.

Near Groom—a mere dot on the map—a notification popped up on Judith's phone.

> **Did you know?**
> At nineteen stories high, the giant cross near Groom is visible from twenty miles in any direction. The steel structure weighs two and a half million pounds. The site includes the fourteen stations of the cross.
>
> Groom is also home to the Leaning Tower of Britten, also referred to as the Leaning Tower of Texas. This was a plain water tower that was to be torn down, but a gentleman surnamed Britten bought it and used it as a landmark for his truck stop. The truck stop closed, but the tower became a famous landmark of Groom.

Mimi would have loved to visit the cross, Judith thought. *How often has she reminded me that grace is all about the cross?*

Daisy seemed lost in her thoughts, and Judith welcomed the silence, though it lasted a mere fifteen minutes. As they passed by a wind farm with close to a hundred gigantic wind turbines, Daisy had some wisdom to share.

"The way I see it, Judith," she announced as if they had been having a conversation all along, "this here is life. You make money from what you're given. Folks here have been given plenty of wind, and someone's makin' money from it. Some guy had a dilapidated water tower, and he made money from it."

She looked over at Judith and declared, "I reckon when I stand before Saint Peter at the pearly gates and he asks me what I had done with what the good Lord had given me, I'm gonna be telling him I got one hell of a body, and I used it to find me a good man."

Daisy giggled at her joke. "I should put that on a T-shirt and sell it. I'll bet ya I'd make me some fine money till I can find me that man."

She pulled out her phone and scrolled through the sites. "Got another bite! Maybe I won't even have to go make T-shirts after all."

———◆———

Judith tried to lean back the seat so she could rest a while, but the seat she had picked had seen better days. It was more of a pancake than a bucket seat. And like Daisy, it only had a Plan A—in this case, to stay upright.

So, Judith sat for a while taking in her surroundings. The guy catty-corner from them whose opportunity she had cut short to sit with Daisy packed a wad of Skoal behind his lip. The minty tobacco smell wafted past Judith.

Passengers' bodies were swaying with the motion of the bus. She watched Lucille's reflection in the rear-view mirror. Even while driving, she wore a sincere smile. Her joy seemed to spill over to the rest of the bus.

Lucille's lips were moving. *Was she talking to herself? Saying a secret mantra? Rehearsing the stories she'd be telling her spouse that night?*

A kid sat on the aisle close to the front of the bus. He had a model of a green car on his lap. It looked like a 1960s Chevy Impala—Virgil's original dream car, though he could not afford more than a used Rambler.

Judith closed her eyes and listened to the sounds around her. The steady hum of the engine. The faint drumbeat of the music from a passenger three rows ahead, which spilled out beyond his headphones. The muted conversation passengers a few rows back were having. One side of a phone call from a mother on the other side of the aisle.

Judith shifted her focus to her breathing.

In for four.

Hold for four.

Out for four.

Hold for four.

She followed her breath through her body, dismissing thoughts as they came to her.

She had been practicing meditation for a while on the recommendation of her chiropractor. She tended to carry the stress from her work with her, and meditating helped to alleviate some of that stress.

Will Mimi make it much longer?

Dismiss.

Breathe.

Am I happy?

Dismiss.

Breathe.

Johnny's adorable dimples, little punctuation marks around his smile.

Dismiss.

Breathe.

By the time Judith opened her eyes, Daisy had leaned back her seat and was fast asleep, still holding her phone, her key to finding Mr. Right. Or if not Mr. Right, Mr. Next.

Judith reached for the bottle of water in her purse, took out her phone, and got lost in work.

Looking up, she noticed the sky looked like the sky in the painting by John Constable she had hanging above her sofa.

Shamrock, TX

"Ladies and gentlemen, we have a big fan of the movie *Cars* on board, so we're taking a tiny detour, taking Route 66 through the town of Shamrock, Texas," Lucille announced. "The art deco Conoco gas station and the U-Drop Inn was the inspiration for Ramone's House of Body Art, right buddy?" she said and glanced over at the kid with the green car on his lap. He nodded enthusiastically, smiling from ear to ear.

"This is not an official pit stop, but if anyone needs to use the restroom, this would be a great place to do so. We'll be making a stop in another thirty minutes to drop off and pick up some passengers."

Though Grace likely would not know about the movie, Judith still got out to take a photo. "My grandma has me tell her stories of the folks I meet every day," she told Daisy who had a hard time climbing down the steps of the bus in her tiny skirt. "We've got to take a selfie for her." Daisy happily obliged, flashing her charming smile at the camera.

Relieved that it was not as hot outside as some of the previous pit stops had been, Judith stopped into the convenience store to buy some water.

"Got Perrier?" she asked.

"This is small-town Texas, honey," the cashier replied. "We got cold water, and we got not-so-cold water. You'll find whatever we got in the icebox over there. Lots of different kinds of Coke. But Perrier? Bless your heart."

The sign welcoming them to Oklahoma was hard to miss, as were the signs for the Okie Trading Post. Judith glanced at the notification on her phone to learn more.

> **Did you know?**
> Welcome to Oklahoma, where twenty-five Native American languages are spoken.
>
> The name of the state comes from a Choctaw phrase meaning *red people*.
>
> The state is a major producer of natural gas, oil, and agriculture. It produces the fifth most beef and wheat in the nation.
>
> Movie buffs may be familiar with the Land Rush of 1889 as it was depicted in the 1992 movie *Far and Away*, starring Tom Cruise and Nicole Kidman.

"So, you're an Okie, right?" Judith asked Daisy.

"Not yet," Daisy smiled. "I'm originally from Birmingham, Alabama. I'd tell you I was farm-raised and corn fed, but that would be a lie. My mama raised me by her own self. My daddy, well, to this day I don't know who he is. Truth be told," she whispered, "I don't think my mama knows either."

Daisy took a sip of water, then carried on. "She moved to the city when she could no longer hide her belly from gossip. Got a job in retail and that's the way it's been. In between jobs, we'd live on food stamps, but mama says the good Lord gave her a way with people. She can assess a lady's dress size faster than you can rub two sticks together. She says ladies get prickly when you get their size wrong."

"Sounds like your mother's a clever woman, Daisy."

"Yes, ma'am, but she works herself to the bone, which is why she's told me to be sure to find us a rich man. I can do that. You just watch this space."

Erick, OK to Oklahoma City, OK

When they pulled into Love's Travel Stop near Erick, Oklahoma, Lucille shared a bit of trivia over the PA system.

"You young'uns might not know this song, but for anyone who does, feel free to sing along 'cause this is where Sheb Wooley was raised. When someone asked him what place Erick was close to, he said it was close to extinction."

Lucille chuckled, then carried on. "There might not be much around here, but there's still life in Erick, Oklahoma. For those who love to find treasures at a flea market, you'll want to come back to visit the Sandhill Curiosity Shop."

With that, she cranked up the music to "One-eyed One-horned Flying Purple People Eater" and no one sang along with more gusto than their tobacco-dipping neighbor. He knew every word to the song.

Lucille belly-laughed as she watched her passengers sing along.

Everyone was chattering when they got off the bus at Love's. Some were still humming the chorus to the purple people eater.

"Tweeeeenty minutes, folks!" she reminded everyone as she went to retrieve the luggage of those leaving them, including the neighbor who had been singing with such vigor.

Judith went to see if she could find some cold Perrier and some organic almonds at this stop.

She walked around a little to stretch her legs and called Cara regarding a message she needed her to attend to as well as to confirm the afternoon's meeting. She had not spoken with Cara all week and it felt good to get an in-person update.

Judith was surprised, though, that she had not obsessed about work while on the bus. For the final stretch of the trip, she put in her earphones and continued listening to the book on Audible she had started two days prior.

In response to some of what she learned about the Comanche people, Judith had been reading up on some of the issues, including the Land Rush of 1889, when fifty thousand people lined up to see if they could claim a piece of the two million acres that was up for grabs.

Most of what became known as the state of Oklahoma used to be Indian Territory. In 1830, President Jackson had passed the Indian Removal Act. Native American nations were to be relocated to the Indian Territory. This would give the Southern states land. In exchange, they were promised autonomy.

This forced relocation became known as the Trail of Tears.

By 1889, President Harrison signed the Indian Appropriation Act, forcing Native American nations to be moved to reservations and for the so-called unassigned land to be open to white settlers from the East Coast.

Judith thought of her conversation with Gary two days before. He had reminded her that we had to learn from history so we did not repeat our mistakes. He had also reminded her how often we were oblivious to the pain of fellow countrymen and how much it may be costing the nation.

We're all connected.

Approaching Oklahoma City, Judith ignored the notification on the bus app and listened instead to what Lucille had to share in a more somber tone. Lucille reminded the passengers of the events of the bombing on April 19, 1995. "The Oklahoma City bombing has put this city on the map for something they'd rather forget: The single biggest homegrown act of terrorism."

She suggested that folks visit the museum and the adjacent park if they had time. "It's something you simply won't forget."

Judith decided to spend part of her afternoon at the site of the bombing.

Mimi would want me to go.

———◆———

The bus pulled into the Greyhound Bus Terminal in Oklahoma City around lunchtime. While they waited for their luggage, Daisy turned to Judith. "I hope you don't mind me saying, Judith," she said hush-hush, "but there aren't many women I talk to who aren't threatened by me. It's nice that you don't seem to think badly of me. I'm not used to that."

"I've learned a thing or two from you today, Daisy," Judith said with a smile. "Thank you."

"Guys have always been fighting for my attention." She shrugged her shoulders. "That's always made the gals around me jealous. You didn't seem one bit jealous. I appreciate that."

"Your bag, Ms. Gucci," Lucille said as she carefully pulled the suitcase from the luggage hold.

Daisy covered her mouth with both hands when she saw Judith's bag. "Oh, my stars and garters! I should have known Another Gucci! That's the most beautiful suitcase I have *ever* seen!"

"You know, Daisy," Judith said as she smiled, "I believe you have a Gucci bag or two in your future. I wish you well."

———◆———

Judith took an Uber Black to a four-star Ambassador Hotel that Cara had booked for her. She had lunch at the hotel, caught up with Tiffany and Tony, then changed into workout clothes to go for a walk.

"The Oklahoma City Memorial and Museum is just fifteen minutes' walk from here," the clerk at the concierge desk told her. "If you can, try to be there around dusk. Sunset is at seven fifty tonight, but the light starts changing just before seven."

The walk to the memorial was pleasant, especially after multiple days of long rides in an uncomfortable coach.

Judith appreciated the fresh air, and she loved watching the way the clouds danced in the sky.

She did not know anyone who passed in the bombing, nor did she remember much of it being on the news. It happened but a month before her tenth birthday, after all, and a mere three months before the fateful night that took her parents.

Still, she felt compelled to visit, like she owed it to the victims to know what happened and to learn what she could from history.

Oklahoma City Memorial and Museum

Judith was not prepared for the impact the memorial would have on her.

First, she saw the reflection pool and the giant copper Gates of Time and then, the field of empty chairs where the Murrah Federal Building used to stand.

The chairs took the wind out of her sails.

There were 168 empty chairs of glass, bronze, and stone. One for each life lost.

She approached gingerly, pausing to look at her reflection in the water as if to mark a moment in time. Next, she walked to the Gates of Time.

On the eastern gate, the letters 9:01 were etched above the opening. It represented the last moment of peace. On the western gate, facing the pool, 9:03. The first moments of recovery. These two walls frame the moment of destruction, the moment the bomb exploded, and the structural collapse that followed. And on the outside of each gate, these words were carved:

We come here to remember.
Those who were killed, those who survived,
and those changed forever.
May all who leave here know the impact of violence.
May this memorial offer comfort, strength,
peace, hope, and serenity.

There were nine rows of chairs, one row for each floor of the building, with each person's name etched on a chair placed in the row, signifying where they took their final breath.

Among those were nineteen smaller chairs for the children who died in the blast.

Mommy! Daddy! Wake up!

The memory of her finding the lifeless bodies of her parents in their living room echoed the sadness of the rows and rows of chairs.

As much as she wanted to get away, to head back to the hotel, Judith shuffled through the rows of chairs, reading each name and age.

The emotions welling up inside of her were all muddled up. Her chest ached.

There was rage for the senselessness of the act.

Sadness for the losses.

Admiration for those who tried to help and lost their lives in the process.

Empathy for those left behind.

Judith walked back before dark, catching a glimpse of her changed self in the reflective pool on her way out.

If she were to stay until the lights came on under each of the chairs, she risked falling to pieces. She would not allow that to happen.

The words carved in the doors kept swimming around in her mind.

We come here to remember those who were killed, those who survived, and those changed forever . . .

———◆———

It was in the shower that she broke down and sobbed uncontrollably.

For the first time ever, she cried hard for the loss she faced as a child. In another first, Judith felt empathy toward herself for the pain she carried for the past twenty-four years.

She ordered room service. There was no way she could go find a hole-in-the-wall place to eat as Mimi wanted. Not with her eyes puffy from crying. Not while being as fragile as she was. Not that night.

She ate but a few bites of the seared salmon salad before placing the tray outside her door. She poured a cup of chamomile tea, put some drops of lavender oil in her diffuser, took a deep breath, and called Mimi.

Wednesday Night Call

"Judy honey, you called at the perfect time. I just washed my plate and put it in the drying rack. Tell me about your day."

Grace sounded a little tired.

Judith told her about the sights along their way, about the giant cross and of passing the town of Groom and wondering if the town was named after someone who was left at the altar.

She also told her grandmother about Daisy and her plan to go find herself a "more permanent" sugar daddy in Oklahoma City. "She really was a piece of work."

"Whoo-boy! That's a little gal headed for trouble. Sounds like she's gettin' above her raisin'. She didn't ask you for any money, did she?"

Laughing, Judith answered, "No, no. She wasn't that type, Mimi. But I'd say she possibly is the most overly confident person I've ever met. And I've met more than my share. Even so, I found her to be ever so entertaining."

"Well, you need to be careful out there," Grace warned Judith. "A pretty girl like you needs to be on guard so nobody takes advantage of your good nature. With a gal like that or a guy like that feller from yesterday, you never know . . ."

"Mimi," Judith said in an equally serious tone as that of her grandmother, "I've learned how to take good care of myself over the years. I appreciate your concern, but you don't need to worry about me. And Johnny? He isn't that type, either. Enough about that. Tell me about your day."

"It was just another day in paradise. Let me see . . . I fixed some oatmeal for breakfast. Read the newspaper and ran some laundry. Made me a bowl of tomater soup and a grilled cheese sandwich for lunch, then watched my shows. Lordy! My afternoons just wouldn't be the same without my shows."

For as far back as Judith could remember—even before she moved in with them—visits to her grandparents' home would be punctuated by Mimi watching *General Hospital* and *Days of Our Lives*.

"Rachel came by later to check on me and brought me some groceries and a big chicken dinner from the Cracker Barrel."

Grace did not easily break with tradition. Whenever she and Virgil had money to splurge, they would have dinner at the Cracker Barrel.

"Other than that, I've just been waiting for your call. You know this is my favorite part of my day now. Listening to your adventures. You do such a good job telling your stories, honey. Every night I go to bed and say my prayers for you. Then I fall asleep thinking about your stories. That makes for a real good day, Judy . . ."

"You know what, Mimi? This has become my favorite part of the day too. Making this trip by bus has been a stretch for me. I'm used to staying in my comfort zone and being in control. But I'm beginning to realize how much I've been limiting myself in the process."

106

Grace reminded Judith that this is something she has done since she was a little girl. "Judy, Virgil and I knew you were special. It broke our hearts that we weren't able to provide for you like you deserved. We were so poor, the ducks would throw bread at us. Only you would know how much trouble that caused for you in school. We always felt guilty for not being able to do better by you.

"But you showed 'em all," Grace added with pride. "Look at you now. Judy girl, be proud. You did what you had to do for yourself, and you did it all."

"Maybe, but you and Granddaddy were my constant during my life," Judith replied. "When everything else was spiraling, I always knew both of you would be there for me. And you were. Especially you."

After her earlier meltdown in the shower, Judith was afraid she might be overcome with emotion again. She took a deep breath in and exhaled slowly. "I had forgotten how much it meant to me to talk with you about things. Can you ever forgive me for how self-centered I've been?"

"Now, you stop with that foolishness," Grace responded lovingly. "Look at you. Ain't nobody from either side of our families that have done as well as you have. God gave you something special. If you'd done anything less, you'd disappointed Him."

"Have *you* been disappointed, though? That I'm not married and don't have children?"

"Honey, we both know that's never been something that's been at the top of what you had to have," Grace assured Judith. "I also know that you've never let the expectations other folks have of you make a difference. You've always marched to a different drummer. *That* is what makes you special."

Grace continued, "There's nothing wrong with a woman who doesn't need a man or children. Following your own heart to what brings you joy and happiness is what's most important."

"Mimi, you've always been able to put things into perspective for me like no one else." Judith cleared her throat to try and get rid of the emotion welling up. "What am I going to do without you?"

"Ha! You're going to do what you've always done. You're going to get back out there and kick life in the butt. You'll figure things out," Grace responded in her normal upbeat tone and energy. "You learned all I had to teach you long, long ago. There ain't nothing else left for me to teach you, sweetheart. Now, enough of this jibber-jabber. If you don't get some rest, you might not be able to tell me more good stories tomorrow night. Go to bed, sweet child. You know how much I love you."

"I love you too, Mimi. Good night."

Judith lay there for a while. For as far back as she could remember, Mimi's room smelled of lavender—not from some fancy essential oil, but from her favorite soap.

She pulled the plush duvet all the way to her chin, imagining a field full of lavender as far as the eye can see.

We'll figure things out, Mimi. We'll figure things out.

DAISY'S SONG

"You Got a Porch to Go with That Swing?"

Hey, hey baby I like the way you talk.
Hey, hey baby I like the way you walk.
I love how your hips are swinging.
But let me ask you first,
you got a porch to go with that swing?

All the boys in town are talkin',
about the way that you've been walkin'.
All the girls are dissaprovin',
about the way that you've been groovin'.
So, let me ask you now,
you got a porch to go with that swing?

Hey, hey baby I like the way you talk.
Hey, hey baby I like the way you walk.
I love how your hips are swinging.
But let me ask you first,
you got a porch to go with that swing?

All the boys think that you're just teasin',
but when you're with me you're pleasin'.
All the girls hate how you're a struttin'.
Their jealous eyes at you are cuttin'.
So, let me ask you now,
you got a porch to go with that swing?

Hey, hey baby I like the way you talk.
Hey, hey baby I like the way you walk.
I love how your hips are swinging.
But let me ask you first,
you got a porch to go with that swing?

But let me ask you first,
you got a porch to go with that swing?
You got a porch to go with that swing?
You got a porch to go with that swing?

CHAPTER 9

An Uphill Road

Janice and Bobbie Sue

Six adults—all stern-looking men—were sitting in the Freeman family's living room in Franklin. It was the fancy living room, the one reserved for visits from the pastor or other important friends.

The visitors were elders from Janice Freeman's church. It was a tightly-knit, independent church. In its inflexible world, everything was either totally right or totally wrong. In other words, it was their way or the highway. Her parents had called them to see if they could talk some sense into the twenty-two-year-old's head.

God knows, they tried. They all did. Janice's parents, her grandparents, her favorite cousin, her siblings. They all cornered her at one stage or another over the last year, trying to pour sand on a fire they knew would get out of hand before long.

Janice would hear none of their pleas, insisting that she loved Robert Wilkerson. It did not matter that he did not share her beliefs, or that he had no beliefs at all.

"Love is love," she insisted. "And once we're married," she defended her choice to each of the armies of well-meaning opposers to her and Robert's relationship, "he'll come around. He'll come to church with me, even if he doesn't want the wedding to be performed in a church. I know he'll come around . . . eventually."

By the time the elders were called in, Janice had dug in her heels deeper than a Texas oil rig. She loved Robert, she insisted. They were to get married the next month, come hell or high water. He was charming, successful. And he loved her.

"You won't be welcome back home," the lead elder announced.

Janice saw the pain on her mother's face when her father echoed those words. "Elder Earl is right. If you go ahead with the marriage, you are no longer a Freeman." He added a final blow, "You'll be dead to us."

The men must have thought the threat would shock Janice back into reality. It did the opposite. Sure, she cried when she hugged her family and walked to Robert's BMW, taking only a single suitcase full of things she thought irreplaceable. Things you would grab in a fire.

Robert would buy her everything she needed to start over.

They'll come around eventually, she believed.

They never did.

Her occasional phone call home was sent to voicemail. Emails never received a read receipt. Later, when she sent them photos of their new granddaughter, they were returned with REFUSED written on the face of the envelope—in red ink, no less.

God knows how many nights Janice cried herself to sleep, wishing things were different. When—courtesy of another woman—Robert deserted her for greener pastures—who knows where—she knew she could not go back home.

Her family would not accept her, and they would never accept Bobbie Sue.

For them, grace was something God—and God alone—could extend.

Janice found a job as a server at a local dive, working her smile and friendliness to try and make enough tips to make ends meet. A neighbor offered to watch Bobbie Sue after school, but Janice was stuck taking only daytime slots when the tips were smaller. Still, she had a job, and for that, she was thankful.

For a long time, Janice refused to set foot in a church, angry at God for the hand she was dealt, at her parents for disowning her, at the woman who stole Robert from her, at herself for thinking she knew better.

But in the end, it was a neighborhood church community that carried her through the darkest times, helping when times were tough. From their example, she learned what it meant to have compassion, to walk through challenging times with someone.

They asked no questions about her child's father. None about why her family could not help. They offered no judgment. Instead, they simply loved Janice and Bobbie Sue and stood with them in the ways Janice needed.

God knows life was hard, but the support the church offered was the lifeline that kept Janice from giving up.

They extended grace, helped her see the difference between religion and faith, the kind of faith that could endure a storm.

Janice still prayed for a better tomorrow, though all indications were that life would remain a never-ending struggle.

It was not fair to Bobbie Sue. But there was nothing Janice could do about it except work hard, then do the same the next day.

"God, help us," she'd plead night after night.

But Janice did not know if she believed God really would.

Six Years Later

"It started with her crying, wanting to be carried home after a walk to our favorite park," Janice found herself explaining to Dr. Barrett, a pediatrician at Mercy Hospital in Oklahoma City. "I haven't carried her since she was, what, three? Four?"

She looked down at her daughter. Bobbie Sue was tired and lay her head on her mother's lap. "Maybe it started before that. It could have been before that—come to think about it. She's been tired, falling asleep on the drive home from school, and struggling to get up in the morning. I figured it's a growth spurt."

The doctor listened, taking notes. "How about the nosebleeds? When did those start?"

"May 31st. On my birthday. We were sharing a donut when, out of the blue, her nose started bleeding. We were able to stop it after ten minutes or so. But you know it's hot in Oklahoma, nosebleeds are nothing uncommon in the summer."

"How often did the nosebleeds occur since then?"

"Sometimes once a week. Sometimes every other week."

"Did you ever have to take her to the ER to stop the bleeding?"

"No."

"You mentioned bruising."

"Yes. That started in the summer. Again, I figured it's just, you know, being a kid. In June, Bobbie Sue got a bicycle from friends at church. She was learning to ride without training wheels. Falling and bruising is part of the package."

Janice took a deep breath and lovingly stroked Bobbie Sue's curls, the child resting her head on her mother's lap. "I should have paid closer attention, but I *know* my child is safe. No one's hurting her. You can imagine the panic I was in when DHS showed up at the door asking questions. The moment the social worker left I took Bobbie Sue to the free clinic. They're the ones who referred me to you."

The doctor got up and prepared the examination table. "Hop on up, Bobbie Sue. Let's see what's going on."

He did a thorough examination, then suggested they run some labs.

"Doctor," Janice objected, "I would do anything to figure out what's wrong with Bobbie Sue, but . . ." She hesitated, searching for the best way to phrase it. "Right now, I can barely afford to put food on the table and pay rent. I don't know how I'd be able to afford tests."

The pediatrician slowly nodded his head as he looked up a number on his phone. "Here's the number for the Sisters of Mercy. Sister Frances will be able to get you set up with their benevolence fund. Once you're approved, the fund will cover the tests and treatment."

———◆———

Sister Frances called Janice a week later. "You're all set, Mrs. Wilkerson. You don't have to worry about a thing."

That same afternoon, Janice had Bobbie Sue back at the hospital so they could take whatever blood they needed to figure out what was wrong with her little one.

A few days after that, Janice got a phone call from Dr. Barrett's office, asking if she would be able to stop by their office at the end of the day.

"Of course." She could feel her heart thumping in her chest.

"If possible, please come alone."

This can't be good. God, help me.

———◆———

There was no small talk when Janice took a seat at Dr. Barrett's desk.

"Mrs. Wilkerson, we ran the full gamut of blood tests. We did a complete blood count to measure the number of red blood cells, white blood cells, and platelets. We did that to rule out any issues with Bobbie Sue's blood. Unfortunately, what we found only led us to dig deeper."

Janice had to remind herself to breathe while she listened to the pediatrician.

"We did a smear to look at how her blood cells look and noticed a very high number of white blood cells—much higher than the normal range."

"Does that mean she has an inflammation of sorts?" Janice enquired.

"I'm afraid the findings from the smear are highly suspicious for leukemia."

Janice's ears were buzzing. She watched the doctor's lips move, but she did not hear a word.

"So, to confirm," she finally heard, "we'll need to do some bone marrow tests and an MRI."

———◆———

Janice was amazed at Bobbie Sue's strength throughout all the tests. First, several more vials of blood were taken. Next, after administering a local anesthetic, the doctor inserted a hollow needle through the bone in Bobbie Sue's hip and into the bone marrow. Finally, he withdrew some of the liquid bone marrow.

Janice could see the grimace on her daughter's face as the big needle was pushed into the bone, yet the little one did not make a sound. Thankfully, the complete process was over in a matter of minutes.

"We're strong, Mommy," Bobbie Sue had assured her mother before the MRI.

Janice wished they did not have to be *this* strong.

———◆———

It was mid-morning on Monday when Janice saw a missed call from the hospital. She had been struggling to get her car started that morning, and Janice was on the verge of tears even before she called back.

She had not even been able to get Bobbie Sue to school yet.

Can you give us a break? she pleaded with God, hoping Dr. Barrett would tell her his earlier concerns were unfounded.

"I wish I had better news," the pediatrician told her.

Janice sat in her car, bracing for what was to come.

"Bobbie Sue has acute lymphoblastic leukemia," she heard the doctor say. "The best course of treatment would be chemotherapy."

Janice's heart was pounding. Bobbie Sue looked at her with questioning eyes.

"We can do the treatment here," Dr. Barrett continued, "but it would be better for us to send you to St. Jude in Memphis."

"When?"

"How quickly can you pack up your life here in Oklahoma City?" Dr. Barrett asked.

Janice's mind was racing as she thought through everything. "Four days. We could be ready by Thursday."

Once the doctor hung up, Janice lay her head on the wheel and sobbed while Bobbie Sue lovingly patted her mother's knee. "We'll be okay, Mommy."

But Janice knew better. She had known hard days in her life. What was to come would be worse by a country mile.

CHAPTER 10

God Knows

Janice, Bobbie Sue, and Judith | Oklahoma City, OK to Memphis, TN

Judith's eyes were still puffy from crying, and a low-grade headache reminded her of the unusual experience the night before. Crying was not in her nature.

She was still in her fancy workout clothes when she headed to the hotel dining room. The stretch to Memphis was a long one, and she wanted to get some good protein in as most places the bus stopped often did not have much more than a simple meal and high-carb snacks.

She could smell the bacon as she got off the elevator on the seventh floor and could hear the muffled sound of conversation and heavy cutlery on plates.

The *maître d'* took her to a table with a view of the city. Judith glanced toward the memorial, took a sip of her coffee, and while waiting for her server, jotted a few thoughts in her notebook—things she wanted to unpack more with Dr. Sanders.

How I felt when I saw the sea of chairs.

That sign carved into the gates.
How have I been changed by my parents' death? By Granddaddy's?
When Mimi dies, who will know or love me?

By the time her cheese omelet arrived, Judith had finished her yogurt. She had added to her list several insights from her conversations with Daisy, Johnny, Gary, and Sara.

Judith was glad that she had only two days left on the bus, but she was grateful for the people she had met along the way.

———◆———

"Were you here during the bombing?" Judith asked her Uber driver, Rhonda, on their ride to the bus terminal. The air was heavy with humidity despite the early hour.

Rhonda told Judith of her niece who worked in the building and survived but whose little one in daycare did not make it. "It's always the hardest on those left behind, isn't it?" she asked.

"I am sorry for your loss," Judith responded, and they sat in silence for the remainder of the trip.

Judith had picked up a magnet in the shape of a chair from the hotel gift shop on her way out. The chair was inscribed with the word REMEMBER. Judith finally tucked the magnet into her tote as they rounded the corner to the bus terminal. The sunlight reflected off the Oklahoma River.

"It's gonna be a hot one," Rhonda stated the obvious as she helped Judith unload her bag. "I hope you'll come back to see more of our city someday."

———◆———

"Welcome to Scenic City Bus Line. Heading to Memphis?" the driver wanted to know.

"Sure am."

He introduced himself as Adam. "We don't have a full bus today, so help yourself to whichever seat you fancy. I see you've been traveling with us for a few days," he said as he inspected her ticket. "Today's stretch is longer, so we'll push past our typical two-hour stop. First stop will be on the other side of the Oklahoma-Arkansas border."

Judith did not mind that the distance covered would be double than it had been on previous days.

The quicker I can get to Nashville, the better.

She was also relieved that he was the first driver not to comment on her luggage or ask her if it were her first trip by bus.

The air on the bus was much more comfortable than that outside.

The first open row was about halfway to the back of the bus. Judith placed her tote in the window seat, placed the bottle of Perrier in the drink holder, and sat back, closing her eyes for a moment to take in the sounds around her.

The giggling of a little girl made her open her eyes. The little one of about six was making a beeline down the aisle toward Judith, her bright red sneakers as jolly as her personality. She was limping a little.

While adults often felt intimidated by Judith, kids were rarely put off by her strong demeanor. Judith hoped the girl and her mom would sit across the aisle.

"You're pretty!" the little one exclaimed as she came to a stop, looking Judith in the eyes. "I like your clothes." Except, with her two front teeth missing, it sounded like she said *cloves*. She stretched out her words like saltwater taffy.

She put one leg in front of the other. "Look! I got new shoes."

"And *you* are even prettier than those shoes," Judith responded with a smile.

The girl smiled from ear to ear, showing off her missing front teeth. "I am six years old. My name is Bobbie Sue. What's yours?"

"I'm Judith."

Bobbie Sue's mom caught up. She was maneuvering multiple small bags down the aisle.

"I'm sorry, ma'am." The mom looked tired, like her clothes. Clean but worn. "She can be a handful," she said.

"Not at all." Judith gestured to the seats across the aisle from her. "Why don't you sit next to me?"

"Are you sure?"

"Absolutely. And please call me Judith."

"Thank you, ma'am . . . I mean, Judith. I'm Janice."

"Miss Judif," Bobbie Sue giggled with delight as she and her mom settled into their seats.

Janice took out a disinfectant wipe from a bag in her purse to wipe the dot of jelly from her daughter's threadbare shirt. She turned back to Judith while Bobbie Sue looked expectantly out the window as the door closed and they slowly started moving.

Oklahoma City, OK to Fort Smith, AR

"It's been a long morning, doesn't feel like it's only seven o'clock."

From the look of things, Judith suspected that the duo has had a few long years behind them. "What a little angel you have," she remarked.

"She's my world . . ." Janice responded politely. There was a look of pain in her eyes that had not been there earlier.

Did I say something wrong?

"I'm headed to Nashville. How about you two?"

"We're going to Memphis, Tennessee," Bobbie Sue said as she poked her head out from the other side of her mom.

"Are you going to visit Grandma and Grandpa?"

The girl looked up at her mommy, not sure how to respond.

"Actually," Janice replied, "we're headed to St. Jude Children's Hospital." She handed her daughter a book from one of the bags.

"Oh . . . I'm so sorry," Judith said softly.

Janice lovingly placed her hand on her daughter's head, stroking her hair. "She has acute lymphoblastic leukemia, or ALL," she explained. "We just found out on Monday, but our doctor in Oklahoma City said that we've caught it at an early stage, and with the miracle-working doctors at St. Jude, her prognosis is good."

"I'm glad you caught it early," Judith said, unsure of what the best response in a situation like this would be.

"So am I." Since her daughter's diagnosis a short four days ago, Janice had discovered the value of talking about it with others, so she continued, "Did you know that at St. Jude we won't have to pay a dime for her treatment? They even provide us with food and lodging during her stay."

"I didn't. I mean, I've seen their TV ads, but I've never really paid attention. That is incredible."

Bobbie Sue looked up from her book, leaned over, and without a glimmer of fear said, "I got *coolemia*. Mommy says that maybe after we've been at St. Jude for a while that my hair may fall out."

Looking at her mom and then back at Judith, she giggled. "She said I'll be the prettiest bald-headed little girl in all of Tennessee. She said they would have *sooooo* many hats for me to choose from to wear. I think I'll be looking for a red one. Red's our favorite color, right Mommy?"

Trying to be strong for the little one, Janice smiled at her daughter.

"Oh, Bobbie Sue," Judith said, swallowing to clear the lump in her throat. "I can just picture you in a beautiful red hat. And it will match your shoes. Your mommy is right. You *will* be the prettiest little girl in Tennessee."

"Thank you, Judith," Janice said quietly. "You are too kind."

"I just can't imagine. Will you have any family coming to be with you?"

Janice took a deep breath, "It's a long story, but the short answer is no. It's just Bobbie Sue and me. All we've got is each other."

It grew quiet between them.

———◆———

For a while, Judith just listened to the deep hum of the diesel engine and the muffled sound escaping from a fellow traveler's headphones.

They passed by the town of Okemah, Oklahoma, and the driver, Adam, enlightened the passengers with a story about the town's most famous former resident. "This man has been acknowledged to have influenced the work of Bob Dylan, Johnny Cash, Bruce Springsteen . . . Anyone know who he is?"

Silence.

"Frank Sinatra?" a young voice from a few rows behind Judith shouted.

"Nice try, but no go," he laughed, seemingly happy that *someone* played along. "This was the home to singer-songwriter Woody Guthrie. Even if you don't know his name, I'll bet you know his most famous song. Feel free to sing along."

"Maybe they should change the company name to the Karaoke Bus Line," Judith muttered.

Adam turned on "This Land Is Your Land," and Janice and Bobbie Sue sang along, as did many of the other passengers.

The scenery outside made even Judith proud of what a beautiful land she lived in.

When they crossed a tributary of Lake Eufaula, a notification popped up on her phone.

> ### Did you know?
> Lake Eufaula is the largest lake in Oklahoma.
>
> From rock climbing to rappelling to skydiving, the area is heaven for folks who love the outdoors.
>
> Oklahoma has eight state parks, including the Little Sahara State Park with 1,600 acres of sand dunes.

Judith pulled up a map on her smartphone and was amazed at how this was the polar opposite of her world back in Los Angeles. There were huge stretches between towns, and the names of towns and villages were ones she would have to tell Mimi about. Sour John, Notchietown, and Greasy were just a few of the names she made a mental note of.

She put away her phone again so she could pay attention to the world around her.

It's what Mimi would want, she reminded herself.

Judith did not mean to eavesdrop but could not miss the one-sided whispers of a young man on his phone, perhaps two rows behind her— *the guy who shouted "Frank Sinatra!" maybe?*—explaining to his parents how he was going to become famous in Nashville.

It sounded like it was a conversation they had had many a time. He knew someone who could get him in at the Listening Room Café, he said.

While Judith had a solid belief in hard work, she had also experienced first-hand the benefits of someone opening a door for her that led to her establishing her own business. It was also why she constantly kept an eye out for promising staff who were not afraid to work hard and give them extra responsibilities or opportunities.

———◆———

The wailing of a siren approaching interrupted Judith's thoughts. The bus pulled over briefly for an ambulance to pass.

"When I'm big," Bobbie Sue leaned over to tell Judith, "I'm going to be a doctor."

"You are?"

Judith glanced at Janice who shrugged and said, "Doctors. She's become all too familiar with them recently . . . They've been a godsend."

Janice helped Bobbie Sue to lean her chair back and covered her in a blanket from one of their bags. In a flash, the little one was asleep.

"It's been hard on her, but she's been such a trooper."

"It would seem to me you've *both* been troopers."

"She's the strong one, really. I'm here to support her. I wish things were different, that my family would help out, but they don't even know she's sick. They've never met her and unless God does some miracle in their hearts, they don't want to, either. So, it's just us . . ."

"I am sorry . . . I can't imagine how hard that must be." Janice simply raised her eyebrows and nodded slightly. "Do you work from home so you can take care of her?"

"I wish. I've tried getting into the virtual assistant space—especially to help folks with research—but it's hard to have consistent clients if you're not connected to a university. I've been mostly waiting tables since her dad left. But a job like that doesn't come with benefits, so I have no FMLA or long-term disability."

"My boss is nice, though," she continued. "He said I can come back to my job when we're back from Memphis, but since I don't know how long the treatment will take, I gave up our apartment and put the little we have in storage this week. At least that's cheaper than paying rent, right?"

"I'd imagine it is."

"I'll be looking at jobs in Memphis or even Nashville while we're out there. After Bobbie Sue's treatment, it would be easier if we lived closer to a hospital for a while—whether St. Jude or even Vanderbilt Medical Center."

"Do you have an online résumé?" Judith wanted to know. "Just in case I hear of something while I'm at my grandma's place."

"That's so kind of you. I do have one. I've been looking for extra jobs to help make ends meet."

"So, you're going to visit your grandma?" Janice enquired after she gave Judith her contact information. "Is Nashville home for you?"

"Yes on both accounts," Judith said kindly. "I grew up with my grandparents in Nashville. My grandma was just recently diagnosed with leukemia, but in her case it's terminal, so I'm heading there to spend some time with her and meet with her doctor to see what we can do to help Mimi."

For the next hour, as the interstate crossed through farmland and patches of woodland in the distance, Janice and Judith spoke about leukemia and how it is impacting them and their loved ones.

"Mimi thought the aches and pains and the bruises were just part of growing old," she told Janice. "But then she started losing weight, getting short of breath, and having recurring nosebleeds. She finally got so uncomfortable with the bone pain that she went to see her doctor."

Judith grew quiet. "It was just days ago when she called me to tell me she had acute leukemia. I thought we'd have time to fight it, but her doctor told her it was terminal. I'm determined to find a way to help her, though. There's *got* to be something more we can do."

Janice was silent for a while. "If cures for leukemia are ever found," she finally said, "they'll probably come out of St. Jude."

Janice told Judith about the research St. Jude was conducting and their success rates. "Of all the children who come to St. Jude to be treated for ALL, they have a 94 percent survival rate. It was only 4 percent when they first opened."

"Seriously? Now *that's* encouraging," Judith said. "I'll be praying for Bobbie Sue to be among that 94 percent."

"Thank you. We're blessed to have caught it this early."

"How did you catch it, if you don't mind me asking," Judith enquired.

"It started a few months ago with nosebleeds, then she started bruising for no reason at all, similar to your grandma, it sounds. The slightest bump would cause terrible bruising. I didn't think too much of it, until her preschool called DHS to investigate. Talk about a fiasco." Janice shook her head. "Hurting her is the *last* thing I would do."

Judith was silent, realizing how far removed she had become from the day-to-day struggles families face.

"After the unannounced visit by a social worker, I realized how lethargic Bobbie Sue had become. This little Energizer bunny of mine couldn't muster up the strength to play. So, I took Bobbie Sue to the local free clinic, and they referred me to a pediatrician at one of the hospitals. He ran tests and, well, here we are, heading to Memphis for treatment."

She showed Judith the spiral notebook where she had begun tracking every aspect of Bobbie Sue's condition, every statistic from her temperature to her blood oxygen level, every detail about suggested treatments.

"I feel like I've had a crash course in pediatric leukemia. I'm becoming quite the expert, though I wish it weren't necessary."

What Judith saw at that moment was a mother who did her darndest to help her child, someone who was meticulous at what she did.

———◆———

With Janice turning her attention to Bobbie Sue, Judith turned back to her phone to read up on St. Jude Children's Research Hospital.

The actor Danny Thomas had vowed he would build a shrine to St. Jude should he ever become successful. That shrine was the children's hospital. He opened the doors to the original star-shaped facility in 1962.

Today, the hospital treats almost nine thousand patients every year. Their goal is to improve the survival rate of children with cancer and other catastrophic diseases.

Judith's mouth hung open when she read that despite three million dollars per day operating cost, patients and their families never receive a bill from St. Jude for anything.

That rhymes with what Janice told me earlier, but how the heck do they cover the costs?

She continued paging through the hospital's website, learning that the hospital and research center relied on generous donors, grants, and insurance, when available, to cover the cost of treatment. But 80 percent of the funds came from public donations—a dollar here, ten dollars there, and a bunch of nineteen dollars-a-month donations.

Judith knew that her time in Memphis was short, but she decided she wanted to see the place for herself someday soon.

———◆———

They took an exit off the I-40 shortly before crossing the border into Arkansas, "the Natural State," as the welcome sign pointed out. Never having driven through this part of the country, Judith had been pleasantly surprised by the beauty of Oklahoma.

If Arkansas is even more beautiful, I may want to pay a visit someday.

As they drove into the town of Fort Smith, Bobbie Sue tugged at her mother's sleeve and pointed at an eye-catching mural of a Native American girl aiming to shoot an arrow. "So cool, right Mommy?"

"It is beautiful, honey," Janice agreed.

Through his rear-view mirror, Adam noticed Bobbie Sue being enthralled by the large-scale art. "For the art lovers on board, Fort Smith has worked hard at sprucing up their town over the past several years. Every year, they commission more artwork. You'll notice several of the pieces as we pass through. For now, though, we'll be making a twenty-minute stop to drop off some passengers and pick up a few new ones."

The bus pulled in at the Fort Smith National Historic Site. "Twenty minutes, folks!" the driver reminded them.

"Are we there yet, Mommy? Is this St. Jude?"

"Not yet, sweetie. We're stopping here to pick up some other passengers."

———◆———

There was an ice-cream stand close to where the bus had parked, and Judith overheard Bobbie Sue asking her mom if they could get some ice creams.

"I was just thinking the same thing," Judith said. "Would it be okay if I got us each a small cone?" she asked Janice. "I think we'll need to finish them before we'd be allowed back on the bus, though."

"I think we could handle that challenge, right Bobbie Sue?" Janice responded.

The six-year-old giggled with delight when she was handed a small cone with strawberry ice cream.

Judith also got them some bottled water. "So, you want to be a doctor someday?" she asked, picking up the earlier conversation with Bobbie Sue.

"Yep. Or a paramedic—that's a *big* word. I want to help other kids to get better like my doctors are going to help me," she said as she took the last bite of the cone. "That was yummy," Bobbie Sue declared.

Before Janice could reach for a wipe, Bobbie Sue wiped her sticky hands on her shirt. "Thank you, Miss Judif."

They walked to wash up before getting back on the bus for the next stretch. As Bobbie Sue pulled up her sleeves so they would not get wet, Judith noticed the small brown-purple spots of petechiae on the little one's arms—a sign of a blood-clotting disorder or minor trauma.

Mimi hadn't mentioned this being an issue for her. But then again, she probably wouldn't say anything about it, anyway.

Judith braced herself for what she might find the next afternoon when she would be home.

Fort Smith, AR to Little Rock, AR

On their way back to the I-40, Adam made sure to pass by some more murals. Bobbie Sue liked the bright red ones the best. "Look, Mommy!" she called out in delight. "Our favorite color."

The state motto seemed to be true, even just judging by the little they could see along the interstate. North and south of the highway were signs for national forests.

"Have you ever been to Branson or Lake of the Ozarks, Judith?" Janice wanted to know.

"I'm afraid I haven't. We didn't get to travel when I was a child, and as an adult, I've been busier than I'd like to admit. But this trip has made me want to see more of our country. Why do you ask?"

"We used to go there for family vacations. Branson had the best concerts, and the lake is *incredible*. Big Cedar Lodge is heaven for folks who love fishing. You don't strike me as the fishing type, though . . ."

"How could you tell?" Judith laughed.

Janice smiled back, her confidence coming back as the miles wore on. "It's a great place to go and relax. I haven't been there in years, but I don't imagine it's changed much." She reminisced about the concerts they used to attend in Branson every year.

I wonder which is more challenging: Growing up poor and then making money, or coming from money but then losing everything, Judith wondered.

Judith's heart ached for Bobbie Sue and the bullying she might face at school—or may have already faced. She became even more determined to keep an eye out for a potential job in Memphis or Nashville for Janice. It was evident that Janice was not afraid to work hard and had excellent social skills.

A notification popped up when the bus approached Little Rock.

> **Did you know?**
> Little Rock is the state capital of Arkansas and home to the Clinton Presidential Library.
>
> Little Rock got its name from a small rock formation on the south bank of the Arkansas River. This rock used to be a landmark for river traffic.

"We'll be making a stop at the Cracker Barrel to drop off and pick up guests," Adam announced. "Forty-five minutes should be sufficient to get some lunch. Please be back on the bus before two fifteen. Thanks, folks."

Judith asked Janice if they would join her for lunch at the Cracker Barrel. It'd be her treat. "Cracker Barrel was my grandparents' favorite place to eat. My grandma swears by their chicken dinner."

"Can we, Mommy? Pleeeeease?" Bobbie Sue begged.

Janice looked a little embarrassed. "I packed lunch . . ."

"I'd *love* for you to join me," Judith insisted. "It's not like I have any other company, and I enjoy yours."

Janice relented.

"I hear their pancakes are pretty good," Judith said and winked at Bobbie Sue.

Cracker Barrel

"I've been reading up on Little Rock," Janice told Judith while Bobbie Sue was dousing her confetti pancakes in syrup. "It's just two hours from Memphis, so it's a feasible option for me to find a job here too. Looks like the University of Arkansas might have some admin positions available."

"Are you interested in working at a university?"

"For sure," Janice replied. "If I can find a suitable position, a university seems like a solid option. They are usually stable employers, and they offer benefits. Some even offer significant scholarships to the children of faculty and staff." She took a bite of her Southern fried chicken. "Oh my gosh, this is *so* good! I haven't eaten at a Cracker Barrel in ages. Thanks again for the invitation."

"Mommy, I *like* Clackabarrow," Bobbie Sue added, then turned her attention back to her pancakes and the picture she was coloring.

"With this little one's career goals," Janice continued, "I'd better be sure I can send her to college. Of course, she's still very young. Who knows if she'll still want to go to medical school when she finishes high school? To be honest, it's *my* dream for her to do exactly that—get a proper education, I mean, no matter what field she decides on eventually."

Janice shrugged as she continued, "I know we shouldn't project our unrealized dreams onto our children, but I think wishing for your child to have a good education may be forgiven."

Judith nodded in agreement, "Have you ever looked into Vanderbilt in Nashville?"

"The hospital?"

"No, I mean the university."

"No, but I can add it to my list. Their med school is highly regarded, isn't it?"

"It sure is. It may not be a bad idea to check whether the university may have positions available."

Little Rock, AR to Memphis, TN

They crossed the Mississippi River to enter Tennessee.

> **Did you know?** *her phone pestered her.*
> Tennessee shares a border with eight states, as does bordering Missouri.
>
> Tennessee's nickname is the Volunteer State, thanks to thirty thousand volunteers from this state signing up to fight in the Mexican-American War in 1846. (President Polk was hoping for less than a tenth of that nationwide.) It is believed that this response was a result of the death of Davy Crockett, who represented Tennessee in the House of Representatives.

Though Judith found the tidbits interesting, she was in her home state. The app probably would not teach her anything she did not already know. So, she deleted it from her phone.

———◆———

It was not yet four o'clock, and the city traffic was nothing compared to what Judith was used to in L.A.

"Let's see who can guess the answer to our second musical trivia question of the day," driver Adam announced.

"Elvis Presley!" an enthusiastic older lady yelled out before the question was even asked.

"Well, it seems like we got ourselves an Elvis fan, ladies and gentlemen." He took a slight detour en route to the Greyhound Station to pass by Graceland.

"Graceland has its own airstrip, in case any of y'all ever wants to fly in for a visit," he joked, and put on Elvis' famous song, "Hound Dog."

"This song alone sold four million copies in the US," Adam told his passengers.

Mimi would love it if I could visit, Judith thought. But she was determined to spend some time at St. Jude instead.

"Will you be heading straight to the hospital, or are you going to the guesthouse first?" Judith asked Janice as they wound their way to the bus terminal near the airport.

"They're expecting us at the hospital. Bobbie Sue will receive her first infusion as soon as we can get to St. Jude."

"If you don't mind me asking, how are you planning to get from the bus station to the hospital?"

Janice was busy collecting all the stuff a parent of a young patient must juggle when traveling, "I think we'll take a taxi; I'll have to check what's available when we get to the station."

"Would you mind if I went with you? My hotel's close to the hospital. You can hop into the Uber I'll take. And I'd be happy to help you with your luggage," Judith offered. "Plus, it may not be a bad idea to have someone by your side for this first step. That is, if you want me to. I don't want to intrude."

Janice's eyes welled up. "I would very much like that. Thank you, Judith."

St. Jude Children's Research Hospital

Once they had Bobbie Sue checked in for her first treatment, Judith said her goodbyes. "Is there anything I can do to help?"

"Just please keep us in your prayers, Judith," she said. "God has never failed us, and He's not about to now. We'll be fine, I'm sure. But another person praying for us can't hurt." She hesitated a bit before adding, "If you do stumble upon a job in the area, though, please don't hesitate to let me know. I'll send you my résumé, like I promised."

Judith hugged Janice. "I haven't been praying that much, but I'm getting back into the swing of it," she confessed. "You can count on me praying for you and Bobbie Sue, though."

She took Bobbie Sue's hand in hers. The little one was looking tired, but she still smiled.

"Thank you for picking the seat next to mine today, Bobbie Sue," she said. "You have no idea what a gift that's been to me."

Bobbie Sue let go of Judith's hand and put both arms in the air for a hug. She hugged Judith tighter than she had been hugged in years. Then Bobbie Sue planted a big kiss on Judith's cheek. "Thanks for coming with us, Miss Judif."

"I wouldn't have it any other way," Judith assured her, stopping short of promising to see her again. Once she got to Nashville, her focus would be on Mimi, so regardless of Judith's best intentions, she would not make a promise she did not know she could keep. Especially to a child.

She stopped by the gift shop and bought a fridge magnet of an angel for Grace.

———◆———

It was dark by the time Judith checked in at the Sheraton. She needed to clear her mind, so she headed straight to the gym to work out. But the exercise bike's wheel was not the only thing spinning. Judith's mind was busy. She kept thinking of the images she saw along the walls at St. Jude—former child patients who were now healthy, thriving adults.

She thought of Bobbie Sue and the path ahead of her, recalling some of what Janice had told her.

She also thought of the conversations with other passengers, the constant anger she experienced beneath the surface.

"What is it that you're angry about, Judith?" Dr. Sanders had asked on one of their first visits.

"It makes me angry when people don't catch on and I have to stop and help them catch up. It's so inefficient. Why can't they just pick it up the first time?"

"Is life always about efficiency?"

Silence.

"Tell me about a time when you felt loved."

It did not take much thinking. "I *always* feel loved when it comes to Mimi. She sees me. She sees who I really am . . . always has. I remember a time in high school when I brought home a stray dog. Granddaddy wasn't too impressed, but Mimi? She looked at me with tenderness. She saw my kindness."

"Do *you* see your kindness?"

———◆———

135

Judith grabbed a bite to eat in the concierge lounge—the lobster bisque and a glass of an oaky, buttery chardonnay—then headed to her room. After a shower, she poured a glass of Perrier and turned her focus to her email.

Getting a lot done in a short amount of time was one of Judith's superpowers, and this day was no different. When she focused, everything else faded out of sight.

Judith called both Tiffany and Tony to get an update on the current project and to encourage them. "It means the world to me not to have any concerns while I'm gone," she assured each of them.

Next, she called Cara. After synching on action items from messages the day before, she asked Cara to gather information on donating toward the work St. Jude Children's Research Hospital was doing.

"Just *one* more day left on the bus," Cara said jokingly. "I'll bet you're ready for this to be over."

"I am, but the past five days have been better than I expected. I've met amazing individuals and learned a lot from them—to my great surprise, I may add."

Cara was not used to her boss sharing anything personal. She did not know how to respond, so she simply told her that the details around the limo transport for the trip from the Nashville bus station to her grandmother's home would be sent to Judith's phone.

Judith poured a cup of chamomile tea, added a few drops of lavender oil to her travel diffuser, took a few deep breaths, and called Grace.

Thursday Night Call

Grace was staring at the photos on her fridge, happy moments were frozen in time, held up by random magnets people had given them over the years.

There was a photo from the fourth of July parade in downtown Nashville, Virgil and Judith beaming with joy. And there was one of her and Virgil at the same event, surrounded by flags and a crowd of smiley faces. Of the three of them at the Tennessee State Fair. Of Judith in high school at her first STEM event where her love of programming was ignited. There was a banner at the bottom of the photo: Nashville Science, Technology, Engineering, and Math 2002.

"Oh, Judy," she said to the girl in the photo, "how I've missed you, child. Just knowing I still have you out there in California has been the only thing that has kept me going."

She kissed the tip of her fingers and gently placed them on Judith's photo. When the phone rang, it startled her back into the present. There was only one person who called this time at night. Grace made her way to the living room.

"Howdy-doo, Judy girl," she answered a little out of breath from hurrying.

Judith laughed at Grace's greeting. "And a hearty howdy-doo to you, Mimi. It's good to hear a smile in your voice tonight."

Grace sat up even straighter. "Just one more day till I see that beautiful face of yours. I have every reason to be smiling."

"Indeed. Just one more day, Mimi. Before I tell you about today's adventure, tell me about your labs."

"Let's see what Rachel wrote down . . ." Judith could hear the rustling of paper. She could envision her grandma adjusting her wire-rimmed glasses. "Well, my O_2 was fine. But my hemoglobin was down to 6.9, which they didn't like, so they gave me two units of blood and a bag of platelets."

Judith interrupted. "Blood *and* platelets, Mimi? That's not good news. How are you feeling?"

"About the same as I did all day. Usually, it's the next day when I feel a little boost from the infusions. Tomorrow will be a good day. How could it not be? Tomorrow, I'll be huggin' and kissin' my Judy!"

"You have no idea how much I'm looking forward to that, Mimi."

"I've been telling the doctor and the nurses all about you coming to visit," Grace assured Judith. "They're all excited for me. They said now I'm all tanked up until I go back on Monday. We've got the whole weekend not to worry about appointments. Enough about me, though. Tell me about your day."

"Today, Mimi, I met one of the most inspirational women I believe I've ever met," she said as she began telling Grace the story of Janice and Bobbie Sue.

Grace interjected, "From what I've heard about St. Jude, there're a lot of angels there disguised as doctors, nurses, and a heap of other folks taking care of them young'uns and their mamas and daddies, givin' them love and hope." Pausing, she added, "Love and hope. There's not enough of that in this world. Over the years I've learned more about St. Jude Children's Research Hospital than you would ever guess. If there's ever a cure for leukemia in this world, mark my words, it'll come from angels there at St. Jude."

"That's what Janice also said," Judith responded. "By the way, we had lunch at the Cracker Barrel. I had—"

"Fried chicken!" Grace said at the same time as Judith. The two laughed.

"I sure did. I know it has long been your favorite, and you said I should eat the kind of things you'd like."

"Well, you know it takes me two days to finish one serving, so I have still some in my Frigidaire," Grace told her.

"If that fridge of yours could tell stories . . . How long have you had it?"

"Let's see. We bought it about four or five years after you moved in with us," Grace said. "That would make it—"

"Twenty years? Good grief, Mimi."

"Isn't it wonderful how sturdy they used to make appliances, honey?"

"I guess you're right. I still can't believe you wouldn't let me buy you a new fridge." Judith shook her head at her grandma's obstinance. "Well, Mimi, you'd better finish that chicken tomorrow morning. There's no eating leftovers while I'm home. I'm going to take you to all the best restaurants you've ever wanted to try."

"Or *never* wanted to eat at," Grace quipped. "You know the best meal for me is a meal shared with you, honey. It don't matter if it's just a plate of boiled potatoes, if you're here, it's a good day and a meal fit for a queen."

Judith shook her head at her grandmother's optimism. "You know, Mimi, I had a lot of time today to think . . . I'm beginning to realize that what I think are my worst days would be many other people's exceptionally good days," she told her grandmother. "Have I become so self-involved?"

"Now, don't you go believin' somethin' about yourself that ain't true. You are kind, Judith Lee. Sometimes it just takes cleanin' one's glasses to see the truth for what it is. You got a lot of people dependin' on you for their livin'. Them jobs you give them help feed their families. That's a lot of responsibility." There was no stopping Grace tonight. "But you're not only responsible. You care. You may have a strong back, child, but you also have a soft heart . . ."

Tell me about a time you felt loved, Judith remembered Dr. Sanders's question again.

"Mimi, I cannot wait to hug your neck tomorrow. Just *one* more night."

"Don't get ahead of yourself now, honey. You still have one last day on the bus, one more person to tell me about."

"Sure do. Now, let me guess what you will be doing after we hang up the phone . . ." Judith teased.

"I know! I know! I'll be snug as a bug in a rug and lights out just as soon as Jimmy Fallon goes off."

"You are incorrigible, Mimi."

"I ain't got no idea what that word means," Grace said while wiping tears of laughter from her eyes, "but if you say that's what I am, then I guess it's true. Good night, Judy girl. Be sure to say your prayers and get some rest."

"I will. Good night, Mimi," Judith replied tenderly. "I love you."

"I love you too, honey."

———◆———

"God, please heal Bobbie Sue," Judith said softly as she looked out the window of her hotel room, a suite on the top floor of the Sheraton. Above and beyond the highway, shining brightly against the night sky were the illuminated words: St. Jude Children's Research Hospital.

"There's not enough love and hope in this world," Grace had mused earlier.

It was raining softly, and the streets below reflected the city lights. A red-brick cathedral across the street caught Judith's eye.

It seemed sturdy and resolute in a sea of turmoil. The soft rain lent an air of magic to the world far below. She felt the tension of the day leave her shoulders, and her body relax.

"God, would you show me what it is you want me to do to help Bobbie Sue and Janice . . . and how I can help St. Jude so they can find a cure for leukemia?"

When she had left the hospital earlier, she had an overwhelming sense of hope for Bobbie Sue, remembering the numbers Janice had cited earlier that day—a 94 percent survival rate for pediatric patients with ALL.

"Oh, may that please be true for Bobbie Sue," she prayed.

Judith stood ready to draw the curtains and head to bed. "There is love and hope out there, Mimi," she said quietly. "And there is faith."

As she crawled into the plush bed, the smell of lavender filling the air, one final thought came to mind before Judith fell asleep.

How is it that that child picked me as her neighbor today?

JANICE'S SONG

"She Remembers When He Loved Her"

She sits in silence as she watches all the people walking by,
and they're all so very careful, not to look her in the eye.
Her worn-out clothes are clean 'cause she still has got some pride.
Another day, and still no job, but God knows, she has tried.

And then she remembers when he loved her before he went away.
A marriage broken, like her heart, she lives from day to day.
It angers her that she would still feel this way and she puts it from her mind,
but when she least expects it, she remembers when he loved her.

So, home she walks so slowly and to her daughter waiting there.
The disappointment showing 'cause she knows that life is just not fair.
Why should her child suffer, just 'cause Daddy left his wife?
It's not the way she pictured spending this part of her life.

"Don't worry now, we'll be alright," says little Bobbie Sue.
"Jesus, in the Bible, says he'll take care of me and you."
She smiles and hugs her little girl and tells her that she's right.
They eat a bite, read from the Book, and say their prayers that night.

A new day brings new hope for the job that she might find,
but the worry from the mounting bills weighs heavy on her mind.
She finally gets a job waiting tables in a dive.
The pay's not good, the hours are long, but at least they will survive.

Enough time has passed that at long last, she's given up her dream.
Now she knows he won't return and make it all okay.
So, with new determination, she approaches each new day.
Still, she remembers when he loved her . . . before he went away.

CHAPTER 11

New Year's in Vietnam

Albert

The squad enjoyed being back at their base for a change. It was Tet, the Vietnamese Lunar New Year. January 30, 1968. Staff Sergeant Jackson—or Big Al, as he was known to his men—played poker with two of his squad. Life was good. After all, they would be sleeping on mattresses that evening.

But in 'Nam, good times never lasted, especially if you served in the 1/9 Marines. The 1st Battalion, 9th Marines, 3rd Division ended up in harm's way so often that members had a one-in-four chance of going home in a metal box.

They woke up after midnight to the sound of deep booming explosions that came rolling in from the direction of the coastal city of Da Nang. Big Al sighed, "Guys, that doesn't sound good. Back to sleep. We're going to need all the rest we can get till we get called."

The distant explosions continued unabated.

Before sunrise, Alpha Company got the call. "So," battalion commander Colonel Mackey—call sign Geezer—informed them, "With a bunch of our allies being on leave for Tet, the Viet Cong and the North Vietnamese Army have decided that this was the perfect time to invade all forty-four provinces."

A mutual groan rose from those assembled. "You'll be flying to Da Nang to join Bravo Company. Good luck. You've got this!"

———◆———

In nearly every village they flew over, huts were burning. There were bodies floating in rice paddies, and they noticed a couple of shot-up NVA trucks. The copilot tapped Big Al's helmet and handed him a radio headset. "Sarge, Geezer's on for us."

Big Al signed on. "Geezer, this is Bear. Over."

The battalion commander informed him that a flame-throwing tank—or Zippo, as they called it—had gotten separated from its squadron northwest of Da Nang. Big Al's squad was tasked with finding and recovering the tank and crew.

———◆———

The squad leader and his men were heading to the Zippo on foot when an improvised explosive device went off. The blast knocked Albert and five Marines to the ground.

The men scrambled up the short creek bank into the tall elephant grass, dirt and shrapnel still raining around them.

"Stay low," Albert gestured, "and stay here! I'll be right back."

His ears were ringing from the blast. For a while, none of them would be able to hear well. He saw the tank crew crawl out of the tank. There was a lot of blood. The tank commander and driver could not walk. But they were alive, and that was all that mattered at that moment. The gunner, though shaken, somehow emerged unscathed.

"Over here!" he barked, unsure of whether troops from the NVA were nearby.

Albert signaled two of his men to go lend a hand and get the injured men to cover. Meanwhile, he and the other three Marines pushed forward through the elephant grass, confirming that there were no NVA troops in the immediate area.

"All clear!" Albert signaled. His squad gathered with the tank crew to evaluate their injuries.

The blast's concussion had transmitted through the tank's chassis and had broken a foot of the tank commander and an ankle of the driver.

It could have been much worse. They knew they were lucky to escape with their lives.

The tank and all its equipment, including its radio, had been rendered inoperable.

With the adrenaline finally subsiding after knowing his men were okay, Albert felt a burning pain in his left shoulder. The fabric of his salty cammies was shredded, and blood oozed down his arm.

"We'd better take a look at that," one of his men insisted.

Albert pulled back the fabric. "I'll be fine," he said. "Hurts like hell, but a few stitches are all it'll need when we get back to base camp."

He turned his attention to the two injured men from the tank. "You're going to need help. We're about ten klicks from base camp, and there will be NVA between here and there. We'll call for an airlift."

"Sorry Big Al," the radio corpsman said, holding out the radio with shrapnel poking out, "Looks like we're on our own. My radio is toast." It had taken a hard hit and had saved the Marine's life.

"Damn!" Albert exclaimed. He wiped the sweat from his forehead as he gathered his thoughts. He had to contend with the burden of two injured men, but at least—with the addition of the tank gunner—his squad now numbered seven able-bodied men, himself included. "Okay. We're on our own. Here's the plan," he told his squad. "I'll run point, and you men help the injured guys. The longer we're out here, the more likely we're going to run into trouble, so let's gut up."

Albert led the men past hedgerows and across dry rice paddies as they struggled to keep up with him. Their survival depended on speed and luck, and as luck would have it, Albert ran into Route 8B—a rarely-used dirt road barely better than a trail—that led to the base camp, but he knew this was a route along which the NVA sometimes lay in wait for an ambush.

Albert led his men parallel to the road through the overgrowth, sacrificing some speed rather than exposing them.

———◆———

They were over halfway to base camp when they came upon a small hamlet. To get to the other side, the group was forced out into the open.

Within seconds, shots rang out striking two of the men. Albert returned fire, followed by fire from his men. But before they could take cover, Albert felt an enemy round graze his right thigh, and his right forearm jerked as a bullet passed through it.

He fell backward onto one of his injured men, grabbed the man's M1903 Springfield with its grenade discharger and rapidly rolled into position. Using only his left arm, he took aim and fired.

The hut where the handful of enemy soldiers had been hiding was turned to rubble.

Albert quickly applied a tourniquet to his forearm and turned his attention to his injured men. One had been struck in the calf muscle, and the other had been grazed just above his kneecap.

"We've got to move and move fast—*now!*" Albert shouted.

He grabbed and supported one of the newly-injured Marines while the other uninjured men took care of the second Marine and hoisted the tank commander and the driver from the ground, working to keep up with Albert.

"I've got you guys, but you've got to help me as much as you can," he barked as he almost dragged his team members across another rice paddy, heading straight to Route 8B.

Albert knew the enemy soldiers would quickly overtake them if his group continued through the hedgerows and elephant grass, so their only chance was to risk being exposed on the open road, scrambling to get back to their base.

Now, it was a footrace. But it was a footrace that soon came to a grinding halt.

———◆———

Albert's regular point man, Tiny, had scouted ahead. He returned with bad news. A large group of enemy soldiers would be upon them in a matter of minutes. Big Al immediately sprang into action, issuing orders to his men.

Steve—the squad's six-foot-five giant and machine-gun specialist— stationed himself well off to the right. He deployed his M60's tripod and lay flat on his stomach.

On the opposite side of the road was Ronnie, the squad's grenadier, occupying a similar position. He had the planned range dialed in on his M79 Thumper and grenades lined up next to him.

Big Al and the remaining Marines were spaced well apart in a support formation.

The trap was set, as was the kill zone.

The minutes dragged by like hours.

Ronnie was the first to spot the enemy. Hand signals were passed down the line. They were coming straight down the road. Four fingers indicated their number was estimated around forty. Seconds later, Steve confirmed the same.

Big Al had been through more firefights than he cared to remember. But knowing what was to come made it worse. He rested his index finger next to the M16's trigger, trying to breathe slow and deep . . . and quietly.

Forty enemy soldiers? Forty? God, help us.

———◆———

Ronnie looked on from his hiding place as the enemy advanced unaware of the squad's location.

Ten more yards . . . five . . .

There was a hollow *thump* as the first grenade left the M67's barrel. For seconds, the grenade flew silently through the air. The moment it exploded the startled enemy started shooting.

As instructed, Big Al's squad remained motionless.

Ronnie quickly dropped grenades just behind the enemy line at ten-second intervals, thus shepherding the NVA troops into the kill zone. The rifle fire drowned out the subtle launch noise.

The signal from Steve's observation post came down the line.

It's time.

Steve sent bursts of bullets from his M60 into the kill zone below. The remaining Marines selectively picked out exposed NVA soldiers and took them down with single or double shots.

They were mowed down by gunfire within seconds.

Big Al led the able-bodied squad members into the kill zone, shooting as they went, stepping over bodies until they had nothing left to shoot at.

Silence.

Big Al raised his fist to halt the squad then dove to the ground screaming, "Down!"

A massive explosion shook the ground. Big Al rolled over and pumped two bullets into an NVA soldier slumped against a rock. He had noticed at the last moment that the dying soldier picked up something that was connected to a wire.

The squad corporal reported back that the kill count was forty-seven. There was no sign of any survivors. "But who knows who else may be out there? We can't hang around, Sarge."

The safety of the base was another two klicks away.

———•———

Colonel Mackey was nervously pacing the HQ when a comms officer called him over. A Colonel Raines—call sign Dango—was looking for him on the open general-forces channel. Colonel Mackey picked up the mic and announced his presence.

A cocky voice boomed through the radio static in response, "Geezer, this is Dango. Ya' know I've never liked the whole one-nine Marines walking dead thing. If you asked me, I'd say it was all a load of hogwash. But I'll be damned if nine almost-dead men did not just walk into my base here! You may want to send a bird or two over to pick 'em up, one of them with red plus signs on the side, if you catch my drift. By the way, if the one-nine ever got tired of this Bear fella, you can pass him on to me. I think you owe him a cold one when they carry his sorry ass from the bird on your side. I s'pose he'll have to hold it with his left hand. Anyways, he says to tell you Bear says hello. Dango. Out."

———•———

Through four years of combat in Vietnam (1966–1969), the 1st Battalion, 9th Marines, became a legend by sustaining the highest casualty rate in Marine Corps history, earning the nickname the Walking Dead.

Albert—because of his exceptional valor and continued leadership—became one of the most decorated soldiers during that era.

CHAPTER 12

Scarred

Albert and Judith | Memphis, TN to Nashville, TN

Despite the comfortable bed, Judith woke up multiple times overwhelmed by guilt for not having done more to help Mimi. She was not one to dwell on the past, but she knew she could not get around the fact that projects, deadlines, and responsibilities were poor excuses for simply not being there for her grandmother.

She had tried to convince Grace to come to Los Angeles the moment she started showing signs of her health failing, but her grandmother would have none of it.

"This is where my people—my church family—are, Judy," Grace objected when Judith brought up the possibility.

Why Judith did not come to see Grace sooner, she did not know. Of course, she knew that coming to visit would make no difference medically, but that is no reason not to come. Was it because she felt incapable of doing anything to help her grandmother? Or was she simply afraid, and if so, of what? Facing the reality of her past? Dealing with another death? Facing the fact that she would be left behind with not a single surviving family member?

Judith wrestled with these questions, tossing and turning much of the night. By the time her alarm went off, she forced herself out of bed, not yet accustomed to the two-hour time difference with her home in L.A. It was still raining outside.

Despite the restless night, Judith was at peace knowing she would see her Mimi within just a few hours—and that the end of the bus trip was in sight. She looked like a million dollars by the time her Uber Black picked her up from the hotel.

"Did you get a chance to visit the Civil Rights Museum?" the driver—a petite, silver-haired, Caucasian lady named Karla—asked.

"I'm afraid not. I've barely been in town for twelve hours," Judith explained. The road to the bus terminal took them past the site, and Karla explained that it was where Dr. Martin Luther King was assassinated.

"If ever you find yourself back in this area, it's well worth the visit along with the Underground Railroad Museum," she told Judith. "The more we can learn from our past, the less likely we are to repeat it," she mused as she pulled into the bus terminal.

* * *

The bus driver was loading luggage into the luggage compartment. When she looked up and saw Judith coming, she got the biggest smile. "Well, well. If it ain't Miss Gucci. How have you been, girl? Headin' to Knoxville today?"

"Lucille! What an unexpected pleasure. I'll be getting off the bus in Nashville, actually."

"Well, it is my pleasure to take you there. I'll bet you're ready to be done riding the bus."

"Oh, you have *no* idea just how ready I am," Judith agreed with a smile.

Lucille took Judith's suitcase. "I've got your Gucci. It'll be a full house in there soon. Please be careful. The steps might be a bit slippery from the rain."

Of the spots still available, Judith picked an aisle seat next to an older African American gentleman.

"Mind if I joined you, sir?" she asked, noticing the Disabled American Veteran logo on his cap.

The man smiled warmly. "I don't mind if you do," he said as Judith placed her tote on the floor and got seated.

"Am I on a hidden camera or something?" her neighbor asked with a slight grin.

"I'm sorry? I don't understand."

"Ma'am, I've been taking this bus from Memphis to Nashville for more years than I care to count," the man explained, "and I've never seen a lady dressed as fine as you on board. Not on *this* bus."

Judith chuckled. "No, sir. There are no hidden cameras. My grandmother had asked me to take the bus as a special favor for her—a dream she's had that she won't be able to make come true, except through me . . . I'm heading to see her today." She extended her hand, "My name is Judith."

As he shook her hand, the man replied, "My pleasure to meet and share this ride with you, Judith. My name is Albert, but my friends call me Big Al. I'd be happy for you to call me that too."

"Well, then, Big Al it will be. And I'm also traveling to Nashville." Gesturing at Albert's cap, Judith added, "I'm honored to be traveling with a veteran. Am I right in guessing Vietnam? If so, I believe the appropriate phrase—even if it's a few decades late—is 'Welcome home.' "

Albert was taken aback by her gesture. His eyes shone with gratitude, "I appreciate you saying that. As you seem to know, that's what we Vietnam vets say when we greet each other. Most people say, 'Thank you for your service.' "

Judith smiled, thankful she had chosen the spot next to Albert.

Memphis, TN to Jackson, TN

"Look at that. Right on time," Albert said as he looked at his watch. "Lucille runs a tight ship. Yes, she does."

The bus headed north toward the I-40 East.

"My late granddaddy, Virgil, served during World War II in the South West Pacific theater—in the Philippines, specifically," Judith explained. "He made sure I knew some protocol insofar as the military goes."

"Under General MacArthur, I assume?"

"That's right."

"Army, or Navy?"

"Army," Judith confirmed. "How about you?"

"Marines."

"*Semper fi.*"

"Oorah!" Albert responded, beaming. "Your grandpa taught you well, young lady."

———————◆———————

For a few minutes, Albert was quiet. Judith looked out the window. *In about four hours, I'll be home.*

She could hardly wait.

Judith imagined that Grace was making sure everything is just so for the visit—that is, if she was feeling well. Though her home was simple, Grace kept it immaculate.

"Everything has a place, and there's a place for everything," Grace used to tell her when she was little and might forget to put away an item she had used. It did not take long for this mindset to become part of Judith's worldview, like so many other Mimi-isms.

"Anything worth doing is worth doing right the first time," was another saying Grace shared with Judith a thousand times. The corner of Judith's mouth turned upward as she realized what a constant teacher Mimi had been to her, shaping her from an early age.

"You know," Albert pulled Judith back to the present, "we didn't hear 'Welcome home' much back when we got back to the States after our tours of duty in Vietnam. So, thank you, Judith."

Judith was surprised by the positive impact such a simple remark had on Albert, realizing he had been reflecting on her comment.

"You are very welcome," she said, "and thankfully, attitudes have changed toward the men and women of the military who make sacrifices that most of us can never imagine and usually will never know about. You mentioned that you take this bus often," Judith continued. "What brings you to Nashville regularly, if you don't mind me asking?"

"I don't mind at all," Albert responded. "My daughter Michelle lives in Murfreesboro, just south of Nashville."

"I know Murfreesboro. Granddaddy took me to Stones River once to watch a Civil War reenactment. A lot of history was made in that town."

"You got it. So, I take the bus from Memphis to Nashville, and Michelle drives up to Nashville to get me. I usually visit for a week or so every now and then."

"That sounds wonderful. What a gift."

"Indeed. My wife passed about ten years ago, so these trips help keep me to stay connected to my family, including my grandkids. Michelle has two boys."

Albert pulled out his wallet and showed Judith photos of his grandsons, and one of Michelle and her husband.

"They all keep on me about needing to move there close to them, but I keep telling them that's a matter of good initiative but bad judgment." He chuckled. "I was born and raised in northwest Mississippi, just south of Memphis. After leaving the Marines I bought a small house in Memphis."

"GI Bill?"

Albert raised his eyebrows slightly. "Sadly, no. Those benefits weren't distributed equally if you know what I mean."

"I do, unfortunately."

"I've lived in that same house ever since. Carried my bride over that threshold. And we carried our daughter into that home as a newborn," Albert continued, not wanting to dwell on the issue. "That's where we raised Michelle, and that's the house that my wife passed in. If I have my way, that's where I'll pass too."

Albert looked at Judith. "How can I leave memories like those?" he asked. "No can do."

"That's what Mimi told me when I tried to convince her to move to Los Angeles," Judith explained.

Albert laughed a long, drawn-out laugh. "Your grandma is a wise woman, Judith. Why you young people think you can just uproot an old tree and hope it blooms again in a new place, no one knows."

He paused for a moment, then continued, "Anyway, I usually schedule my trips to visit when I have an appointment at the V.A. hospital there in Murfreesboro."

The questions Judith had wrestled with for much of the previous night came back to mind, as did the guilt for not coming to see Mimi more often, especially since Granddaddy passed.

"Big Al, do you have any idea how lucky you are to have a daughter and family who are as loving and supportive? It's a rare thing."

"Indeed. I count my blessings every night during my prayers."

"I'll bet you do," Judith said and smiled at the memory of her grandfather kneeling at the side of his bed in prayer.

"But that's not the only thing I talk to the good Lord about," Albert added with a concerned look. "The rest of those prayers are for this country I'll be leaving behind for my family. I won't lie to you: I worry."

"About what, Big Al?"

For the next several miles, Albert shared with Judith his concerns for how the country had changed. "Don't get me wrong," he said, "some of the changes are good. I'm not suggesting that the good ol' days were all good. No ma'am. Dr. Martin Luther King didn't die for no reason. Things had gotten better for the most part, but there's still so much work to do."

Judith listened intently.

"I know our country isn't perfect, but I have bled for this country and have seen many men do the same. I cared enough to be willing to die protecting the United States. Indeed, many I served with laid down their lives."

An even more serious look came upon Albert's face. "But these days? It's like we've taken a step back in terms of civil rights. I fear for my grandsons, I do."

Albert pulled a book from his bag. "I've been reading *Just Mercy* by Bryan Stevenson. Perhaps you've seen the movie?"

"I haven't yet."

"Well, this guy says it the best," he said as he turned to an earmarked page. " 'We are all implicated when we allow other people to be mistreated. An absence of compassion can corrupt the decency of a community, a state, a nation. Fear and anger can make us vindictive, abusive, unjust, and unfair until we *all* suffer from the absence of mercy and we condemn ourselves as much as we victimize others.' He goes on to say, 'We *all* need mercy. We *all* need justice. And perhaps, we *all* need some measure of unmerited grace.' "

"That is powerful."

"Thing is, I told you I'm afraid when I think of how we thought we had come a long way, thinking back on the civil rights movement and all we had gone through. But so much still has to change. However, nothing will change unless we have compassion, and I believe we cannot have compassion toward others unless we have compassion toward ourselves . . .''

Judith listened as Albert continued. "Once we tap into compassion, we can move from fear and anger toward mercy, toward justice, and toward grace."

Albert was not done yet. "It's when you find grace that you can extend grace. I don't know about you, but to me, that's a journey. Just when I think I've made it, that I've got the compassion piece down, I run into an obstacle and find the anger boiling up inside of me."

"Mind if I took a photo of the quote?" Judith asked after a while. "I definitely want to read the book, but until I do, there's a lot packed into those few words. It's like you said, it's a journey, and to be honest, I still have quite a long road ahead of me yet."

———

The rain let up and the sun broke through as they headed further east. It turned out to be a gorgeous September morning.

"Isn't this turning out to be just the perfect day to be making new friends and visiting family?" Judith observed.

"Seems to me like *any* day's a good day for that," Albert said with a smile.

Judith laughed and nodded in agreement. "Sure, can't argue with that."

"First stop of the day, folks. Just pickin' up a couple of passengers, then we'll be pushin' for Nashville. Tweeeeeeenty minutes," Lucille said as they neared Jackson. She took the exit and pulled in at the Casey Jones Village.

Casey Jones Village

"I'm going to get a coffee," Judith told Big Al. "Can I get you one? Do you take cream and sugar?"

"How kind of you. No cream, no sugar. Thanks, Judith."

She returned with two coffees and a cup of grapes each for her and her neighbor.

"Do you know who Casey Jones was?" Albert asked.

"I don't believe I do."

"Well, Jones was a locomotive engineer, and in April 1900 he was driving the train from Memphis down to Mississippi when he ran into a stalled train. His heroic actions saved the lives of his fireman and all the passengers on board, at the cost of his own. This here was where he and his family used to live."

"I'm surprised I've never heard his story," Judith mused.

"There are some songs about him, and his name has made it into pop culture. Now that you know about Casey Jones, you'll know when you hear a reference," Albert said with a smile. "And you'll remember our bus ride to Nashville."

Jackson, TN to Nashville, TN

"Would you mind telling me a story or two about Vietnam?" Judith asked once they were back on the I-40.

Albert hesitated, "It's not something I talk about much, but there were also some good things that happened. I don't mind telling you about those."

For the next several miles, Albert related stories of the 1st Battalion, 9th Marines, where he had served as a staff sergeant.

"We did our best to defend our northern outpost and our fellow Marines. This body of mine's been through a lot, which is why I get to go visit the doctors at the V.A.," he said with a faint smile. He rolled up his right sleeve to show Judith a scar on his right forearm from a story he had told her.

"Scars remind us that we're fallible," he said. "But it's the scars we can't see that remind us of how strong we are. They're the hardest to heal. And we don't have to fight in a war to have those."

They both fell silent.

———◆———

"On a lighter note," Judith said shortly after they had crossed the Tennessee River, "can you imagine living in a town called Bucksnort?"

Albert laughed out loud. "I wonder how close you had to be to a buck to hear him snort."

"How about living in Only?"

"Only? Good lawd."

The two laughed as Judith told Albert about some of the town names along the way.

"You mean to tell me you've been on this bus for five days? How many miles would it be?"

"By the time we roll into Nashville? Almost two thousand miles."

"Has it been worth the trip?"

Judith hesitated, giving his question thought before replying. "You and I both know there are more time-efficient ways to get across the country, so in that sense, no," she admitted. "But like you said earlier, Mimi's a smart woman. This trip forced me to connect with people in ways I haven't in years—maybe ever. It wouldn't surprise me if this trip wasn't so much for *her*. She knew this was her last chance to lure me back into the real world. She's clever, in a sneaky sort of way."

Judith could not help but chuckle at the realization. "So, the short answer would be yes, it's been absolutely worthwhile."

———◆———

The closer they got to Nashville, the deeper the sense of hope there was in Judith's spirit. She had hope for her Mimi's path forward, and hope for her own life, a rekindling of her connection to life, really.

Dr. Sanders would be delighted to hear about some of the breakthroughs. She'll also be quick to remind me that it's not about pleasing her, but about my own well-being.

"This is my old stomping ground," she told Albert when they passed the exit for Vanderbilt University.

"Do you ever think of moving back?" Albert wanted to know.

"Can't say I do. My company's in L.A., so making a move wouldn't be that simple. But if the doctors can find a way to help Mimi, I'll be back more often, for sure."

They passed the Country Music Hall of Fame and Music City Center before turning toward the bus terminal. "Don't know if you're aware of it, but from the sky, this building looks like the body of a guitar," Judith told Albert.

"Well, how about that? We sure miss a lot when we look at things from one vantage point only, don't we?" he responded with a smile, as if there was nothing special about the remark, as if he was simply pondering aloud.

If I walked past him on a city street, a stranger, would I have imagined the depth of his wisdom and insight? If I saw an African American Vietnam vet, what would my immediate judgment have been?

Judith could not know for sure, but she had an uneasy feeling that she would have defaulted to some kind of stereotype.

If someone stood behind Mimi in line at the supermarket checkout, would they have any notion of the mountain of love and mercy held in her fragile body? Our prejudice blinds us to the truth.

It turned out to be a picture-perfect afternoon for September. The billowing white cumulus clouds slowly drifted across the brilliant azure-blue sky. They pulled into the bus terminal just in time for an early lunch for those who were continuing onward.

"We'll be here for one hour, folks," Lucille announced on the PA system. "For those of you disembarking here, thank you for your patronage, and we hope to see you again on a future trip."

160

"Looks like you got to know Big Al," Lucille said as she placed Judith's bag in front of her.

"And I'm glad I did," Judith said with a smile. "As am I to have gotten to travel with you, Lucille." She extended her hand to shake the driver's hand, but Lucille opened both arms.

"What's with shaking hands? Let me give you a huuuuug," she said with her trademark jubilance. "It's passengers like you who sustain me each day, missy. Thank you. And may God bless you."

Judith noticed the young man she had heard talk to his parents about following his dream. Here he was in the most iconic music city in the nation. He picked up his guitar case and his bag and started walking toward the Walk of Fame Park just a few blocks north of where they were.

Albert grabbed his duffel bag and turned to Judith. He put out his hand, and she shook it with a smile.

"Thank you for giving me a lot to think about today, Big Al," she said.

"This has been the most memorable bus ride to Nashville I've ever had, Judith," he responded. "You have no idea how much I appreciated your respectful comments about my service. May God bless you and yours."

Judith pulled her hand back from Albert and hugged him. "And you enjoy your time with those who love you the most."

As Albert took his leave, Judith turned to walk away. She paused to look back. There was the bus, the station, the people. Tears filled Judith's eyes as she smiled, realizing another part of her journey was over.

ALBERT'S SONG

"My Country 'Tis of Thee"

My country 'tis of thee.
Sweet land of liberty
where have you gone?
Back when I grew up
riding a pickup truck
so grateful for my luck
of thee I sang.

Life was much simpler then,
filled with brave, honest men
and women too.
Vietnam and World War II,
they fought for me and you.
They saw the battle through
for country's love.

Now egos rule the state,
we mustn't hesitate
to right the ship.
When did we lose our way?
My heart says now to say

it's time for us to pray.
We still love you.

Dear Father God above,
you've blessed us with your love,
to Thee we pray.
Please God, don't hesitate
to save our homes and state.
We pray it's not too late,
our God, Amen.

PART 2

CHAPTER 13

Welcome Home

Judith scanned the parking lot for her ride. Remembering Johnny's punchbowl remark, she smiled broadly as she spotted the long, black limousine in the bus station parking lot. The driver stood next to it holding a sign with her name. This was certainly not a sight seen often at a bus station.

As she approached the limo, the heat rose from the asphalt pavement. The driver nodded and touched the bill of his cap as he took her luggage. "Welcome to Nashville, Ms. Lee. Let me get that for you. My name is Walter."

"Thank you, Walter," Judith responded and stepped toward the door that Walter opened for her. She settled into the air-conditioned comfort.

Lucille watched from a distance. She laughed out loud when she saw Judith walk to the limo. "Well, look at that," she said to herself. "I knew that lady was *someone*, but who'd've thought a *limousine* like that would be picking up one of *my* passengers. Probably payin' more for that one ride home than for the past two thousand miles!"

———◆———

A Perrier was waiting for Judith at the exact temperature she liked—fifty-five degrees—and both a steaming hot and an icy cold towel in a tray beside it. Judith picked the cold towel to wipe her hands, the aroma of peppermint oil filling the air.

After placing her suitcase in the expansive trunk, Walter got into the vehicle. "Depending on traffic, we're only about fifteen minutes from East End," he announced.

Judith knew that, of course. She knew this town like the back of her hand. She could also tell you exactly how long it would take to get from the East End neighborhood to West End Avenue, where Vanderbilt University was. In regular traffic, that route took thirty-eight minutes, which included nine minutes of walking to the bus stop, one transfer, and twenty-two stops along the way.

Walter maneuvered the lengthy limo out of the parking lot and into the street.

"If you don't mind me asking, Walter, where are you from?" It was not like Judith to be engaging in conversation with her limo drivers, but after a week on the road, she found herself more curious about the people around her.

"I don't mind you asking, ma'am. I'm from Knoxville," he responded.

"I mean, originally."

"I was born and raised in Knoxville, ma'am," he said with a smile. "But if you are referring to my heritage, my ancestors are from Taiwan. We've been in the US for two generations, though. My mom was born here, as was I. Hence, I'm from Knoxville."

He continued, "And if you don't mind me asking ma'am, where are *you* from?"

Judith caught the irony of the moment and smiled at Walter in the rear-view mirror. "Nashville, but I live in L.A. And if you're referring to my heritage, we're originally from England, I'm told."

"Would you say you've retained some of your English traditions?" Walter was careful not to overstep.

"Goodness, no!" Judith laughed. "I have no idea what it means to be English. How about you?"

"Very much so. Despite my grandparents having moved here when Japan invaded Taiwan during World War II, they and my parents are still Taiwanese at heart. We all live together, and at home, my grandparents speak Taiwanese, and my parents speak mostly Mandarin. I'm embarrassed to admit that I speak neither. Like I said, I'm American."

Judith wondered about her chief marketing officer, Tony. She knew he was from Singapore since she hired him immediately after he had gotten an MBA from Duke, and her company had sponsored his application for a green card. His sales and marketing team sometimes teased him good-naturedly about his clipped accent.

Does Tony have extended family in the US? And does he speak—Judith realized that she did not know what languages Singaporeans might speak other than English—*Mandarin, perhaps?*

They passed all the familiar places that made Judith feel at home. When they crossed the Korean War Memorial bridge, Judith thought of her conversation with Albert about some of the fears he had regarding his grandsons, which made her wonder about her chief operating officer, Tiffany, who was also African American.

Does Tiffany have any such fears? I don't really know my staff, do I?

Walter pulled up in front of Judith's childhood home almost exactly fifteen minutes later. The Craftsman-style house looked smaller and a little more run-down than Judith's memory of it.

Grace did not have her flower boxes overflowing with bright purple wave petunias like she always did. She had warned Judith about that. "Next year, I'll plant twice as many," she had told her earlier in the summer when her energy started to fizzle.

Walter opened the door for Judith and retrieved her luggage.

"May I carry your luggage in for you, ma'am?" he asked.

Judith smiled. "No, thank you, Walter," she said. "I've got it." Handing him a generous tip, Judith slipped the tote over the suitcase handle and began pulling her luggage up the walk.

Before she was even halfway up, Grace flung open the front door. "Oh, my Judy girl! Is it really you?" she exclaimed; her arms outstretched. "Come hug me so I'll know you're real!"

Judith gave her grandmother the biggest hug. "Yes, it really is me, Mimi! It really is me."

Rachel stepped onto the porch.

"You must be Rachel," Judith said as she extended her hand. Taking Rachel's hand into both of hers, she said, "What a pleasure to finally meet you in person."

"I feel the same, Miss Judith," Rachel responded.

"Please just call me Judith."

"Well, Judith, let me take your suitcase."

"Come on in, Judy," Grace said, slipping her arm into Judith's. "We have so much to talk about and catch up on. We've got lunch ready."

Grace, Judith, and Rachel lingered at the kitchen table after finishing their meal of country-fried steak, green beans, macaroni and cheese, sliced tomatoes, rolls, and sweet tea.

"There's nothing like Mimi's cooking," Judith told Rachel. "Even the fanciest restaurants in L.A. cannot hold a candle to it."

"Well, sweetie, you know what I always say. My secret ingredient is love," Grace insisted. "But I couldn't have made all this today without Rachel's help."

"I can't take much credit," Rachel pushed back. "Miss Grace was thrilled to be cooking for you. My role was pretty much handing her the ingredients she asked for. She must be running on adrenaline."

Rachel had enjoyed listening to the rapid-fire back and forth conversation between Judith and Grace as, minute by minute, the two years since they last saw each other fell away.

Judith reached to dish up just one more spoon of the mac and cheese as Grace watched her with adoring eyes, savoring the moment. "Now, save some room for dessert," she warned Judith with a smile. "I've got Blue Bell strawberry ice cream in the freezer."

"Blue Bell strawberry ice cream? I'll have a little bowl later, Mimi. I'm stuffed. Thank you both for the best meal that I've had in two years."

"Well, it's been a while since I whipped up a big meal," Grace responded. "Glad to know I can still do it. Now, Judy, don't think I've forgotten about that big baked ham dinner we're gonna cook up soon. *And* that lemon meringue pie! Rachel, it goes without saying that we expect you to join us."

"Oh, you couldn't keep me away. Just say the day and time and I'll be here. For now, though," Rachel said as she got up, "I'd better get going. Rob invited me to go see a movie tonight." She winked at Grace.

"That's the fella your friends introduced you to just the other day, right?" Grace said with a twinkle in the eye.

"That's the one. We'll see how it goes. Let me clear the table before I go, though."

Judith immediately objected to Rachel's further help, saying, "No, no. I've got it from here. I can't thank you enough for today, and every day."

Rachel took her place setting to the sink before walking back over to the table. "Miss Grace is my favorite," she told Judith, placing her hand on Grace's shoulder. "She is pure human sunshine. Let me know if you'd like me to pick you up for church on Sunday, Miss Grace. If I don't hear from you, I'll just pick you both up Monday at nine to go to the clinic for the lab work. If you need anything else, please don't hesitate to call me. Thank you for allowing me to share this homecoming meal with you."

As the front door closed behind Rachel, Judith surveyed the table and kitchen. "Mimi, it won't take me long to clear everything and clean up in here," she told Grace. "How about you go on into the living room and rest for a few minutes, and I'll join you in just a few."

Grace hesitated briefly. "Actually, that sounds like a good idea. I may have used up too much energy fixin' this food," she admitted. "I'll go and recharge my battery while waiting for you."

Grace got up and slowly tottered toward the living room. Judith watched her with a wistful smile, tinged with sadness, realizing what's to come.

———◆———

When Judith got back to the living room, Grace was asleep, sitting at the end of the sofa next to the end table that holds the phone.

Judith took the opportunity to go and unpack her luggage in her room. The twin bed looked even smaller than Judith remembered, but the decorations were still the same ones she had put up in college. She picked up her old camera and looked through the lens, smiling as good memories snuck up on her.

Judith sat at the edge of the bed. During her last visit, she had ordered an extra-plush mattress topper for same-day delivery—one for her, and one for Mimi.

"You don't own stuff, Judy," Grace had objected fiercely. "Your stuff owns you." But Judith insisted, adding some high thread count bed sheets for both rooms.

———◆———

She put a load of laundry in the washer and made some hot tea before joining Mimi on the sofa.

"Have I been dreaming, or are you really here next to me?" Grace asked lovingly when she awoke.

"I'm as real as that country-fried steak you made," Judith said and took her grandma's hand in hers. She loved how soft and wrinkly those hands were and was thankful not to notice any petechiae. "I've missed you, Mimi. I'm sorry it's been a while."

"Oh, it's okay sweet pea. I'm just glad you're here now," Grace assured her.

A framed photo of Judith stood next to the phone, alongside a smaller photo of her grandparents. "That's such a nice picture of you and Granddaddy. I remember the day I took it."

Grace glanced at the photo. "That was always my favorite of Virgil and me. It was a homecoming Sunday right after church. We were outside under the trees gettin' ready to eat," she said. "I had just set my lemon meringue pies on the table with everyone else's food when Virgil called me over so you could take our picture with that little camera we just got you for your birthday. You were *so* proud of that camera. Do you still take pictures these days?"

"Not so much. The camera on my cell phone takes better photos than my last camera did, and I always have my phone with me. I took a few photos on the trip, though. Let me show you."

Judith went to get her phone and came back with a brown paper bag in hand as well. As she scrolled through the photos, Mimi squealed with delight at the photo of Judith and Sara in front of the Roadkill Café.

"That's exactly how I imagined Sara would look. Now, remind me again where she was heading."

"She had just escaped a bad relationship and was going home to Flagstaff to start over."

"We all need a second chance sometime, don't we?" Mimi commented.

Judith pulled out the brown paper bag with the handful of fridge magnets. "When we were at that first rest stop on Sunday, I had an idea to pick up a few magnets along the way for you. Let me see," she poured the magnets onto the coffee table.

Judith picked out the Route 66 magnet and set it aside. "I picked this up from the museum at the Roadkill Café, a little reminder of the journey."

"Judy, you know you didn't need to buy anything," Grace objected.

172

"I know, I know," Judith smiled. "These are just so you can think of your crazy request every time you take something from the fridge."

Judith scrolled to the next photo. "This is Gary," she said as she showed Grace the photo of the two of them on a corner in Winslow, Arizona. Gary was holding the small cedar chest.

"That was the gentleman who went to scatter his wife's ashes in Albuquerque, right?"

"That's him. He reminded me a lot of Granddaddy." Next, she showed Grace a photo of the hot-air balloons. "I told you you'd love seeing them," she said and placed the hot-air balloon magnet next to the first one.

"I don't think I would ever have the courage to go up in one of those things."

"You've done braver things than that, Mimi. You said yes to raising a ten-year-old at a time when your friends were sitting at home crocheting blankets for their many grandbabies."

"You turned our world upside down, Judy Lee, in the very best of ways," Grace assured Judith. "And I would have it no other way."

"Speaking of brave things," Judith said as she placed the magnet of the teepee next to the earlier ones, "Gary taught me a lot about the plight of the people who lived here before us, how brave they were in fighting for their land. I won't go into all the details now, but I know that I'll forever see the Native American nations and their cultures through different eyes."

Judith scrolled to the next picture. "On a lighter note, this one's from Tuesday when we stopped in Amarillo." She showed Grace a picture of her and Johnny at the Cadillac Ranch. "Hold on, I have a magnet from there too," she said as she separated the Cadillac tails from the rest of the small pile.

But Grace was more interested to learn about the man in the photo. "This is the fella who had been in the accident, right?"

"That's him, yes. His name's Johnny."

"Looks like you two had some fun exploring Amarillo," Grace said and winked at Judith.

Am I blushing? Or is it just hot in here?

"We did," Judith said, scrolling to the next photo of her and Daisy at the art deco gas station in Shamrock, Texas. "And this is Daisy, the gal who's committed to working her charms to find a rich man who'll take care of her for the rest of her life."

"I hope you told her that money's not everything in life. Look at Virgil and me. Barely had a cent to our name, but we were rich in love, right?" Grace reached into a drawer in her end table and took out a picture. "Look what I found the other day."

Judith glanced at the photo of her grandparents. The black dress Grace wore in that photo was unlike anything else her grandmother owned, looking more like the type of gowns Judith was accustomed to wearing to black-tie and red-carpet events in L.A. The bodice sparkled with shimmering sequins and was covered in a matching jacket with a narrow satin lapel and sheer sleeves stretching to her wrists.

Judith could imagine that for that one night in Chattanooga, in Grace's mind she was a beautiful queen being escorted by her handsome King Virgil. Mimi looked like an angel in that picture. "Rich in love? You certainly were."

As Judith scrolled on, there were several photos from the memorial in Oklahoma City.

"Hold on, honey. You're going too fast," Grace said. "What are these of?"

"It's a memorial for the Oklahoma City bombing." Judith stopped at the photo of the doors with the inscription on it.

"Would you read that to me?" Grace asked.

"We come here to remember those who were killed, those who survived, and those changed forever . . ." Judith stopped reading and took a deep breath to fight the tears she felt coming on. She placed the magnet of the chair alongside the growing line, then scrolled to the photo of the sea of chairs.

Grace looked at the image for a while before she said, "*That* is certainly moving." She reached into her pocket for a handkerchief and dabbed a tear from her cheek. "But I don't want to cry right now."

"Neither do I," Judith was glad to declare. "A photo of Bobbie Sue will put a smile back on your face." The only photo she had was one she took at the Cracker Barrel. Bobbie Sue was beaming at the sight of the confetti pancakes.

"What a beautiful child she is," Grace noted. "I can see why she stole your heart."

Judith smiled as she took in some of the joy the six-year-old exuded. "I wonder how they're doing, how she's feeling today. Yesterday was her first infusion."

"Well, if it's anything like my experience, she'd be feeling better today than she had in months."

Judith turned over the angel magnet and told her grandmother about how impressed she was with St. Jude. "Being in that building almost felt like walking on holy ground," she said. "The work they do there is nothing short of God's work, don't you think?"

"I couldn't agree more, honey. So many children's lives have been transformed there—and to think the parents don't pay a dime."

Judith turned to the final photo, one of her and Albert that they took at the bus terminal while waiting for their luggage.

"This was my neighbor today. He's a Marine and a Vietnam veteran," Judith explained. "He comes to the V.A. in Murfreesboro and stays with his daughter and her family for a while before going back home. They're down in Murfreesboro too."

"He seems like a kind man," Grace observed. "Honey, you have no idea how it warms my heart to have heard the stories of the people you met and to be able to put faces to their names. It looks like you made some friends this week."

"That I did. I never thought I'd say this, Mimi, but it's been good to be forced to slow down some, to meet ordinary people, to listen to their stories," Judith admitted. "If you told me a week ago that I'd see parts of my own story in the lives of six random strangers on a cross-country bus trip, I would have thought you lost your mind."

Grace gave Judith a knowing look. "Was there anything in particular that stood out for you about the trip?"

Judith thought for a moment. "It's not something that I've just realized this week," she said. "I've been meeting with a therapist—Dr. Sanders—for about a year now, and something we've been talking about became very clear to me this week."

Grace listened as Judith continued. "You know me better than anyone, Mimi. You know that I can be hard on myself and on others."

Grace nodded. This is something she had talked to the Lord about but could not raise the topic with Judith.

"One thing Dr. Sanders has helped me see is how I try to protect little Judy who found her parents unresponsive and called nine-one-one. Over the years, I've beaten myself up about that night, Mimi. I used to believe that it was my fault that they died . . . that my incompetence got in the way," Judith said, her voice quivering.

"Honey, there was nothing you could have done," Grace assured her again, her eyes full of tears.

"I realize that now, I do," Judith replied. "But ten-year-old Judy didn't know that. Dr. Sanders has been helping me to find ways in which I could become an ally to my younger self. Part of the journey has been to see how much grace has been extended to me . . ."

She took a deep breath. "This week, I think I realized for the first time that I've not been given grace just for me to keep it. I had the chance every day to extend grace to others. To the bus drivers who made silly comments on how I was dressed and about my fancy luggage. To my seatmates, my Uber drivers, people at the restaurants where I ate."

Grace kept holding Judith's hand, seeing before her the sweet child who had grown up by years in the span of a week.

"At the memorial two days ago, I came to see each one of those chairs as a chance to extend grace," Judith continued.

"We can be kind to others, but first," Grace said with a knowing look in her eyes, "we have to be kind to ourselves."

"Precisely," Judith responded, ready to move on.

Though Grace wanted to hear more, she was not going to push Judith.

———◆———

The two visited until it was time for dinner, and they moved back to the kitchen.

Judith placed the magnets on the old refrigerator door, next to Mimi's favorite magnet of Winnie the Pooh. "We didn't realize we were making memories; we just knew we were having fun," it read.

"Virgil bought me that on our trip to Chattanooga," she reminded Judith. "I can't tell you how much my good memories have kept me going since Virgil passed."

As Judith dished up some leftovers for them, Grace continued, "I hope you're stackin' up a pile of good memories out there in California."

Judith smiled awkwardly. "There are a few. It's been necessary for me to focus most of my time on the company. But I enjoy what I'm doing," she said. "All my best memories are from being here with you and Granddaddy, though. I realize now that we really didn't need much besides each other."

"You know what I always say, Judy," Grace said. "You don't own your stuff—" and Judith joined her in finishing the sentence, "Your stuff owns you."

"You know, Mimi," Judith confessed, "for so many years, all I could focus on was what we did *not* have."

There was a pregnant pause before Grace shared knowledge that only comes with age, experience, and wisdom. "The trouble is that most folks spend so much time gathering stuff that they don't enjoy what really matters—enjoying experiences with those they love," she said. "That's why I've never let you buy me a new house or remodel this one. I didn't even allow you to buy me a new Frigidaire." Grace looked at the refrigerator, "Though I probably should have listened to you about replacing it," she added with a gleeful cackle.

"I should have just had one delivered like I did with those bed sheets and mattress toppers," Judith teased her grandmother as they finished up the light dinner after spending the entire, glorious afternoon catching up. She could see that Grace was tired—possibly too tired for her nightly ritual of watching Jimmy Fallon.

"Maybe I can fix us some omelets for breakfast tomorrow morning," Mimi offered while Judith cleaned up.

"That sounds wonderful. I love you, Mimi," Judith said as she gave Grace a big, long hug. She laid her cheek on Grace's shoulder as she had done so many times over the years.

Grace gently rubbed Judith's back, the way she always responded to these hugs. "I know, child," she responded. "I know without a doubt. I love you too."

———◆———

Back in her room, Judith opened her closet. She took a step back scanning it, surprised to find her old clothes still hanging there, exactly as she had left them.

Turning and wistfully surveying the entire room, she wrapped her arms around her shoulders in a hug.

For now, Judith was home.

CHAPTER 14

Reflections

By the time she was in middle school, Judith knew where every consignment store in the area was. She knew which ones typically had the best selection and which days were sale days.

Once, early in her high school sophomore year, perfectly dressed Virginia Franks dared to make a snarky comment in the school cafeteria about Judith's outfits.

"Well at least I don't have to have my initials embroidered on my shirt so I'd remember who I am," Judith punched back at full volume. "I *know* who I am!"

That was the last time a classmate dared to say anything about Judith's wardrobe. Except in college, where she was considered cool for the deals she was able to score at what Judith referred to as "the GW."

Before leaving for California for her first job, Judith went to the Goodwill store one final time to buy a few business outfits, then left most of her old wardrobe at home. It would not take long for her to begin earning enough money to hire a personal stylist and a personal shopper.

Staring at her wardrobe that Saturday morning brought back memories of hours spent in the library, of heated discussions about politics and environmental issues. George W. Bush defeated John Kerry in her sophomore year, and Judith recalled heading down South with class-mates to help with cleanup after Hurricane Katrina.

That was the first time she ventured outside her self-created bub-ble, exploring opportunities for new experiences. On that trip, she befriended Joel, an engineering student, and had a crush on him for months to come. But nothing ever came of it.

Judith slipped on her favorite pair of cuffed jeans from back then—they still fit—and a well-worn flannel shirt.

Grace was still asleep, so Judith quietly got to work in the kitchen. She got a pot of coffee brewing and started preparing their brunch.

"I thought I heard a mouse scurrying in here this morning," Grace said as she came into the kitchen wrapped in her fuzzy, pink robe. "Oh, Judy, you're fixing your pancakes! Gracious goodness, how I've missed them."

She looked over at the skillet on the stove. "I thought I smelled bacon. Mmmm. My mouth is watering. Where'd you find the bacon?"

"I picked some up on my run," Judith said as she looked up from the mixing bowl. "Did you sleep well, Mimi?"

"I sure did. How about you, honey?"

"Couldn't have slept better," Judith fibbed. She was not going to tell her grandmother that her mind was busy much of the night thinking about what more she could do to help.

"And look at that! I think I recognize that flannel shirt and jeans of yours from college days. I can't believe they still fit you."

"I have good genes," Judith said as she smiled and winked. "How about you make yourself at home and let me pour you a cup of coffee."

She placed the cup and a pen beside *The Tennessean*. Grace scanned the obituaries, then turned to the crossword puzzle page while sipping her coffee.

The familiarity of the scene warmed Judith's heart.

Judith joined Grace at the table. "I can hardly believe I was able to remember my pancake recipe," she said as she doused the pancakes in warm maple syrup before adding the bacon to their plates.

Grace wrinkled her brow. "You don't fix them at home?"

"When I first moved to California, I sometimes did. But nowadays, I usually just have a smoothie on my way to the office, or some yogurt and fruit."

Grace raised an eyebrow. "And for lunch and dinner?" she asked.

"For lunch, my assistant, Cara, gets me a salad on most days," Judith explained. "I have a proper meal every evening."

"That you cook for yourself?" Grace wanted to know.

"I wish! You know I love cooking, Mimi, but I honestly don't have time to cook during the week. I have a housekeeper who also takes care of that for me," she explained. "She saves me a ton of time."

Grace placed her hand on Judith's. "And what do you do with all the time you save? When do you relax, honey?" Grace asked.

"When I work out," Judith said, "I guess . . ." Judith did not sound too convinced, nor could she convince her grandmother.

"Eat. Exercise. Work. Sleep. Repeat," Grace pointed out. "It doesn't sound like you have much of a life if that's how you spend all that saved time, sweetie pie."

"It's odd, Mimi," Judith reflected. "When you are in the middle of it, it seems so normal. And the days just all seem to run together."

Judith took another sip of coffee, then continued, "I've been way outside my comfort zone during this entire bus trip. Yet, I've had many, many experiences that are unforgettable."

"That's called livin', Judy girl," Grace said as she took another bite of bacon. "And you need a good dose more of it. Nothing wrong with a good routine, just as long as you control it and not let it control you."

"Wise words by Grace Lee," Judith said with a smile. "We can print a book full of those!"

Grace and Judith finished their breakfast, and Grace sat back in her chair as Judith topped off both their coffee cups with the steaming brew.

Grace looked down at her empty plate and said with a chuckle, "If Virgil was here with us this morning, he'd look at my plate and declare, 'Well, you're a member of the Clean Plate Parade today!' "

"What's funny," Judith smiled as she cleared the table, "is that we rarely ended a meal with any food on our plates! It was too valuable to us. How about you finish that crossword puzzle while I finish cleaning up here."

"That'll work," Grace smiled. She had already completed most of the crossword puzzle, her mind still sharp as a tack. "Here's one I need your brain for, though. Seven letters. Rising from the ashes."

"Do you have any of the other letters yet?"

"Let me see," Grace said and adjusted her glasses. "It ends in an *X*."

"Phoenix?"

"Got it! Team Lee is back in the crossword game," Grace laughed with delight, then paused. "You know what I'd like to do today?"

"No, what Mimi?"

"I'd like to go through old pictures with you. Then you can write on the back of 'em so you'll remember when they were taken and such."

"That sounds like a fine idea. How about you go get ready? Once I'm done in the kitchen, I'll get the picture box."

She watched as Grace placed both hands on the table to leverage herself into a standing position. "Do you need a hand getting ready, Mimi?" It was hard seeing her grandmother struggle.

"I'll be fine. I just feel a little short-winded this morning," Grace explained. "Guess I overdid it a little yesterday."

Grace slowly walked out of the kitchen with one hand on her chest. Judith watched her taking a deep breath with some effort, realizing how rapidly the effects of the disease were accelerating.

◆

Judith opened the living room windows to let in fresh air. It was a perfect late-summer Tennessee morning. The loud chirping of a male cardinal made Judith stop and listen.

"Isn't that just the most beautiful sound?" Grace said as she came in and made herself at home on the sofa.

"I've missed hearing birds in the morning, especially cardinals," Judith admitted as she joined Mimi on the sofa and pulled the photo box closer. They had kept photos in this box for as long as she could remember.

One by one, Grace pulled pictures from the box and provided a narrative about the who, when, and where of each. Occasionally, Judith jotted a brief note on the back.

Laughing with amusement, Grace handed Judith another picture. "And this one is me at the overlook up there at Rock City," she explained. "I don't know if Virgil and me saw seven states from up there, but it was the highest up I'd ever been. What a view! Virgil bought me some fudge and a Moon Pie at the gift shop, and we got a Rock City bumper sticker for our old car."

She paused briefly, remembering. "Lordy, what a time we had down there in Chattanooga. You know people down there say they can tell who are tourists by the way they mispronounce the town name, leaving out the 'a' in the middle."

"Well, maybe I'll visit Chat-'ta-nooga someday," Judith joked. "You have countless good memories from that trip with Granddaddy."

Grinning naughtily, Grace leaned in and whispered, "Yep. It was the most fun we ever had with our clothes on." She roared with unbridled laughter.

Faking embarrassment, Judith placed an open hand over her mouth, exclaiming, "Oh, Mimi! Really!" as she burst into laughter too.

Wiping her tears of laughter, Grace reached into the box and a more serious look appeared on her face. "Well, this here's a good picture to end with. This was my favorite picture of your momma and daddy.

That's *you* right there they're holding." She stared at it, then handed it to Judith. "Remember this one?"

"It's been a while since I saw it last, I'd almost forgotten," she answered uncomfortably, almost in a whisper. "They look happy . . . and healthy."

"They were, honey," Grace said softly. "Your momma always said bringing you home from the hospital was one of the happiest days of their lives." She cupped Judith's cheek with her hands. "Oh child, how they loved you."

"Not more than they loved the drugs that would kill them, though," Judith responded bitterly.

"Oh, sweetie pie," Grace continued softly, "they *always* loved you. That *never* stopped."

"They didn't *love* the painkillers, honey. The painkillers had a hold on them. They were addicted. None of us knew back then how bad the pills were that the doctor gave your daddy after he hurt his back at the warehouse or that he got addicted. Back then no one understood the danger of opioids. Doctors prescribed it like it was candy. We were *all* impressed at how much better they made your daddy feel. So, he gave your momma some when she was in too much pain during that time of the month."

"Mimi, do you know how scared I was in the months leading up to their deaths?" Judith asked. "No child should see their parents high on drugs. And no child should find their parents unconscious, let alone *dead*."

"You're right about that, honey," Grace assured Judith. "And I am sorry that it happened that way. None of us realized that your momma started takin' the pills every day. It was downhill for your momma and daddy from there. They were real sick, Judy."

Judith wiped away a tear, "You know, that has been the darkest day of my life by far. I've never been able to block that image from my mind. A little girl being faced with that . . ." Judith stared out the window for a moment and then continued, "I just sat there. Doing nothing. I waited forever before calling nine-one-one, hoping they'd eventually get up and all would be fine again—even though I knew better. I didn't want to believe it."

Grace dabbed her eyes with her old lace handkerchief and affirmed, "No child should ever see what you saw, Judy . . ."

Tears were streaming down Judith's face. "I was so lucky that I had you and Granddaddy, so lucky. If it weren't for you—"

"No, Judy," Grace interrupted her, "you weren't lucky. You were blessed. As were we."

Grace took a deep breath, then steered the conversation in a new direction. "Speaking of being blessed, will you go to church with Rachel and me tomorrow morning? Rachel usually picks me up at nine."

"Well, sure Mimi," Judith said with some hesitation, "that sounds nice."

"That's my girl," Grace said before Judith could change her mind. "Now let's put all these pictures back in the box so you can take them back home with you later."

For both Judith and Grace, their morning together became another memory to be stored away like the pictures in the box.

Judith took the box up to her room. On returning to the living room, she found Grace fast asleep, so she quietly turned around and went back to her room to empty out most of her closet, holding on to just a few favorites. She would drop off the rest at the GW later that afternoon.

"Judy honey," she heard Grace call sometime later.

"You didn't get to watch Jimmy Fallon last night, did you?" Judith asked as she sat down next to Grace.

"Oh, honey, you know I never miss him," Grace said. "But I was too tired to keep my eyes open."

"Well, I wish he knew that you are his biggest fan. How about we hang out here for a while and watch last night's episode?" Judith proposed.

"But Jimmy's only on weeknights, remember?" Grace objected.

"Today is special," Judith said and winked. She opened Hulu on her laptop. "We can watch last night's episode here," she explained.

Though Grace was thoroughly confused by how Judith was able to have them watch the previous evening's episode—on a computer, no less—she did not object.

For most of the afternoon, the two of them watched old episodes of Jimmy Fallon's *Tonight Show* while Grace went in and out of sleep.

———◆———

Judith quietly went through a box of papers Mimi had mentioned earlier in the week, but her thoughts kept drifting.

"What are you doing with all that time you're saving?" Mimi had asked her earlier. Judith also wrestled with the guilt of not having come to visit earlier and not having done more to get her the absolute best treatment.

It did not matter that Grace and Rachel had both assured Judith that nothing more could have been done to help Grace—Judith was not convinced.

Perhaps I could try convincing Mimi to go to Florida to try naturopathic treatment, she thought. But she knew Mimi only trusted her doctors at Vanderbilt.

"I'm not leaving Nashville, honey," Grace had insisted when Judith brought the option up a few months ago regarding treatment for her worsening arthritis.

———◆———

Judith and Dr. Sanders had spoken about her sense of responsibility not long ago, how she felt responsible for Mimi, to get her the care she needs, and how she felt responsible for not helping her parents sooner.

"Let's say, hypothetically, there's a ten-year-old girl standing next to you. What's your expectation of her?" Dr. Sanders asked.

"With regard to?"

"A matter of life and death."

"I wouldn't expect anything of her," Judith said. "She's too young to be tasked with issues of life and death."

"Precisely. The level of responsibility you place on your ten-year-old self is unreasonable. It was not yours to carry."

"And yet, I was expected to do just that."

"Who expected that of you?"

Judith was quiet for a moment. "I wish I could change that."

"Change what?"

"The past."

"*Can* you change the past?" Dr. Sanders asked.

Judith did not answer.

"Of course, you cannot, even though you'd like to." The therapist continued, "And the future?"

"I can't change the future, but I can influence it."

"What does that look like?"

"By how I respond to events and in choices I make."

Dr. Sanders smiled reassuringly. "So, what are the choices before you?"

———◆———

As Judith sat with the box of papers next to her, she contemplated what choices lay before her.

I can acknowledge the grace Granddaddy and Mimi had extended to me. And I can extend grace to Mimi by being here for her, by helping her get the help she needs to get well.

It was hard seeing her Mimi this worn out, but in between going through paperwork, Judith went to sit in the rocker in Grace's room, and the two visited about this and that.

"Honey, could you please look in my top dresser drawer?" Grace asked. "There's a manila envelope under my folded nightgowns."

Judith found the envelope and took it over to Grace. "No, I want you to look at that," Grace insisted. Judith sat on the side of Grace's bed and pulled out a document from Benton & McDougall, a local law firm.

"That there is my advanced directive," Grace said quietly. "My will is also in the envelope."

Judith looked at the piece of paper, then back at Mimi. She did not know what to make of the information.

"When the time comes, I don't want there to be a fuss or any unnecessary measures taken," she explained.

"What do you mean by *unnecessary?*"

"I don't want to be in the hospital connected to machines and tubes . . ."

Judith felt her heart racing. "Mimi, I don't care what it costs or—"

"Honey," Grace interrupted, her voice as calm as before, "I don't want that. I am ready . . ."

Judith struggled to process the information.

Don't you leave me too! The thought took Judith by surprise. *Don't abandon me!* Her chest tightened. She could not think about this right now.

"I made us some chicken soup," Judith told Grace to get the elephant off her chest. "Would you like me to bring it here, or are you ready to get up for a while?"

"I'll join you in the kitchen on one condition . . ."

"Anything you want, Mimi," Judith assured her.

"How about we play a game of Rook after supper?"

"Great idea. You'll need to refresh my memory on the rules, but I'd love to play."

After supper and one round of Rook, Grace was ready to head back to bed. "My cup is running over, Judy," she said earnestly.

"As is mine, Mimi. As is mine."

———————◆———————

That night, Judy visited Judith in a dream again. She was sitting under the apple tree in the backyard.

"Don't leave me," Judy said, her bottom lip quivering.

"I'm right here, Judy."

A huge tear rolled down Judy's cheek. "Why's Mimi leaving? Don't let her leave."

"Judy, I'm here, okay? You are not alone. You don't have to be afraid." She reached down, wiping the tear from her cheek, then tucked a wayward curl behind her ear. She cupped her hand lovingly under Judy's chin to raise it, then looked Judy squarely in the eyes. She took Judy's hand in hers. "You don't have to be afraid," she repeated. "I'm right here, and I won't let go of you."

Judy cried hard, and Judith simply held her until she calmed down, gasping, then taking a deep breath. Her shoulders relaxed, and she leaned her full weight against Judith. "I won't let go of you, okay?" Judith said again.

She sat back so she could look Judy in the eyes again. "Judy, a time will come when we'll need to let go of Mimi." Judy's eyes grew wide. "I'll be right here. Remember that, okay?"

———————◆———————

The Sunday morning sun produced dancing rainbows on the kitchen wall. It beamed through butterfly-shaped prisms hanging in the double window above the sink.

Fresh out of the shower after her morning run, Judith had prepared coffee and was getting ready to prepare omelets when Grace eased into the kitchen. She was taking slow, deep breaths as she walked carefully toward the kitchen table.

"Mimi! Here, let me help you," Judith said as she moved quickly to support her grandmother as she sat down at the table. "Are you okay?"

"Oh now, I'll be fine," Grace dismissed Judith's concern. "Just havin' a little trouble catchin' my breath, like yesterday. I'm afraid we're goin' to need to take a rain check on church."

She was smiling bravely and attempting to reassure Judith that she was fine, adding, "There's nothin' wrong with my appetite, though! Can you fix those omelets without me helpin' you?"

Judith kissed Grace on the forehead. "Can you do your crossword puzzle without me helping you?" she teased. She poured Grace some coffee and brought it over along with the paper and a pen, then focused on cutting up ingredients for the omelets, giving Grace space to catch her breath.

Grace skimmed the obituaries for anyone she might know, then pushed the newspaper aside. "I'm sorry we can't go to church this mornin', honey. You, me, and Virgil, we never missed a service."

"Oh, I remember our weekly ritual," Judith confirmed as she chopped up some tomatoes. "It was Sunday school, then church, dressed in my Sunday best."

"You had one pair of patent leather shoes we bought you not long after you came to live with us," Grace remembered. "We paid for those over several months while they were in layaway. You were *so* proud of those shoes."

"You made sure I changed into other clothes the moment we got home, before Sunday dinner," Judith said while grating cheese. "It's funny hearing myself talk about lunch as *dinner*," she mused. "If I'd invite someone in L.A. to dinner, they'd assume it was the evening meal, not lunch. Or if I'd invite them to supper, they'd probably tease me for being so Southern."

Judith paused, then added, "Isn't it funny how when things change you miss some of the smallest things?"

Grace nodded her head in agreement, replying, "That's just the way the world works. Times change and so do we. Sometimes that's good, and sometimes, not so much."

Grace's words hung in the air while Judith focused on preparing the omelets.

———

"I've got a Sunday School story for you, Judy," Grace said with a grin as Judith brought over their breakfast.

"Well," Judith said as she retrieved two juice glasses and filled them with fresh orange juice. "Let's hear it."

"The Sunday school teacher wanted to use squirrels as an example to teach about workin' hard and savin'," Grace started. "She told her class of young'uns, 'Now, I'm gonna describe somethin' and want you to raise your hand when you know what it is.' The kids were excited. They wanted to show her what they knew."

Grace continued with a twinkle in her eyes. " 'I'm thinkin' of something that lives in trees and eats nuts,' the teacher said. No hands went up. 'It can be gray or brown, and it has a long bushy tail.' Still no hands. 'It chatters and sometimes flips its tail when it's excited.' "

"Finally, one little boy shyly raised his hand, and the teacher breathed a sigh of relief. 'Yes, Henry?' 'Well,' Henry said, 'I know this is Sunday school, so the answer is supposed to be Jesus, but it *sure* sounds like a squirrel to me!' "

Judith erupted into uproarious laughter, covering her mouth too late, snorting orange juice, and spewing it across the kitchen floor. This made her laugh even more as she ran to the sink to grab a dishtowel.

"Oh, my! I wasn't expecting *that*," Grace laughed. "What a hoot! That one tickled my funny bone too. I can't tell you how much I've missed hearing you laugh, Judy. It does my old heart good."

Judith hugged Grace before placing the juice-stained dish towel in the sink. She filled her tiny juice glass again. "I had forgotten how you could make me laugh," she said. "What a gift that is."

"We've always given each other plenty of laughter and love, haven't we?" Grace replied.

"Not everyone can say that, Mimi. You know, no matter what was going on around us, you and Granddaddy were always there, loving me."

"And we always will be sweetie pie," Grace confirmed. "You won't be able to see us, but we'll always be in your heart."

"Mimi," Judith said. "What is half-moon shaped, filled with yummy veggies, bacon, and cheese, and is getting cold?"

"Our omelets!" Grace laughed. "Let's eat."

Despite her excitement about the food, Grace barely made a dent in the omelet.

———◆———

As the day progressed, Grace continued to struggle with catching her breath. "Mimi, how about you go lay down? I'll come check on you in forty-five minutes," Judith suggested.

Grace objected at first, wanting to be where Judith was. But she gave in. "That sounds like a wise choice."

When Judith poked her head into Grace's room later, her Mimi was fast asleep, so she left her and carried on with tasks around the house. Just before noon, Grace emerged from her room.

"I can't believe I've slept most of the morning," Grace observed. "You know it's not like me."

Judith apologized for not having yet fixed dinner. "I wasn't sure if you'd be up," she said, "but I can fix you something right now. What would you like? How about—"

"I'm not really hungry," Grace interrupted. "Maybe just some soda crackers with butter?"

Judith was concerned about Mimi's lack of appetite but decided not to make a big deal of it. Grace had said before that she had some good days and some bad days. This seemed to be the latter.

Grace went to lay down again soon after, and Judith went to Whole Foods to buy some fresh apples and a few other items she knew Grace would enjoy.

By the time Grace emerged again, the lights were turned low, the music of Glen Miller's orchestra was playing quietly, and there was a large bunch of pink roses in the living room.

"You know just how to warm my heart, Judy girl," she said as she walked into the kitchen. "And look at you, so at home in the kitchen."

"I had forgotten how much I enjoy cooking and how relaxing it is for me," Judith admitted. "When I get home, I'm going to make some time to cook my own—" she smiled and leaned toward Grace, "*supper.*"

Judith dished up a bowl of hot, homemade applesauce that Grace had canned the year before. "Here's a little something to tide you over while I cook you some salmon," she said.

Grace had some of the applesauce and declared, "This is perfect, thank you. I don't need anything else . . . except perhaps a second helping. This is delicious!"

Judith sat down with a small bowl of her own. "Mimi, I'm glad we have your lab work tomorrow morning," she said, "and your doctor's appointment. This shortness of breath of yours is concerning."

"They said this'll be part of the deal at some point with the leukemia," Grace explained. "There aren't enough red blood cells to carry a sufficient supply of oxygen. That's why I need them blood transfusions. They give me the bag of platelets to help prevent gettin' nose bleeds and such."

She chuckled at herself, adding, "Listen to me. I'm pickin' up that doctor lingo pretty good. Ha!"

Judith ignored Grace's attempt at levity, put her hand over Grace's, and said softly, "You're pretty amazing. No doubt about that. Now," she continued, "Rachel said she'll pick us up tomorrow morning at nine. Is there anything you need from me to help you get ready in the morning?"

"No, I'll be fine," Grace assured her. "But I think I had better go on to bed so I'll be ready for tomorrow. Sorry to be such a party pooper, honey. Is that okay with you?"

"Absolutely," Judith said. "It's a big day tomorrow." She helped Grace get up from the table and make her way toward the master bedroom.

While Grace got ready for bed, Judith changed the bedsheets and moved the roses to the bedroom for Grace to enjoy.

"Thank you again for that applesauce, sweetie pie, and for these roses. They smell like—" Grace buried her nose in the flowers, "like honey and sunshine . . . and like sweet dreams." She hugged Judith and kissed her on the cheek, whispering, "I love you, Judy girl. See you in the morning."

"I hope you sleep well. I love you too, Mimi."

After leaving Grace's bedroom, Judith tidied up the kitchen and turned off the lights. On the way to her bedroom, she paused to scan Grace's memory wall of photographs as one caught her eye.

It was of her holding a small jar filled with lightning bugs. She remembered one summer evening long ago, running around her Mimi and Granddaddy's backyard catching them one by one and placing them in the jar she had filled with blades of choice grasses and a few small clover flowers, closing them in with the lid.

The jar had holes in the lid. She learned the need for those the hard way the night before, having suffocated the previous catch.

Judith remembered placing the lit jar beside her bed as a nightlight until the next morning.

"God, please be with Mimi tonight, and with Bobbie Sue and Janice, and with Albert, Daisy, Johnny, Gary, and Sara."

Picking up her old journal, she glanced back at pages filled with dreams, concerns, and hopes.

As she turned the page, a notecard dated 2005 fell out. It was written in Mimi's beautiful script.

"Do not be afraid; do not be discouraged. The Lord himself goes before you and will be with you; he will never leave you nor forsake you."

The tears made it hard to read. Judith set aside the journal, turned off the light, and took a deep breath, savoring the familiar smells of home.

CHAPTER 15

Reality

The sky the next morning reflected the mood with which Judith woke up. It was overcast, almost dark. Thundery. And there were no rainbows dancing on the kitchen walls.

Grace waited on the sofa, ready, holding her pocketbook, while Judith tidied up from their morning coffee. Grace's appetite was still not what it was just days before. She ate two bites of buttered toast and half a hardboiled egg and only because Judith insisted that she needed some protein.

Rachel pulled up right at nine.

"Miss Grace, you're looking beautiful, as always," Rachel exclaimed when Judith welcomed her in, though Grace's appearance concerned her. "How are you this morning?"

Grace attempted to be upbeat, but the strain showed in her voice, answering, "Child, I'm fed and ready to go. My Judy is tryin' to fatten me up. That's for sure!" When she tried to get up from the sofa, her body hardly moved.

Judith stepped up to help her.

"Let's get you to the lab, Miss Grace," Rachel said, "and then we'll go hear what your doctor has to say."

Grace took Judith's arm to steady herself as they walked out the door. Once Grace was seated and the car door closed behind her, Judith briefed Rachel.

"I'm concerned," she said quietly. "Mimi's shortness of breath and fatigue have progressed since Saturday. She explained to me what was happening with her blood and platelets."

"We knew this would begin to happen but thought it might take longer for it to start," Rachel told Judith with a concerned look on her face. "I'm glad you are here for her."

———◆———

It was almost noon by the time Grace's labs were completed and they were waiting in the exam room of Dr. Samples, Grace's oncologist. Grace stood in the corner and stared out the window while the other two sat in silence.

She had been issued a portable oxygen tank while in the lab. The high-flow nasal cannula was looped over each ear to hold it in place, and the occasional hiss of the oxygen flow was the only sound in the room.

The door opened, and Dr. Samples stepped into the room with his assistant following. He smiled warmly at Grace.

"Mrs. Lee, it's so good to see you this morning," he said, then added, "and you too, Rachel."

He turned to Judith and extended his hand. "You must be Judith."

Judith stood up briefly to shake his hand. "It's a pleasure to meet you, Dr. Samples. Mimi's a big fan of yours. Both she and Rachel have had such glowing things to say about you."

"She's a true joy," the oncologist responded, glancing at his patient. "Mrs. Lee's beautiful smile and positive energy set her apart."

Dr. Samples sat down at the small wall desk that held a computer. With a few keystrokes, he pulled up Grace's lab work. He frowned as he scrolled through the results, stopping several times to type in comments.

He exhaled deeply as he rolled his stool back from the wall desk, turning to face the three ladies.

The joviality of a moment ago was replaced by concern.

"Mrs. Lee, your hemoglobin is down to 6.9 this morning," he said. "That's what's causing the shortness of breath. The lab had called me saying your O_2 was at 85 percent, which is why I told them to put you on oxygen. You'll have to stay on oxygen."

He looked briefly at Judith saying, "Before you leave today, we'll give you a fresh tank to take with you. We've contacted home health and they will come to your home later this evening with an oxygen concentrator and additional tanks for when your grandmother needs to go out."

He looked at Grace. "We also have a finger pulse oximeter for you to take with you," he told her. "Your O_2 level should always be above 90 percent. If it drops below 90 percent, the output level on your home machine or this tank needs to be increased. We've started your level at two liters."

Pausing briefly, he continued, "You were also running a temperature of 99.9. They gave you some Tylenol for that, and you can continue that as needed."

He addressed Judith. "Her temperature will probably fluctuate, dropping to normal during the day, then elevating during the evening and night. If it goes above 100.7, it's important you call us right away."

Judith nodded as she jotted cryptic notes on her phone.

Dr. Samples turned his gaze back at Grace. "We'll be giving you two units of blood today," he said. "Your platelets are okay, but most of your labs, such as your white blood cell count, hematocrit, and potassium were also low."

Grace peeked over at Judith, who had gently placed her hand on her grandmother's forearm. Grace placed her hand on Judith's.

It was a lot of information for them to take in.

Dr. Samples took a deep breath, then continued, "Based on the very high blast count of your previous bone marrow biopsy as well as today's lab work, it appears your disease is progressing much faster than expected."

Grace's body seemed to understand the news faster than her mind could process. Her eyes welled up.

Dr. Samples glanced briefly at Judith and Rachel to check that they were tracking. He turned his gaze back to Grace. "If it's okay with you, I would like to send you upstairs for another bone marrow biopsy to see what changes have occurred since the last one. I'll call and tell them to fit you in right away."

Grace looked back and forth between Judith and Rachel. Both were visibly taking slow, deep breaths. They tried to be strong for Grace, offering weak, unanswering smiles.

The silence cast a pall over the room as Grace looked down at her wrinkled hands for a moment. She straightened herself in her chair.

Mustering courage, she said, "Well, doc, we knew this was coming." She pushed back a strand of hair from her forehead, then continued. "Would getting another bone marrow biopsy change anything on how you'd treat me? I guess the real question is, is there anything else you can do to fix me?"

Dr. Samples leaned forward, resting his elbows on his knees. He took Grace's hands in his and looked her directly in the eyes. "Mrs. Lee, if you were fifteen or twenty years younger and had this blast count level and lab work, there would be an option or two we could try. But those aren't easy options for the patient, and even for a younger, healthier person, there's a relatively high mortality rate. I have too much respect for you to offer them."

He continued. "As for your first question," he said, "another bone marrow biopsy would probably just confirm your blast count has elevated even further."

Grace absorbed his reply, looking again at her hands, nodding slightly. "Dr. Samples," she asked earnestly, "if I were your mother, what would you do?"

"I would take my mother home and spend as much time with her as possible," he said softly, almost in a whisper. "When the time comes, I would call in hospice to provide any comfort care she might need. And I would enjoy reliving good memories with her. That's what I would do."

Judith's heart was pounding. *Am I imagining things, or are the walls closing in on me?* She struggled to compose herself.

Rachel pulled some tissues from her purse, sliding one onto Judith's lap.

Dammit! I do not want to cry.

Grace looked again at her hands cupped in those of her trusted oncologist. She slightly nodded, smiling sadly. She patted her doctor's hands and said softly, "I appreciate your honesty."

She turned her head toward Judith, declaring with renewed vigor, "Well, Judy girl. You and Rachel heard him. And that's exactly what I want. No more biopsies for me. Not today, not ever. All we need to do is go to the infusion center to get my blood, then head home."

Judith's mind was racing. *Why does it feel like someone's got their hands wrapped around my throat? Is there a two-ton truck on my chest?*

"No!" That was the only word that came out. Judith tried hard to stay present, but the only thing she could wrap her head around was the doctor saying there was nothing else that could be done for Mimi.

Her mouth was dry, and there was a lump in her throat. She tried to swallow.

"Hell no!" she heard herself saying.

For a moment, Judith felt trapped, like she felt the day she had to call nine-one-one, the day her parents died.

She got up.

"Excuse me, Mimi," she said. She glanced at Dr. Samples. "It seems to me that you are *clearly* confused on what we need to do to help my grandmother."

Grace sighed. "Doctor, my apologies. She means well."

Judith's demeanor remained the same. She was fit to be tied.

Dr. Samples kept his composure, smiled politely, and said, "Could we perhaps step into my office? It's right next door." He stood back for Judith to walk through first.

His office door had barely closed behind them before Judith demanded, "What I just heard in there is *not* what needs to happen. I am *not* okay with it."

Grace and Rachel could hear every word Judith said.

Dr. Samples responded in a much slower tempo and at a much lower volume. His eyes were kind despite Judith's anger.

"What part aren't you okay with, Ms. Lee?"

"I'm not okay with us not helping her to get better, us not finding a cure. I'm not okay with you just walking away saying there's nothing else we can do. Essentially what you're saying is to go home and die."

The oncologist looked out the window for a moment, then tenderly looked at Judith again. "Ms. Lee, if you'll bear with me, please. You remind me of Byron Wagner."

"What?" Judith exploded.

"I'll explain. There's a point to the story for us here and now," Dr. Samples responded carefully. He gestured for Judith to take a seat.

Judith sat down, glared at the oncologist, and waited.

"When I was about ten years old, I would pass this house on my way home from school every day."

Why is this guy telling me a story about him being ten and walking home from school?

"I would pass that house every day. There were these bigger boys who lived there, and they would come out and tease me . . ."

This has nothing *to do with my grandmother. Doesn't he get it?*

201

"One day, they came out and started beating me up. I was all by myself until all of a sudden, there was Byron Wagner. He was just two years older than me, but he beat up those boys and told them, 'Don't you ever touch my friend again!' "

He continued. "Everyone needs a Byron Wagner to defend them when there's an injustice. Just like every grandmother needs a Judith to defend them when they are weak . . ."

Judith's breathing slowed down a bit.

Dr. Samples carried on in his calm tone. "There are a few things I want to make sure you and I agree on regarding your grandmother. Do you believe I intend to hurt her?"

"No."

"Do you believe if there were a cure that I would *not* give it to her?"

"No, but how, I, how . . ." Judith stammered. She exhaled slowly.

"It seems to me *both* of us are advocates for your grandmother. We want what is best for her. True?"

"Yes."

"Okay. So, could it be that some of what's happening right now is that this is a big shock and that you didn't expect any of this news today?"

"I didn't . . ." she swallowed again to clear the lump in her throat, but the words wouldn't come out.

"I get that," he said with a gentle smile, eyes glistening. "How blessed Miss Grace is to have you in her life, especially right now. You love her *so* much, and it shows."

Dr. Samples reached out his hand. Judith looked down, handing him her hand. He squeezed it, saying, "Well, now that we've agreed that we both love your grandmother and would do anything in the world to help her, could we agree to make sure she exits this life as graciously as she lived it? Could we agree on honoring your grandmother's wishes regarding what the next steps would be?"

Judith surrendered. "We can," she said. "Thank you, doctor." She meant it. It was a strange position for her to be in, to be disarmed by someone else's superior logic—in this situation at least. And she was grateful. "And my apologies. I was out of place."

"You're welcome, but no apology required. I really do believe that we all need a Byron. And by the way, I'm still friends with Byron today."

———◆———

When the two of them walked back into the exam room, the oncologist looked at Rachel, then back at Judith, "Your grandmother is fortunate. She has a wonderful support system with you and Rachel. Not all people are so lucky."

"I'm not *lucky*, doctor," Grace said with a smile. "I am *blessed*."

Dr. Samples nodded, then continued, "I would recommend you continue with the Monday and Thursday lab work for blood or platelets, as needed, until whenever you decide to bring hospice in. At that point, they will take over care."

With that, he stood up slowly and shook Judith and Rachel's hands. As he turned to Grace, she reached out and gave him a big hug.

"You're a good man, Dr. Samples," she said, her voice cracking. "Thank you for everything. May God bless you."

"I wish there was more we could do," he said, clearing the emotion from his throat. "This is a terrible disease. I hate it. We've had advances in treatment, but we still have so far to go. There are some trial treatments in the pipeline getting very promising results, but there's so much more research and development of treatments needed . . ."

His voice cracked and he excused himself, leaving the room.

His assistant stepped up, extending her hand toward the hallway, "Ladies, if you will follow me, please."

———◆———

Checking in at the infusion center, Rachel guided them to the family room nearby as the wait would be long. She excused herself for a moment.

"Judy honey, it seems that you got yourself tied up in a knot," Grace said once they were alone. "What's going on?"

"It just felt like we were giving up too easily, Mimi," she explained. "But I get it now. Not that I want to, but I do."

She hugged Grace tightly. "I wish there was more we could do . . ."

"You're doing all you can, Judy," Grace assured her. "You being here with me is the best gift in the world."

On the table was an unfinished Thomas Kinkade jigsaw puzzle waiting for the next visiting patient to find more pieces that fit.

They started looking at the puzzle and the pieces remaining to be placed, happy to have something to take their attention from the real world during their wait.

For the life of her, Judith could not place a single piece. The conversation with Dr. Samples kept playing in her mind.

———◆———

"Grace Lee?" a tech called as she opened the door to the family room.

Grace smiled, holding up her hand. "That's me."

Judith helped Grace up, and they followed the tech out the door and down the hallway to the third of three pods in the infusion center. Each pod had about twenty small infusion rooms.

"You'll be in room eight today," the tech offered, adding, "The nurse will be with you in a minute."

Grace settled into the large vinyl recliner.

Judith sat down in a chair in the corner of the small room, watching Rachel help Grace get comfortable, covering her with a warm blanket given to her by the tech. Rachel brought her some crackers and juice.

Since they had missed lunch, she also brought a couple of packs of peanut butter crackers for herself and Judith, but this time it was Judith who did not have much of an appetite.

Not long after, Grace's nurse rolled a portable computer stand into the room. She exchanged pleasantries with everyone, then checked Grace's plastic medical wristband that had been placed there when she was checked into the lab earlier that morning. After taking Grace's vitals, she excused herself to place the order for the bags of blood.

"The blood normally takes about forty-five minutes to arrive," Rachel told Judith.

While they waited, Grace turned on the television mounted high on the wall and switched channels to "Judge Judy." They all stared at the small screen, but none of them took in a word of the drama unfolding in the courtroom.

Don't leave me, Judith heard the words deep in her soul.

"You won't be able to see us, but we'll always be in your heart," she remembered Mimi's words.

When the images from the dream two nights before came back to her, Judith held her breath as snippets from the dream played out in her mind.

"You don't have to be afraid," she watched herself say to her younger self. "I'm right here, and I won't let go of you. A time will come when we'll need to let go of Mimi, but I'll be right here. Remember that, okay?"

As tears welled up for the umpteenth time, Judith scooted her chair closer and held Grace's hand.

The transfusion procedure played off like a scene from a movie.

The nurse reappeared, positioning her computer at the doorway. On a tray on the computer stand lay the first bag of blood for Grace.

The nurse stuck her head into the hallway, calling loudly, "I need a check!"

Almost immediately a tech appeared. "Ready," she said.

Looking at Grace's wristband, the nurse asked Grace her name and date of birth, which the tech confirmed against the label on the bag of blood. Next, the nurse took the bag of blood, reading out the numbers on the label while the tech compared them to the numbers from the blood bank's record.

"You're good to go," the tech confirmed before walking away.

"You have a port, correct?" the nurse asked Grace.

"I do, right here," Grace said, motioning to just below her left collarbone.

After the nurse prepped the port, she inserted the needle from the bag of blood that was hanging beside the chair. She adjusted the flow and announced, "I'll be back to check you in five minutes, then it will be about an hour or so till the first infusion is complete."

"Thank you," Grace replied gently, but the nurse was already out the door.

Grace, Judith, and Rachel stared blankly at the television screen. Grace's oxygen supply buzzed and hissed in the background.

Judith gently rubbed Mimi's hand. *"A time will come when we'll need to let go of Mimi,"* the words kept turning in her mind. *"But I'll be here . . ."*

The loud beeping of the flow meter jerked Judith back to reality. The first infusion was complete. The nurse repeated the entire procedure with a second unit of blood. An hour later, it was completed.

The tech removed the needle and sanitized Grace's port, then taped it shut. She replaced the oxygen with a full new tank. "All done, Mrs. Lee," she said with a comforting smile. "You can go home now."

———◆———

"You girls must be starving," Grace declared by the time they got into the elevator. "Let's go get something to eat."

While they appreciated the thought, Judith suggested that they simply pick up something on the way home. "I think we're all ready to be home."

The other two did not object.

———◆———

It was late afternoon by the time they walked back into the house, exhausted.

Judith placed plates and silverware on the table and unpacked boxes from a large Cracker Barrel bag. "Country-fried chicken with corn, green beans, and biscuits. Sound okay?"

"It sounds heavenly. Oh, I wish Virgil could join us for dinner. He sure loved Cracker Barrel's chicken," Grace reminisced.

Rachel rolled the oxygen tank and parked it next to Grace as she took a seat at the table, breathing with effort.

"I wish I could have met him, Miss Grace," Rachel said as she dished up a plate for her and Grace.

"Granddaddy was a gentleman to the core," Judith told Rachel, taking just a spoonful or two of vegetables.

The three ate in silence, the reality of the day adding a heaviness to the room.

"I had better get going," Rachel said as she cleared her plate. "It's been a long day. I hope you rest well tonight." She leaned over and gave Grace a hug.

With Judith standing right there, it seemed awkward not to hug her, too, so Rachel reached out and hesitatingly, awkwardly smiling, gave Judith a quick hug.

"Thank you for all you do, Rachel," Judith told her. "I don't know what we would have done without you today."

"You are welcome. You get some rest tonight. Please don't hesitate to call me, no matter what the hour. Home health should be here any moment with Miss Grace's oxygen machine and supplies," she said as she headed out. "Good night, Miss Grace. Good night, Judith."

———◆———

Judith sat down at the kitchen table with Grace. She sat looking down, her hands folded, rubbing the top of one thumb with the other.

"This day didn't quite turn out the way we expected, did it, Mimi?" she said without looking up.

Grace had been quietly watching Judith, seeing the sadness on her face. "We got thrown for a bit of a loop there, Judy girl, but that's okay." She paused briefly. "The good Lord has us in the palm of his hand, so it's alright sweetheart."

Judith looked up, tears gathering in the corners of her eyes again. "With everything that's happened recently and getting this news today, how can you be so calm and collected?" she asked.

Grace looked tenderly at Judith. "I want you to listen up now, okay? This is important," she said softly. "There are things in this life that we can control and things we cannot. When we have things happen that we can't control, too many people spend way too much time frettin' over them."

The corners of her mouth raised into a slight smile. "When you're feelin' lower than a bow-legged caterpillar, that's wasted time. Life's too short to waste time on frettin'. So, the answer to your question is, you just do what you got to do. Ever'day. Just get through it. Tomorrow will be better. Wasn't that what you done in school when you was gettin' picked on? You just did what you had to do."

"I guess . . ." Judith hesitated. "I guess I did."

"It's *exactly* what you did, honey," Grace confirmed. "And that's what we're doin' now. We're doin' what we got to do."

She paused for a moment, looking at Judith with her ever-loving eyes and with a slight, sympathetic smile, then continued reassuringly, "It's gonna be okay, Judy girl. You made that long bus journey here for me, and now you're gonna be here with me as I finish my journey. Then you'll continue yours. *That*, sweetheart, is God's plan."

Tears were flowing down Judith's cheeks. "But all the years I've been away—"

Grace interrupted Judith. She reached across the table, taking Judith's hands in hers. She waited until Judith looked into her eyes. "Hush now, child," she admonished her softly. "Virgil and me, we always knew you were just doin' what you needed to do. You had your own path to take. We never doubted your love. Not ever. Not for one second. I need you to remember me tellin' you this. Heart to heart."

She paused for a moment, then asked, "You gonna remember?"

Judith attempted a feeble smile, answering, "Always, Mimi. Always. Thank you."

She let go of Grace's hands to get a Kleenex.

"When you've wiped off them tears, I have another story for you," Grace told Judith.

"I'm all ears," said Judith as she poured them each a glass of water. She loved watching Mimi tell stories. She watched the sparkle in her eyes and the ways she spoke with her hands.

"A preacher once gave everyone in church a red balloon," she started. "He told them to blow 'em up and write their name on the balloon. Next, he took everyone into the event center and told them to toss the balloons into the room. There were well over a hundred red balloons."

Grace took a sip of the water. " 'You have one minute to find your balloon,' he told them. There was chaos as ever'one was searching, but not a single person found their balloon. 'Now,' the preacher said, 'pick up any balloon, and hand it to the person whose name is on it.' Wouldn't you know it," Grace said, "It didn't take all but two minutes and ever'one in that room had their own balloon again."

She looked at Judith, "Them balloons are like peace, Judy girl. We'll never find it if we only look for our own peace. But if we care about helping other people find peace, we'll find ours too."

Judith reached over and held Grace in a long, long hug. "Thanks for handing me some peace today, Mimi."

A knock on the door interrupted their hug.

"That must be them home health folks with my new equipment. You go on and let them in," Grace said. "I'll sit here and catch my breath."

CHAPTER 16

Amazing Grace

Judith sat staring at her phone. She could not even muster up the energy to deal with her email.

So much for efficiency.

She called her therapist's office. "I need to schedule a call with Dr. Sanders, please . . . The earliest opening . . . I know she doesn't do phone consultations, yes . . . It's an emergency . . . Thank you . . . If there's a cancelation sooner, will you please let me know? . . . Thank you, bye."

She typed the details of the appointment into her phone. The days had all been running together, so she paused to check what day of the week she found herself in.

It's only Thursday?

Pushing aside the three unopened copies of *The Tennessean*, she poured a cup of coffee and sat down on the sofa.

No amount of breathing exercises or essential oil wafting through the room was helping. She could not even get herself to go for a run.

She was barely wearing any makeup and had been wearing the same flannel shirt for three days.

Her mind would not stop replaying snippets of conversations and dreams from the past few days.

*"When the time comes, I don't want there to be any unneces-
sary measures taken . . ."*

"What you're saying is go home and die."

*"Let's agree to make sure she exits this life as graciously as she
lived it . . ."*

"Don't leave me."

*"A time will come when we'll need to let go of Mimi. But I'll
be right here."*

*"You won't be able to see Virgil and me, but we'll always be in
your heart."*

*"You just do what you have to do. Ever'day. Just get through it.
Tomorrow will be better."*

Judith stared at the photo of Grace and Virgil on the end table for a
while. She inhaled slowly, picked up her cell phone, and texted Rachel.

> Pls cancel Mimi's labs.

> Will do. Everything OK?

> She's not up to going to the infusion center today.

> Would it help if I come by to help?

> No need. Thanks.

> OK. How are her vitals?
> Any temp spikes?

> Only slight rises. Nothing above 100.3.
> Increased O2 again last night to keep her above 90%.
> 3rd night in a row.

What do you have the O2 at?

8 liters.

Barely maintaining 90%.

Struggles with breathing when she moves.

How about her sleeping?

Eating?

Liquid intake?

Lots of sleeping since Monday night.

More than being awake.

Only ate a bite or two since Cracker Barrel.

Barely been drinking anything.

Pause

The little booklet I gave you . . .

It lists what to expect and watch for as someone's body begins to shut down.

Have read it, yes.

It may be time to call in hospice . . .

Long pause

Maybe tomorrow.

Not today.

I get it.

She's always been the rock of our family.

No surprise.

I hate seeing her this way.

So do I.

Know what's amazing?
She's never complained.
Not a single time. Not once.
How does she do that?

She's a remarkably strong and special person.

I've always known that she's special, but OMG!
She's been more concerned about me than herself.

No surprise at all.

G2G.
Need to check on Mimi.
Sounds like she's stirring.
Thanks for canceling her appointment.
And for being there for us.

The evening shadows stretched into darkness as night fell outside Grace's little home. Judith opened some windows, letting the early fall air in.

She poked her head into Grace's room.

"Well, look who's awake," she said quietly. She made herself at home on the side of Grace's bed. "How are you feeling?"

A smile slowly came over Grace's face. "I was just laying here counting my blessings," Grace said, speaking slower than usual, taking deep breaths. "It has been a *very* good day . . . and I have no pain at all . . . but I am ready to get up for a bit." Deep breath. "Can you help me, honey?"

Judith had to listen carefully to hear every word.

"Of course." Judith helped Grace from the bed and into her rocking chair, then adjusted the cannula tubing. She wiped a wayward curl from her grandmother's forehead. "You look amazing for someone who's been sleeping most of the time for three days straight. You must be hungry. How about I bring you some crackers and applesauce?"

"Maybe just peppermint tea."

Judith got up and adjusted Grace's pillows. "One cup of peppermint tea coming right up." She kissed Grace on the forehead.

"And the photo of Virgil and me in Chattanooga. Oh, and . . ." Judith paused, waiting for her grandmother to finish. "Can you get Johnny Cash music on that fancy phone of yours?"

"Can do." Judith smiled tenderly at Grace as she pulled up a Johnny Cash playlist on Spotify, turning the volume down low so she would be able to hear Grace call if needed.

While making tea, Judith filled a bowl with warm, soapy water.

"How about I help you freshen up?" she said as she put the tea on the dresser. "Would you like that?" She turned on a bedside lamp.

Grace sighed with relief. "Very much."

The sound of the washcloth being dipped into the water and being wrung out joined that of the buzzing and hissing of the oxygen concentrator. In the distance, you could hear some sirens passing.

While Grace sat brushing her teeth, Judith put fresh sheets on the bed. Next, she carefully helped Grace change into clean pajamas.

The room smelled of lavender and peppermint toothpaste.

"Look at you," Judith said with a smile, "you look like a new woman."

"I think I should lay down."

215

Judith helped Grace, then adjusted the pillows and the tubing, noticing a slight blue tint to Grace's lips.

She started to place the photo of her grandparents on the bedside table, but Grace shook her head and held out her hand. Judith handed her the picture.

"When the time comes, I want you to bury me in this dress," she told Judith, pointing at the beautiful gown in the photo from that magical night so long ago.

Judith nodded and filed the comment away as something she will remember to do someday. It was not yet time to talk about things like that.

She quietly cracked the window open to let some fresh air in and moved the rocking chair right next to Grace's bed. She took a seat, placing her hand on that of her grandmother.

Grace looked a little worn out, but she had a glimmer of energy— more than she had had in days. She looked at Judith with great tenderness. "Tell me about your bus trip again, would you?"

"Which part?"

"The very best part."

Judith thought for a moment. "When I boarded the bus that first day, I would never have thought I'd say this, but the best part was the people I met . . ."

Grace gave a satisfied sigh. She took a slow, deep breath. "Do you know why I asked you . . . to take the bus to Nashville?"

"Well, you said it's been your dream to see the places along the route."

"Honey . . ." Grace said with a smile, "I coulda checked out a book if I wanted to learn about the places." Grace took another deep breath, then carried on. "Life's journey . . . ain't about the destination . . . The only thing that matters . . . is the people you meet . . . and who touch your life." Deep breath. "And the people whose lives *you* touch. That's the way the good Lord works. It's the people . . . Don't ever forget that."

"I won't, Mimi," Judith said. "I won't forget."

"If it ain't got a soul, it don't matter."

Judith squeezed Grace's hand. "If it ain't got a soul, it don't matter," she repeated thoughtfully.

For a while—*a minute or was it thirty?*—the two remained silent, Judith gently stroking Grace's hand with her thumb.

The buzz and hiss of the oxygen concentrator blended with the evening sounds drifting through the window—crickets, the occasional lonesome call of a whip-poor-will, and Johnny Cash singing,

"Softly and tenderly, Jesus is calling . . ."

Peace settled in the room like a warm blanket.

"Calling for you and for me . . ."

The curtains gently moved.

Is it the breeze?

Judith looked up, goosebumps sliding down the back of her neck. "What were you saying, Mimi?"

Oak leaves rustled.

Crickets.

Buzz.

"Come home, come home . . ."

The atmosphere in the room has changed.

Judith got up gingerly, leaning over. "Mimi?" she whispered.

She placed her hand on Grace's chest. Nothing moved, nor could she feel a gentle thump of Grace's heartbeat.

"Mimi?" She gently shook Grace. "Mimi!" Tears started running down her cheeks. "Mimi, please don't leave me. Not yet!"

Judith wrapped her arms around Grace's shoulders, lay her head on Grace's chest, and wept.

———◆———

Another copy of *The Tennessean* joined the earlier copies on the kitchen table, untouched. By Saturday afternoon, Judith willed herself to go for a walk. It was a beautiful, cloudless day. Returning from the walk, she picked up the paper from the swing on the porch, then opened the front door.

"Judy girl, you're just in time for coffee," she expected to hear.

But the house was silent.

No laughter from the kitchen.

No quirky joke or encouraging word.

Not even the buzz of the oxygen concentrator.

Just silence—except for the thoughts Judith replayed in her head.

"A time will come when we'll need to let go of Mimi. But I'll be right here."

"You won't be able to see Virgil and me, but we'll always be in your heart."

The breeze coming through the front door stirred up the smell of the enormous bouquet of calla lilies on the end table, a gift from Judith's staff. "Thinking of you. Let us know if there's anything we can do," their note read.

Judith closed the door and headed to the kitchen. She opened the refrigerator, but it was mostly empty. In a fit of rage, she had cleared it out into the trash the night before. It started with a trio of casseroles, each accompanied by a Bundt cake. Folks from church had dropped them off on Friday the moment the news of Grace's passing spread.

The hole in the Bundt cakes felt like the hole left in Judith's world. That, along with the fact that two of them were pineapple upside-down cakes, is what angered Judith.

"I know your world has just been turned upside down. Here, have a pineapple upside-down cake." Judith conjured up a sassy encounter in her mind.

"Honey, the people care. The gesture is one of love," she could hear Grace admonish her.

218

She stood before an empty refrigerator, not feeling hungry but knowing she had to eat. For the life of her, Judith could not decide what to order for delivery.

I'll just go drive and see what's open where I can order to go.

Picking up the keys to Mimi's ancient Honda Accord, Judith paused to look out the window.

An oriole landed on a boxwood and looked straight at Judith.

"I'll be right here . . ."

A pair of fat gray squirrels played among the branches of the oak tree, shaking their bushy tails and chattering. For the first time in days, Judith smiled as she remembered Mimi's joke from just a week ago. *"What's brown or gray and has a bushy tail?"*

Judith headed out the door. As she drove around her childhood city, a plan started taking shape in her mind.

———◆———

Most of the cars in the church's rutted gravel parking lot—torn up by many years of rainstorms—were from Tennessee. But there were also a few from Alabama, Georgia, Kentucky, and even one from Louisiana, old friends who had moved away.

The foyer of the church was jam-packed as they waited for the doors to the sanctuary to be opened.

"Ooo, you drove a laht to get here," Violette Hebert greeted the Basketts from Kentucky. Despite her and Avit having moved to Nashville from New Orleans twenty years ago, their accents still made heads turn and their Cajun expressions still puzzled their friends at times.

"It's good to see you, Violette," Francine Baskett responded as she gave her old friend a bear hug. "I sure wish it weren't under these circumstances, though."

They reminisced over the hours they had spent in the tiny church serving refreshments at funerals and showers.

"Don' choo know dare, if deez walls could speak, dey would tell of the many hours Grace served here."

"You know that Grace was the first one to welcome us when we moved here forty years ago?" Mrs. Baskett remembered.

"Talk about," Violette said softly.

"And she was the first to show up at our home with a casserole and a lemon meringue pie in hand when Susan was born." She looked to where her husband was catching up with Avit Hebert. "To this day, Charlie would say no one can make a lemon meringue pie like Grace Lee."

"Talk about," Violette repeated, nodding her head.

———◆———

On the other side of the doors, Judith stood alone next to the open mahogany casket at the front of the church.

"I wish you could smell these roses," she said softly. "I think you might tell me the arrangement is too big, though, that I'm making a fuss, and that the casket and the silk lining is over the top . . ."

She took a deep breath and smiled tenderly, determined not to cry.

Grace was wearing the dress from the photo, the one she had worn with Virgil to their fancy dinner that night long ago at the Chattanooga Choo-Choo. It had only been worn that one time.

Grace looked at peace—like she was sleeping. Her hands were folded over a single long-stemmed red rose resting on her black dress. The funeral home director had invited Judith earlier to place the rose, a symbol of the love Grace gave and the love she received during her lifetime.

"I miss you, Mimi," Judith said, her hand resting on Grace's ice-cold hand. "I miss you more than you can ever imagine." It felt strange to talk to what looked like Grace, yet it was not Grace. "Thank you for making me take the bus to come see you."

She paused to read some of the cards attached to the plants and flowers that filled the front of the church—bouquets, wreaths, baskets, posies, orchids, peace lilies, even a redwood bonsai from her team.

The pianist entered and quietly started playing hymns. Though the old upright piano was slightly out of tune, it brought back precious memories of a time and place that had been tucked away almost forgotten in a corner of Judith's mind. Many moons ago, Judith would sometimes stare at the yellowed keys, wishing she could make music come from it.

The funeral director opened the doors, nodding at Judith to take her place at the head of the casket.

People began walking in, filing by the casket to pay their respects, to share stories, and tell Judith how sorry they were for her loss. They spoke in low voices, as if speaking any louder might wake Grace up.

If only it were that easy. Yelling, wailing, begging, sobbing inconsolably. None of that helped on Thursday night.

Judith tried to be present, to be courteous, but the words and the faces were mostly a blur, as had most everything been since the moment Grace left.

Deep breath in.
Hold for four.
Out for four.
Wait for four.
Repeat.

"Thank you," she heard herself say as folks she had known for as far back as she could remember filed by. She saw people's lips moving but for the life of her, Judith could hardly make out a word.

Typical of life in a tight community, they all knew of Judith's success in the business world, and folks looked at her curiously, as if judging whether she was still in touch with her roots.

———◆———

Judith finally took a seat next to Rachel in the front row on the right, the exact spot where she and Grace had sat just two years before at her Granddaddy's funeral service.

It felt surreal sitting in that front-row spot. It was not where she, Grace, and Virgil used to sit. Judith closed her eyes, seeing the three of them sit in their spot—six rows from the front to the center of the left. She could see Virgil leaning over to pass her a dollar to drop in the collection plate.

In the seventh grade, she once thought she could put the dollar to better use at the GW. Virgil noticed, and Judith got a thorough scolding once they got home.

She never once tried that again.

There was a low hum of conversations among friends and acquaintances while the pianist continued quietly playing until the preacher stood before them.

"You doing okay?" Rachel whispered.

Judith simply nodded. She knew if she started to speak now, the floodgates might open. She could not afford that. Not before her talk. Not in front of a sea of people.

"Today," the preacher's thunderous voice pulled her back to reality, "we have come to celebrate the well-lived life of Mrs. Grace Lee."

He slowly scanned the full church, pausing as he met Judith's gaze, then carried on. "Miss Grace, as we all called her, was one of the matriarchs of this congregation. Almost always here when the doors were open, she led by example."

Judith heard an affirming "Yes, she did," from the row behind her.

"Miss Grace was one of those rare people who used words sparingly, but when she spoke, people listened because they knew what she said had meaning."

Rachel glanced over at Judith and nodded reassuringly.

"Recently," the preacher continued, "I received a phone call from Miss Grace asking me to come visit her as soon as possible. I went over the next morning, and as we sat out on her front porch having sweet tea, she told me about her leukemia and the terminal diagnosis. 'I have two specific instructions about my funeral,' she told me. 'Write them down so you don't forget.' "

Folks laughed, and the preacher carried on. " 'Keep it short,' she said, 'And don't make it a pity party.' " The laughter rose even higher as the people looked at one another nodding their heads as if to say, "That sounds *just* like Miss Grace."

The preacher looked at the sea of faces before him. "Each of us knew and loved Miss Grace. There is another kind of grace that we can know, a gift offered to all of us who choose to receive it. In a world that sometimes seems out of control, we are each on our own journey in hope of finding grace."

He paused to let the words sink in. "Miss Grace's journey ended on Thursday night in the arms of her precious 'Judy girl.' " He looked at Judith, "When her soul left this earth, she was welcomed in the arms of Jesus where she found grace and was reunited with all her other loved ones, and with the love of her life, Virgil."

The preacher continued, but Judith's mind wandered. One image after another appeared from as far back as she could remember, of weekends at Granddaddy and Mimi's home, of decorating cookies with the two of them, of moving in and them tucking her in and being the first smiling faces to greet her in the morning. Of them cheering proudly as Judy excelled at school, and of many a conversation around the dinner table about the day's highs and lows.

She saw them standing and applauding as she received her high school and then later her university degree, saw them waving with tears rolling down their cheeks when she boarded her first flight ever and headed to the West Coast.

She saw Mimi on her knees next to Granddaddy's casket when no one else was in the room, sobbing like she had never seen her do, not even the day when they lowered Mama and Daddy's bodies into the ground.

The memories turned to a dream-like vision of Grace dressed in a long, white flowing gown. She looked younger, was not wearing glasses, and stood taller than Judith had seen in years. She was surrounded by a sea of white clouds. Next, a younger Virgil appeared, also dressed in white, looking almost perfect. In the vision, he extended his hand to her saying, "Grace," and she accepted his hand with a smile.

Gazing into each other's eyes, they began waltzing, and Virgil slowly turned Grace as the white smoke drifted in swirls from their movement.

———•———

"Now, please turn to page forty-six in your hymnals as we sing Miss Grace's favorite hymn, 'In the Garden.' " The preacher's instructions pulled Judith back to reality.

Once they were through singing, everyone took a seat, and the preacher invited Judith to the podium. "Many of you know Miss Grace's Judy, uh, Judith," he said. "She wanted to say a few words this afternoon."

Rising quickly from her pew, Judith took the three steps up to the stage, walked to the podium, and looked across the sea of faces, many of whom she recognized.

She took a deep breath to calm her beating heart.

"I'm right here," the words from her dream popped back in her head. Judith could feel her heart slowing to a normal rhythm, her confidence rising.

"Thank you for the overwhelming show of support and love since Mimi passed. The casseroles, Bundt cakes, and other delicious food that you brought was a reminder of the love you all had for her and for me."

Judith paused to fight back the tears that were attempting to dampen her cheeks.

In through the nose. Out through the mouth.

Rachel had reminded her of the age-old trick the day before when they were talking through some details around the funeral. "It activates your parasympathetic nervous system," she told Judith. "That slows your heart rate, lowers your blood pressure, decreases your muscle tension, and restores your breathing to its calm state."

"Mimi was my North Star," Judith continued, measuring every word. "She was my constant that allowed me to survive, find my way, and thrive. Though she's gone, her influence on me—and on many of you, I hope—remains."

She looked up at the ceiling for a few seconds as if searching for divine intervention. "Having been fortunate to have had a front-row seat in the world of Grace Lee—especially for the past twenty-four years—I can assure you that my Mimi was someone who acted on her intentions. She showed her love by her actions."

Judith glanced at the audience, seeing one familiar face after another.

"There were times I felt sorry for myself, especially during my teen-age years. But Mimi would always remind me in the most loving ways how blessed we were, and that we Lees don't do pity parties."

People smiled at Judith lovingly and knowingly. Judith avoided looking at those who were wiping tears, afraid the sight would unleash her tears.

"I've heard it said that we judge others by their actions, but we judge ourselves by our intentions," Judith said, watching as heads nodded in agreement. "The legacy Mimi has left me is that I must live in such a way that those who judge me by my actions find me worthy."

She cleared the lump in her throat.

In through the nose. Out through the mouth.

"The night Mimi—" Judith cleared the lump in her throat again. "Some of Mimi's final words to me were a reminder that life's journey is not about the destination, but about the people we meet, the people whose lives we touch and who touch our lives."

There was barely a dry eye in the room. Judith cleared the lump in her throat again.

"My prayer is that with God's help, I can lead a life worthy of the many blessings he has bestowed on me. And if Mimi and Granddaddy can look down on me, they would see that their efforts to guide me were worthwhile."

Tears started to trickle down Judith's cheeks. She cut her speech short. "Again, thank you, and may God bless each and every one of you," she said and headed back to her seat next to Rachel who handed her a Kleenex.

Silence.

Here and there, you could hear a stifled sniffle. Mr. Hinkle broke the silence with a loud blowing of his nose, leading to muted giggles and more sniffles.

The preacher was about to take his place behind the podium, but one by one, others began standing up, sharing memories of Grace's impact on their lives.

"When you were with Grace, nothing else seemed to matter to her. She gave you the gift of presence" was a theme throughout.

"Sorry, Miss Grace," the preacher said, smilingly looking over at the casket as he stood up a full forty minutes later. "I know you wanted me to keep it short, but this is what happens when you leave a mark on a community."

He looked up at the congregation, thanking them for sharing and for coming. "Let us stand." The preacher picked up his hymnal. "In closing. Let us turn to page sixty-six and sing 'Amazing Grace.' "

Nashville's National Cemetery was just outside of the Nashville city limits, only a few miles from the Grand Ole Opry. Grace's hearse and the funeral procession made the thirty-minute drive from the church as cars and trucks on both sides of the highway pulled over in respect as the procession passed by.

"I'd forgotten about this Southern tradition. It's so different than in L.A.," Judith told Rachel who accompanied her in the family limousine behind the hearse.

The ceremony at the National Cemetery was brief. The smell of dirt having been freshly dug hung in the air. Far off in another section of the cemetery, Judith heard a lawnmower.

Life goes on, I suppose . . .

All those who came to the cemetery paid their respects to Judith one last time, finally leaving only Judith, Rachel, the limousine driver, and some of the cemetery workers.

"Would you wait here for me, please?" she asked Rachel, then walked alone to Virgil's open grave, where Grace's coffin would soon be placed on top of his.

Judith leaned over and dropped a single red rose she had taken from Grace's casket spray of flowers.

"Thank you for all you did for me, Granddaddy. I know you and Mimi are dancing in heaven, and someday, I'll join you both. I love you more than you'll ever know," Judith said with a trembling smile and with tears welling up.

She walked back to the limousine where Rachel waited for her. The driver opened their door as they stepped into the welcome coolness.

———◆———

Back at the church, Judith hugged Rachel in a full embrace, asking, "When you take me back to the house, would you be able to stay for a

227

little while? There are some things I've been thinking about and that I need your help with."

"Of course," Rachel said, still pleasantly surprised by Judith's unexpected enveloping hug.

The two stepped back into the church where Judith gave directions to the representatives of the funeral home about what to do with the various flower and plant arrangements that had not been taken to the cemetery.

Most were to be taken to the Vanderbilt-Ingram Cancer Center in the Vanderbilt University Medical Center where Mimi had received her treatments and infusions. The largest peace lily was to be sent to Dr. Samples' office, with a note of gratitude and thanks from Judith attached thereto. "Her leaving this life was as gracious as she lived it," Judith wrote, "thanks in no small part to you."

She took only the bonsai with her, having the perfect place for it in her home.

Judith ran into the preacher on her way out. "My Mimi would have been proud of you today."

"Judith, she was an incredibly special lady. We were lucky—"

"Blessed," Judith interrupted.

He gave a big smile, having heard Grace make that correction several times throughout the years. "Yes, we were *blessed* that she and Virgil chose to make this their church home. She was such an amazingly kind and loving woman, a woman of action, not merely intention."

"Thank you for fulfilling her wishes today. I'll always remember your kindness to her and to me."

With that, Judith slowly walked to Rachel's waiting car for the drive back to Grace's empty house.

PART 3

CHAPTER 17

The Plan

Exhausted, Judith fell onto the sagging sofa, exhaling with a deep whoosh in an effort to expel some of the day's stress.

"You needed that!" Rachel said as she took a seat on the chair nearby.

"I guess the stress of the past week is catching up with me," Judith said as she pinched the bridge of her nose between her eyes. "Today went better than I had hoped, and I sure am glad it's all over."

"I'll bet," Rachel agreed. "It was a beautiful celebration of Miss Grace's life. I'm sure she would have approved." She smiled reassuringly. "Your tribute was spot on and thought-provoking."

"Thanks. I realize more and more how blessed I am for having had Mimi's influence in my life . . ." She closed her eyes and lay her head back, processing the day. Meanwhile, Rachel pulled out her phone and jotted down some things she wanted to remember.

"Okay, so let's talk about why I asked you over," Judith said as she sat up herself. "You'll need to take notes."

Rachel held up her phone and winked. Judith smiled as she slid a legal pad and a pen across the coffee table. "You might need to go old-school so you can write faster."

Judith took a sip of water before continuing. "So, when I spoke at the church about judging others by their actions and ourselves by our intentions, that was something I've been wrestling with for the past two days," Judith explained. "I meant what I said about wanting to live in such a way that those who judge me by my actions find me worthy."

Judith continued, "My prayer is that I will lead a life worthy of the many blessings God has bestowed on me."

Judith looked at the row of magnets she had pulled off the fridge the day before as she was thinking about one of her and Grace's last conversations and the way forward.

"I've spent all my life focused on the destination, not recognizing that it was the *journey* that was the most important, and the people who cross our paths on that journey. Well, that changes, beginning today," Judith declared. "Rachel, what I'm about to ask of you is going to take a *lot* of your time over the next few days. Would you be able to help me?"

Rachel had worked with bereaved families enough to know that in the weeks following the loss of a loved one, tasks that may have been second nature to them could be overwhelming.

"I can move some things around," she assured Judith. "Whatever you need."

Judith smiled briefly, delighted that Rachel's position allowed for the flexibility they needed for the plan to come together, then slipped into a role she was very comfortable in—that of the one who comes up with grand ideas broken down into the most effective steps toward execution.

"Okay," she began, "here's what I need you to help me with."

Judith spewed a list of things, and Rachel scribbled them down as fast as her hand could write. As Judith's list grew, Rachel's eyes widened.

———◆———

Time seemed to move in slow motion. For Judith, a day would sometimes feel like a week that she had to struggle through. But then, somehow, the next day would zip by in a wink. In the evening, she would be unsure of what day it was and where all the hours went.

On one of those hazy days, Judith headed out to drop off goods at the GW. When she returned, she found an envelope Rachel had left on the porch.

"Miss Grace made me promise to give this to you exactly seven days after her passing," Rachel had written on the envelope.

Judith sat down on the swing, took a deep breath, and opened the envelope. There was a note penned in Grace's beautiful script.

"My Judy," it said. "It has been a week since I left you and rejoined Virgil and your momma and daddy. I'm sure you are happy for me. I didn't have many materials things to leave you, but I wanted to leave you with the words of this poem I had found. When you remember me, remember these words.

Love you forever,

Mimi"

Tears begin to well in the corners of Judith's eyes as turned the page to read:

> *"You cried again for me today*
> *and will tomorrow too . . .*
> *And the pain of losing me, I know,*
> *will always be with you."*

True to Grace's words, Judith broke down crying—again.

She decided to wait until later that evening to read the entire poem.

———◆———

As Saturday morning rolled in, Judith realized that she was getting control of her days again.

The healing would take time—much more time. There would always be a scar, as there should be. But she knew life went on, and she had to live it. For now, she would have to do that one day at a time.

Deep in thought, Judith was sipping coffee on the porch when a shiny red Honda Accord pulled into the driveway with Rachel behind the wheel.

"What a beauty!" she remarked as Rachel got out.

"Can you believe this metallic red? Wait till you feel how she drives," Rachel responded. "There're a mere forty-two miles on the odometer."

"Well, come on in," Judith invited and gave Rachel a Mimi-sized hug.

Rachel could not help but notice that the photo of Grace and Virgil and Grace's beloved pink phone were both absent from the end table.

"I appreciate all you've done this week," Judith assured Rachel.

"So much of it was outside my area of expertise," Rachel admitted. "It was a bit overwhelming to start with. But in the end, I managed to work through it all. Cara helped me out with one or two items. Thanks for connecting us."

"You are welcome. She and I didn't have our usual check-ins this week, so tell me, is everything in place?"

"Well," Rachel said as she pulled a folder from her purse, "I met with one of the best contractors in the area, and he and his team were able to fit the job into their schedule. They'll start the renovations first thing on Tuesday. I figured I might need to have all the other things removed on Monday."

"Good thinking. I packed all the personal items I wanted to keep and had them shipped to my home in L.A. Shipping the bonsai was a little tricky, but I was able to get that done. I took several loads to the GW, but there's still much here—some to be donated, and some to be disposed of. If you could arrange for the rest to be taken away on Monday, that would be great."

"Consider it done," Rachel said. "I've already made arrangements." She continued, "Getting the contractors to add this to their schedule may have been the biggest challenge of the week. But once they heard the story, the owner said they simply had to do it."

Rachel beamed. "As requested, they'll paint it inside and out, update the plumbing, wiring, and all the light fixtures. They'll pull out the carpets and install hardwood floors. And they'll remodel the kitchen and bathroom, as well as install all new appliances."

She slid pictures of the designs she and the contractor had agreed on and laid paint swabs and hardwood samples on the table. "This is what we agreed on. Does it look okay?"

"It's perfect."

"Okay, so, I also met with a landscaping company who'll be doing a redesign of the yard. They even suggested adding a chicken coup in the back if the zoning permits it."

"I love that idea," Judith laughed.

"Once the home is done in a few weeks, the new furniture will be delivered. I met with Shelia, a designer at Magnolia Homes, about that. For now, a provisional order has been placed, allowing tweaks for personal preferences and needs. Shelia insisted on coming up to do a thorough needs assessment. In fact, she insisted on it and won't charge you. She's a passionate lady, and it's clear that this will be a very special project for her. This home will soon be better than a new build. It will be a forever home."

With that, Rachel pulled out a red envelope from her tote. "This is the deed to the house. Miss Grace had already transferred it to you."

"Perfect."

"And this one," Rachel said as she pulled out a second red envelope, "is the title to the new car. You'll just need to sign it on the back for the transfer. All her details have already been completed. It's been gassed up and is ready for your trip. It's a hybrid, by the way."

"Excellent."

"This one," Rachel said as she pulled out the third red envelope, "Cara helped me with. It contains a copy of the documentation for the trust fund. The originals are in safekeeping with the firm. We've been careful to ensure that the documents meet all of the requirements you spelled out. But just to be on the safe side, we've asked the lawyers to include an executive summary, which you'll also find in the envelope."

Judith nodded, took the summary from the envelope, and quickly scanned it. "Perfect, that looks just fine. Thank you."

Rachel continued. "Cara pulled in someone in your office to assist in approaching the university," she said. "She indicated that they identified the senior person responsible for alumni matters, a Dr. Dowlen, who also deals with grants and other financial contributions from former students. Your team was careful not to come across as entitled, and they used what Cara referred to as 'high-grade, nuclear-level diplomacy.' Anyway, it—"

Judith burst out laughing.

"I must tell you, I don't think I always realize just what amazing people I have in my company. Cara clearly tapped Steven to help her with this. He's the smoothest yet most humble salesperson you'll ever meet. And he loves breaking a tense moment in a meeting claiming— with obviously fake bravado that it's time for him to employ his secret weapon."

Rachel chuckled. "Let me guess. High-grade, nuclear-level diplomacy?"

"Exactly."

"Well, apparently Dr. Dowlen didn't need that. Once he heard your name, he was immediately transformed into 'an advocate for the worthy cause of Judith Lee.' "

Judith smiled.

"Dr. Dowlen told Steven to leave it all to him. Exactly whom he spoke to—or which strings he pulled—no one knows. But it ended up at the highest level. Later that same day, a letter from the president of the university arrived in Cara's inbox. Here you go."

Judith eagerly accepted a copy of the letter from Rachel and scanned the contents.

"Wow, Rachel. Wow. I was hoping that they may be able to help in some way, but this? This is the whole package! I *do* support the university generously, but so do others. Vanderbilt University owes me nothing. They helped me by opening the door to get me to where I am today. I owe them a great debt of gratitude. They've already had my wholehearted support, but now . . ." she shook her head in disbelief.

Rachel took in Judith's words, then continued, "Finally, there are these." She pulled out two white envelopes. "This contains a check to pay for a complete paving of the church's rutted, gravel parking lot as well as to purchase a brand-new Steinway piano. Cara drafted a letter to the preacher, which is enclosed. If you'll just sign the letter, I'll drop it off at the church this week."

"The pianist and the choir are in for a surprise," Judith laughed as she signed her name.

Rachel handed Judith the final envelope, remarking, "This is the other check you requested. Tiffany had it overnighted—I was just waiting for FedEx to deliver it this morning. I've been nervous having a check of this size in my possession. To tell you the truth, it's a relief to hand it off to you."

The two women got quiet, looked at each other, and smiled. They felt lucky—no, blessed—to have crossed each other's paths.

They started talking at the same moment.

"Mi—"

"Mi—"

Judith gestured for Rachel to go ahead.

"Miss Grace is probably smiling down on us right now."

"I was going to say the same thing. And she's at peace."

So were they.

———•———

"Rachel," Judith said, "thank you so much for your help with this. From the day I hired you, you have consistently exceeded my expectations—and that's not a compliment I dish out often. Over the past two years during my calls with Mimi, it became obvious what a special person you were to her. And during my calls with you and my time here the past two and a half weeks, it just confirmed what I already knew."

She took an envelope from her bag and handed it to Rachel. Rachel looked questioningly at Judith as she opened it, pulling out a check. Her eyes widened and grew teary as she covered her mouth with her hand.

"Wh—what?"

Judith paused a moment, giving Rachel time to fully comprehend what this life-changing gesture might mean for her. "You were here for Mimi when I should have been, Rachel," Judith said, tears freely running down her cheeks. "It feels inadequate for all you have done for her *and* for me these past two years. Thank you. You have become a dear friend to me—the younger sister I never had."

"I don't know what to say," Rachel whispered, wiping tears.

"No need to say anything. Would you let me drop you at your house on my way out of town, though?" Judith asked and got up to get her bags.

"I've arranged with my friend Rob to pick me up. He should be here in a minute or two."

"The name sounds familiar."

"I was telling Miss Grace about him the night you arrived. We met recently on a blind date, and we're going to explore the Bicentennial Capitol Mall. The park is perfect for a history buff like Rob. He believes that unless we learn from our past, we are bound to make the same mistakes."

"He sounds like a wise young man. Keep me posted on how it goes," Judith said with a wink, remembering how Gary made a similar statement on the bus.

Rachel reached out and gave her a big hug. "I'm still at a loss for words. Thank you for your generosity . . . and for your friendship."

Judith smiled, looked around the room one last time to make sure she had all she needed, threw the tote over her shoulder, and rolled her Gucci bag out the door.

Rachel insisted on waiting for Rob on the swing on the porch.

Judith locked the door behind her and handed the keys to Rachel so she could coordinate with the contractors.

"Make sure they keep the swing, would you?" Judith said as she placed her luggage in the car.

"It's not going anywhere. It's one of my favorite things about this house. It'll get some TLC next week. I was thinking it should get a coat of red paint."

"That is perfect!" Judith exclaimed. "Now, please give me a hug so I can get on the road. It's a beautiful day for a road trip."

———◆———

Judith headed down the street toward the I-40 West.

And so, my journey continues. Just as Mimi predicted.

Her phone dinged at nine, just before she got onto the interstate. It was a message from Cara.

"Your reservation at the Peabody tonight has been confirmed. If you're there before five o'clock, you'll catch the duck march," Siri read. "And you have an appointment for a massage first thing in the morning courtesy of Tiffany, Tony, and me."

Judith accelerated onto the interstate, impressed by how peppy the engine was. It felt good to be behind the wheel again, to be able to decide on a whim where to go or when to stop.

It would take just three hours to get to her destination.

GRACE'S POEM

"My First Days in Heaven"

You cried again for me today
and will tomorrow too.
And the pain of losing me, I know,
will always be with you.
If you knew now what I know now
you'd be so happy instead of blue.

That's why I need to tell you about my first days in heaven.

My first day I sat at the Master's feet, so many questions about life's strife.
"Welcome my child," he said, "Well done, and now we'll celebrate your life."
The good days and the bad days were revealed, as it all became so clear.
The challenges of all life's suffering was my path to lead me here.

My second day I chose to be the rain
gently falling on your face.
This was as close as I could come
to give you my embrace.

My third day I chose to be a rose
With petals full and red.

You picked me, sniffed, and then you smiled
remembering what I said.

My fourth day I chose to be the moon
Shining down on you that night.
You gazed at me through tears
that you tried so hard to fight.

That's why I need to tell you about my first days in heaven.

My fifth day I chose to be the wind
blowing gently through your hair.
You never knew that it was me
but I knew I was there.

The sixth day I chose to watch you sleep
as you tossed and turned that night.
And then I came into your dream
so you'd know all things were right.

The seventh day's today
and I'll decide just what to do.
Just know today and every day
I'll always be with you.

That's why I needed to tell you about my first days in heaven.

CHAPTER 18

Extending Grace

The memories of the bus journey flooded Judith's mind as she crossed the Tennessee River, heading in the opposite direction from the previous time she crossed that river by bus.

When Judith spoke with Dr. Sanders on Friday—thanks to her therapist agreeing to a video consultation—Judith, after unpacking events around Grace's passing, told her about something she had been thinking about since the day she arrived.

"Albert, my neighbor on the trip from Memphis to Nashville, said that we cannot have compassion toward others unless we have compassion toward ourselves. For the past month, I have had two dreams about my younger self. In the first dream, little Judy asked me if I was happy. In the second one, Judy was begging Mimi not to leave, and my current self was telling Judy that I'll be there for her when the time comes to let go of Mimi . . . I think I'm learning to have compassion toward myself."

"Hmm," Dr. Sanders nodded. "And what does that look like?"

"Some of it is letting myself off the hook for not being able to save my parents." Dr. Sanders was quiet, allowing Judith to continue. "I found notes I had scribbled in my journals when I was younger. Over and over, I wrote that I wished I had gotten up earlier on the day I found my parents on the sofa. That if I had gotten up earlier, they would still be alive."

"Would they?"

"Probably not. For so many years, though, I carried that burden, believing I should have saved them. But the truth is that they were addicts. There's nothing ten-year-old me could have done to help."

"That's right."

"So, having compassion toward myself? I think it looks like me extending a hand to my younger self and helping myself out of the lie that I failed to save my parents."

"How would you do that?"

"It's about becoming aware of when I'm believing lies and am hard on myself. It's about cutting myself some slack."

"And what does that look like?"

"Some of it is about the self-talk I have. I can be kinder to myself. And some of it is about asking for and accepting help."

"Tell me more."

"You know I have no qualms telling others what to do. But when it comes to personal stuff, I don't ask for help because I'm afraid it might make me look weak . . ."

"Does it?"

"Make me look weak?"

"Uh-huh."

"I think it makes me human," Judith said with a shrug.

Dr. Sanders smiled, and Judith continued, "So, Albert suggested that once we tap into compassion, we can move from fear and anger toward mercy, justice, and grace. I think it's safe to say that in the past month, my mission in life has become clearer."

"Which is?"

"Finding grace."

———◆———

Judith turned on the stereo, figuring she would connect her phone and pick up where she had left off on an Audible or catch up on some business podcasts. But Rachel had tuned the radio to Nashville's WSM-FM, and the familiar sounds of country music filled the car. Judith cranked up the volume and rhythmically tapped the wheel.

She remembered Saturday nights when Mimi and Granddaddy used to listen to the *Grand Ole Opry* on their old radio. Once in a while, Virgil would remind them that it was the longest-running radio broadcast in the nation. "If it ain't broke, don't fix it, right?" he would say like he often did.

Judith did not have to think hard to recall some jingles. She giggled as she recalled a random jingle and found herself singing it out loud.

Now you bake bread, biscuits, cakes, and pies . . . Oh Martha White's Self-Rising Flour, the one all-purpose flour, Martha White's Self-Rising Flour with hot rize plus!

As she drove, Judith allowed herself the freedom to enjoy the journey—a new experience for her. She noticed some of the place names along the way that she and Albert had laughed about, including Bucksnort. She noticed a few others as well: Cuba Landing, Natchez Trace, and Christmasville Road.

I must tell Mimi—

She felt the twang of pain she would become familiar with during moments when she would make a mental note to tell her grandmother about something she saw but then realized she was gone.

Judith thought of the conversation she and Mimi had about the bus trip. "What's important in life is the people we meet," Grace had wisely reminded her.

Judith wondered about the individuals she had met on the bus, and the bus drivers driving the same stretch of the I-40 day after day. About that kid who had come to Nashville to chase a dream. About Daisy's plan to find herself an Okie millionaire. About Sara making a fresh start back in Flagstaff.

She wondered how Albert's visit with his family had been, and if he had some of the conversations around racism that he had planned on having with his grandsons.

Judith thought about Janice and Bobbie Sue. Two strangers at the time, who ended up seated next to her on a rather unremarkable bus, yet they changed her outlook on life forever.

And she thought about Gary, wondering how he was dealing with the grief of loss. Having now experienced the rollercoaster that followed the loss of a loved one, she asked God to comfort Gary in the moments when unexpected grief would pounce upon him, taking the wind out of his sails.

She thought about Johnny and how comfortable he made her feel, how he stirred up within her desires she had pushed deep into the recesses of her mind.

"Text Johnny," Judith told Siri.

"Which Johnny would you like me to text? Johnny Liu, or Jukebox Johnny?"

"Jukebox Johnny."

The message screen popped up, and Judith dictated a message, letting Johnny know she had scheduled her first double-bass lesson. It did not take long to hear back from him.

Gucci! Good to hear from you.

I'm proud of you for scheduling the lessons.

I'm driving.

Can't talk now but would love to hear about the new job.

Would love to tell you more and hear about the time at home.

Let me know when's a good time to catch up.

244

Will do.

Talk soon.

Can't wait.

A smile came over Judith's face.

———◆———

Judith was well past the midway point when she pulled into a Pilot Travel Center for a quick break. There was a cross-country tour bus—a much fancier one than that which she had traveled on—and Judith caught herself wondering about the stories of the individuals pouring out of the bus.

After the short stop, she punched in the Peabody as a stop en route to her final destination so she could drop off her suitcase.

The final hour of the drive flew by. As Judith pulled up at the hotel, a bellman opened her car door. "Good morning, and welcome to the Peabody. Will you be checking in?"

"I'll be checking in later this afternoon," she explained. "I'd like to leave my bag until then."

"Certainly. And the name the reservation's under, ma'am?"

"Judith Lee."

"Thank you, Ms. Lee. May I deliver your bag to your room, or would you like it held at the desk?"

"You can deliver it to the room. Thank you."

A second bellman rolled a luggage cart over, and they took the Gucci bag from the trunk and rolled it into the hotel.

Judith checked her phone; traffic was light. She would be there in just over five minutes.

———◆———

Judith passed several contemporary buildings, all with playful red accented features. Bright red lettering identified one as the Danny Thomas Research Center. On another building was the institution's red logo, an outline of a child praying.

Judith briefly found herself on Danny Thomas Boulevard. "Turn right, then your destination will be on the right," her phone instructed.

Turning right took her into an underpass with murals on both sides featuring children's artwork. Big, bright, and happy, framed in yellow. There were flowers, a rainbow, and even a chicken.

Judith laughed. She had clearly arrived.

———◆———

Rachel had arranged for a one o'clock meeting with Scott Spencer from the Strategic Partnership office. When she checked in at the main gate, presenting her identification, the guard issued her with a special permit to park in front of the Patient Care Center rather than having to head to the parking garage.

"Mr. Spencer will meet you there. I'll let him know you're here," the guard explained. "Welcome. And thank you for visiting."

Judith eased to a stop in front of the building. As she got out of her car, a man in a suit walked up to greet her.

"Welcome to St. Jude, Ms. Lee," he declared with the warmest of smiles. "I'm Scott Spencer. It's a pleasure to meet you."

"Mr. Spencer," she said, shaking his hand, "thank you for coming out to meet me. And please call me Judith."

"Call me Scott then."

"Thank you, Scott. I appreciate your time and willingness to meet with me."

"No problem, not at all. It's only a pleasure. I enjoy showing people around. I'll take you on a short tour through some of our facilities. The campus is quite expansive, so we won't visit all of it. But I'll tell you about all of our facilities and services as we go along."

"That sounds perfect, thank you."

"Rachel indicated that you'd also like to sit down with me, so after showing you around, we'll head to my office. And then I'll accompany you to your other appointment. Rachel told me what that's about. I get goosebumps just thinking about it!"

Judith smiled. "Thank you. Me too! I'm like a little girl counting the hours to Christmas."

St. Jude Children's Research Hospital

Before they headed inside, Scott pointed out some of the buildings. There was a memorial pavilion dedicated to the founder of the hospital, and a nearby gift shop.

In the distance was a building housing an After Completion of Therapy Clinic and several other clinics, all of which not only provided quality care but also facilitated top-notch research.

Beyond that, a section of another building was visible. "Tri Delta Place is our on-campus accommodation facility for patients and family who visit with us for a week or less. As you probably know by now, housing is also provided free of charge," Scott explained.

There were also two off-campus hotel-like facilities. One catered for stays of up to three months and the other for long-term stays. In addition, the hospital had agreements with hotels and guesthouses for overflow.

Judith found the campus grounds impressive. Everything was modern and extremely neat. But what stood out for her were the beautiful gardens with park benches to which patients and their families could retreat.

"Let me show you the Danny Thomas Research Center," Scott said as he walked Judith into the building. From the high ceiling in the atrium hung the flags of a hundred countries, representing the diverse nationalities among the St. Jude staff.

"This is quite impressive," Judith remarked as she scanned the various flags, "and beautiful."

"Yes, St. Jude—and our mission—has no borders."

Scott led Judith to a half-moon-shaped glass facade. "This links the Patient Care Center and Chili's Care Center. Beyond are a host of other buildings and departments, most of which are interlinked. But we'll focus on the main complex."

As they entered through a revolving glass door, you could not miss the brightly lit welcome station, beyond which a joyful cut-out of children welcomed visitors with open arms. Judith remembered the impression all of this made on Bobbie Sue the evening she checked in for her first treatment.

Scott led Judith further into the complex. Walking down the hallways felt unlike any hospital Judith had ever been in. The paint was as bright as the countenance of the people they passed. Folks greeted them with warm smiles and acknowledging nods.

Instead of tension filling the air, Judith experienced something she could only describe as joyful hope.

"You feel it?" Scott said quietly as he glanced at Judith.

"How did you know?"

"There's a positive energy here that is constant and unwavering," he replied. "Everyone experiences it. We all just view it as a daily gift from God."

The tour was somewhat overwhelming, in the best possible way. Patient rooms were spacious and well equipped, typically featuring large windows that offered a view of the gardens below. The rooms had everything to offer comfort to patients and their families. Beautiful artwork adorned the walls.

Judith's head spun with all she was shown and told about, including the laser treatment they provided patients with deep-brain tumors.

"This treatment has but a fraction of the collateral damage such a procedure would normally involve," Scott told her.

It was but one example of the institution's groundbreaking research, showing their willingness to spare no cost to create solutions to difficult problems. And yet they managed to not burden families with the cost of treatment.

What struck Judith the most were the people—whether staff, patients, or their families. They were brought together by difficult journeys, yet they chose hope. They chose to love and to extend compassion.

The hope, love, and compassion were more infectious than the most infectious disease. Once you've been exposed to the spirit of St. Jude, you left a changed person.

As they began their way back to Scott's office, he led Judith down the hallway that housed the Survivor Wall. It held photos of children who had been patients. Next to each was a photo of that same child, now a healthy adult.

Judith had seen these photos briefly while there with Janice and Bobbie Sue, but she stopped to look at them again. She asked Scott about one grouping of photos.

There were photos of a little girl, and then her healthy adult photo, then to the right was a photo of a little boy, and his healthy adult photo. Positioned between their photos was one of the two of them together with a beautiful little girl.

Scott smiled, "Those are two of our past patients who met here while undergoing treatment as children. As adults, they married. That's their little girl. We are *so* proud of them! And you know what? They now both work with us here at St. Jude."

The Plan: Phase One

After the brief tour, they reached Scott's office. "Here we are," he said as he opened the door. "Please come in and have a seat. Can I offer you some water, a soft drink, maybe some coffee or tea?"

"Some water would be just fine, thank you."

Scott retrieved two bottles of water from a small refrigerator and took a seat next to Judith in front of his desk. "So, from what I read about you—of course, I googled you—you and your company are based in L.A. What brings you to this part of the country?"

Judith sat back. "My grandmother lives—I mean, lived—in Nashville. That's where I grew up. She asked me a few weeks ago to come visit but insisted I come by tour coach." She raised her eyebrows. "I was not happy with the idea, but there was no getting around her request."

Scott listened as Judith continued. "The reason I obliged was that Mimi—that's what I called her—had terminal leukemia. She passed away just more than a week ago . . ."

"I am so sorry to hear that, Judith."

"Thank you," Judith said, taking another sip of water. "Well, on that bus trip, I met Janice and Bobbie Sue. Bobbie Sue told me she had leukemia—or coolemia, as she called it—and that she was coming to St. Jude to be treated. Of course, I had heard about the hospital many a time and have seen countless ads. But I never knew what an impact the research you do here has had worldwide, let alone the number of children who get treated here every year at absolutely no cost to their families."

Scott was used to hearing people tell of their jaws dropping when they learn more about St. Jude, but it still delighted him to listen.

"At the end of each day's journey, Mimi had me tell her about the people I met and the things I saw. When I told her about St. Jude, she told me there are a lot of angels here disguised as doctors, nurses, and caregivers, giving families love and hope."

Judith reached for her tote and pulled out a white envelope. "She said if there's ever a cure for leukemia in this world, it'll come from here." Judith glanced down at the envelope, then looked back at her host. "Scott, I had *never* heard her talk with such conviction as she did that evening about St. Jude."

"We do have an extraordinary research staff—some of the most brilliant medical minds—from all over the world. Our unending quest is finding the keys to unlocking the mysteries of the causes of the various types of leukemia and to figure out how to attack those causes. Ultimately, our goal is to completely eradicate the disease in all its forms," Scott explained.

"In 1955," he continued, "when Danny Thomas first planted the seed that has grown into what you saw today, the survival rate for a child was dismal. Today, that rate gives hope. So, yes, we are a place of genuine hope, but still so far from achieving our ultimate goal of losing *no* child. Fortunately, our cures for children also apply for most adults."

Scott pointed at a photograph on his wall. "One of our most joyous events is our 'No More Chemo' party. When a patient finishes their chemotherapy treatment, family, friends, and staff come together to celebrate. Everyone sings a special song before showering the patient with confetti."

Judith could see the joy on everyone's faces in the photo including the child at the center of it with the bald head. A badge of honor.

Scott paused momentarily before continuing, "Most people have no idea that St. Jude provides open-source access to *all* our research data to *any* research hospital or organization, worldwide, that is also working on cures. We are enormously proud of that. But most of those hospitals and organizations do not reciprocate with their research findings, knowing that they can monetize any cures their researchers develop."

Judith shook her head. "That's unfortunate."

"It's just the world we live in, Judith. It's just the world we live in . . ."

"Well, Scott," Judith said as she glanced down at the envelope again, "I'm not a believer in coincidence, and with everything that has happened over the past few weeks, I'm convinced more than ever that there's a reason for what happens to us, good or bad, and who we meet along life's way."

She hesitated momentarily. "Mimi was a modest woman who gave more than she received throughout her life. And as I said, her life ended because of leukemia. My wish is to honor her, creating a legacy that will live well beyond her life and mine."

She handed the envelope to Scott.

"I wish to make this donation to support the research for a cure for leukemia. There are no special requests or strings attached. I'm confident that your organization will be good stewards of this endowment."

Scott looked at Judith, then at the envelope. He opened it and pulled out the check.

This time, it was Judith who had the joy of seeing someone's jaw drop.

He looked at Judith, then back to the check before mumbling, almost inaudibly, "I . . . I . . . but . . . this can't be . . ." Tears welled up in the corners of his eyes. "A hundred . . . *million* dollars? What . . . ?"

His unexpected emotion touched Judith. "I don't know what information you found when you googled me," she said with a smile, "but I'm the sole owner of my company. And I've been blessed that the company has been extraordinarily successful."

Scott still shook his head in amazement.

"The recent time I have spent with Mimi brought clarity to my life. In seeing how she lived her life, I saw how I could choose to live my life going forward. It's about choices, big and small. This endowment was a big choice—a life-defining one—borne out of compassion. And if Mimi were still here today, that would bring her great joy."

Scott placed his hand over his heart and held it there while telling Judith, "You have no idea what this is going to mean for our research. This will allow us to accelerate the timelines on some of our clinical trials and provide funding to initiate new research on our wish list. The bottom line is," Scott said as he leaned forward, "an endowment of this magnitude will help us move the survival rate even higher."

Judith smiled at the thought.

"Judith," Scott continued, "these are *real* lives that will be saved—thanks to you."

"Thanks for the kind words, Scott, but any praise or credit belongs to Janice, Bobbie Sue, and Mimi—especially Mimi."

"What was your grandmother's name?"

"Grace," Judith said. "Mrs. Grace Lee."

Scott leaned back in his chair and vowed, "Well, I can assure you that Mrs. Grace Lee will be memorialized properly in the near future."

"That's not necessary, Scott," Judith objected, "but it would be a truly kind gesture for Mimi."

Scott told Judith about some of the research that was underway and planned, and how her endowment may be applied to those. But their time was limited as Scott indicated that it was almost time for Judith's next appointment.

They exchanged contact details, and Scott assured Judith that she would be kept up to date with developments at the hospital. Scott would be her one-stop contact at the hospital, and they would love for her to visit and be otherwise involved, at least to the degree that she would prefer.

"This is indeed a special place, Scott. Holy ground, if you will," Judith said as they stepped back into the sun outside the Patient Care Center, "a place of love and hope. What a battle all of you are waging! Thank you for the work you do and for your time today. I appreciate it."

"Well, it's generous people like you who enable us to keep fighting the daily battle. Our goal is to find better treatments and cures," Scott reiterated. "Today is one of those days that will live on in my memory. Your unexpected endowment will have quite an impact and will be cause for celebration when we make the announcement."

He looked at his watch. "My assistant will be bringing them down any moment. This is where you wanted to meet with them, correct?"

"Yes, thank you."

As the doors opened, Scott excused himself. "Here they come. I'll be in touch with you soon to share how we will be memorializing your grandmother . . . and you."

Before Judith could protest the "and you," Bobbie Sue came running, and Scott slipped back into the building.

The Plan: Phase Two

"Miss Judif!" Bobbie Sue shouted in childish delight as she jumped into Judith's open arms. Judith lifted her into a bear hug, the little one's red baseball cap ending up crooked on her head. She looked adorable with the hat matching her sneakers.

Judith put Bobbie Sue down and straightened the cap just as Janice stepped into the sun, taking off her readers to be able to see better.

"Judith? Is that you?"

"It's me indeed," Judith laughed and hugged Janice. "It's *so* good to see you, Janice."

"What a pleasant surprise. It's great to see you too. How's your grandmother doing?"

"She passed away . . ."

"Oh, Judith, I'm *so* sorry."

"Thank you. She had a full and wonderful life, and I've been blessed to have known her for the last thirty-four years. I'll tell you a little more, but let's go sit on those benches so we can visit."

The three of them headed to a couple of benches under some trees nearby.

"Mommy, look," Bobbie Sue said, "that car is as red as my shoes and my hat." She giggled with delight, and Janice lovingly played with Bobbie Sue's ponytail.

"Look at my new hat, Miss Judif. It matches my shoes. And I didn't even have to wait for my hair to begin falling out. Can you believe they just let me pick this one out?"

Judith laughed, leaned over, and placed her hand on Bobbie Sue's cheek. "Oh, Bobbie Sue! How beautiful you look in your new red hat. You're even more beautiful today than when I saw you last."

"I've been thinking of the two of you since I last saw you here. How has the treatment been going?" Judith asked Janice.

"This morning, the doctors told us that Bobbie Sue is tolerating her treatments better than most, which is a *really* good sign." Janice looked down at her daughter. "You've been responding really well to the infusions, haven't you, honey?"

Bobbie Sue nodded and smiled. "And I've made some new friends who have coolemia just like me."

"That is *wonderful* news. I've been praying for you—*both* of you."

"I'm still processing what the doctors said," Janice shared. "It's been good for me to be surrounded by parents who have walked this road and who encourage me on days when I have felt discouraged." She took a deep breath. "But enough about us. You were going to tell us more about your grandmother."

"I remember that, yes."

"Indeed," Judith said and took a deep breath to slow her beating heart. "I had told you at lunch that day that Mimi had me tell her all about the people I met on the bus and the things I saw."

"I remember that, yes."

"Well, when we spoke that night, I told her about you two and about St. Jude. Turned out that she knew *so* much more about St. Jude than I ever imagined," Judith told them.

She looked at Bobbie Sue who was listening with the rapt attention of one much older.

"Your story, Bobbie Sue, made an impact on me," Judith said, placing her hand on her heart. "On our last night together, Mimi reminded me that the people we meet along our journey is what's important." She cleared the lump in her throat.

"There are things in life that happen which we have no control over," Judith continued. "Like the fact that you chose to come sit next to me on the bus."

Bobbie Sue giggled. "We had fun on the bus. And I *loved* the pancakes."

"Pancakes with sprinkles are the best," Judith said with a big smile. "But you know what I remember most about the trip, Bobbie Sue?"

The little one looked at Judith with huge eyes.

"Your mama's dreams. She was telling me about *all* the things she wanted for you and her. You two are a good team."

Judith looked at Janice. "Janice, I wish we had more time to talk about all the details, but with arrangements after Mimi's passing and knowing that you two were in the middle of treatment, I thought much about the things you said about trying to get back on your feet."

Janice looked perplexed.

"You had mentioned the kinds of jobs you were looking for—"

"You received my résumé, right?" Janice interrupted.

"I did. And I passed it along to friends of mine at Vanderbilt University. If you want it, you have a job waiting for you in their office of Alumni Affairs. It comes with full healthcare and retirement benefits."

Janice's eyes filled up with tears. "Judith, I . . . thank you!"

Bobbie Sue looked at Judith, then at Janice, not sure what was happening.

"Mommy got a new job, baby," Janice said, "a great job. Looks like we'll be moving to Nashville."

"You'll be needing a place to stay in Nashville, right?" Judith asked Bobbie Sue.

"Yeah . . ." Bobbie Sue answered, not sure what was transpiring.

"Well," Judith said, looking at Bobbie Sue and then at Janice, "there's a home in the East End neighborhood that'll have a red swing on the front porch. The home is yours if you want it. It was my Mimi's home. By the time Bobbie Sue's treatment is complete here at St. Jude, it will have been completely renovated, furnished, and ready for you two to move in."

Tears were streaming down Janice's cheeks. "What . . . what do you mean?"

Judith pulled a large red envelope from her tote. "This contains the documentation giving you ownership of the home."

"Are you . . . serious?"

"Mommy, what's wrong?" Bobbie Sue wanted to know.

"Baby, we just got a new home! Mommy got a job, *and* we have a home. Our very own home!" Janice said and hugged her daughter tight.

"Now, it's a fifteen-minute drive from your home to the university . . . You'll need a car."

"I have a car, but it's on the fritz. I'm sure there's great bus service in Nashville, though. We'll be fine."

"Yes, there is. But you won't need to take the bus." Judith pressed the remote to the car, and the alarm system beeped. Janice turned her head toward the beep. "That car is yours. It'll go well with the red swing on the porch," she said and winked at Bobbie Sue. She handed Janice the second envelope. "This contains the title, which I've already signed, transferring ownership to you. And here are both sets of keys."

"I . . ." Janice stammered.

"Mommy, is that *our* car?"

"I believe it is, baby," Janice said, wiping the tears that kept flowing.

"It's okay, Mommy," Bobbie Sue said, patting her mom's back.

Janice smiled lovingly. "You're right, sweetie. Everything's okay. These are happy tears."

"I told you Jesus would take care of me and you," Bobbie Sue said. "See, I told you! He wouldn't leave us!"

Bobbie Sue's comment caught Judith completely off guard, and tears started flowing down her cheeks.

She and Janice started laughing through the tears. "We must be a sight for sore eyes!" Judith said, reaching for a Kleenex in her tote.

"You have my number, so we'll be in touch about the move. My friend Rachel will be contacting you. She'll set up a meeting with a designer regarding choice of furniture and the like. Rachel will be at the home to welcome you, whenever that may be. Also," Judith said as she wiped away more tears, "we can talk about the details later, but Bobbie Sue's education's been provided for by means of a trust fund."

She looked at Bobbie Sue. "If you work *really* hard at school, you should be able to go to university someday so you can become whatever you want—maybe even a doctor."

"I can work at St. Jude!"

"I'll bet you could."

"Judith, I don't know what to say . . ." Janice said as the two ladies stood up. Janice enveloped Judith in a hug. Bobbie Sue wrapped her arms around both women's legs and looked up as Janice continued, "Until now, there have been very few good things that have happened in my life except for Bobbie Sue. I don't understand why you are doing this, but since we met you, things have taken a turn for the better for us."

Releasing Judith and taking a step back, she continued, "First the news this morning. Now this. Knowing we *both* have a future that we never could have dreamed of before is amazing. It's going to take a while for it to sink in. I'm afraid I may wake up and discover it's all just been a dream."

Judith smiled, looking down at Bobbie Sue, then back at Janice. "I can assure you that this is not a dream," she said and laughed. "I know you two have to get back in there, so if you don't mind, I need to order an Uber, and then I'll show you your car. How does that sound?"

Judith heard the buzz of a hummingbird as it flew by and hovered mid-air right in front of the benches where the three had been sitting. As quickly as it appeared, it flew away again.

Bobbie Sue ran to the car and Janice went after her while Judith pulled out her phone to order her ride. An Uber Black was just a couple of minutes away.

She headed to the Honda and showed her friends their new vehicle. "Rachel thought of everything—including a booster seat for you," she said and helped Bobbie Sue onto the seat.

"This is the bestest gift in the whole world!" Bobbie Sue declared.

"And you look great in it. Now, hop on out so I can give you a good-bye hug." Judith turned to Janice. "I'll be in touch soon. And when you and Bobbie Sue are settled in your new home in Nashville, I promise I'll come visit both of you. Okay?"

"My head is still spinning, Judith. Yes, we will look forward to your visit. Hopefully in the not-so-distant future. I don't know how I'll ever be able to thank you enough," Janice said and gave Judith another hug.

"You'll have the opportunity to help someone else someday," Judith assured her. "That'll be thanks enough."

Next, Judith knelt to hug Bobbie Sue. Without the two of them knowing, Janice took a photo of Bobbie Sue wrapping her arms tightly around Judith's neck and giving her a big kiss on the cheek.

"Miss Judif! You made mommy and me *so* happy!" she exclaimed as she released her hug.

"Now, will you help your mommy by doing everything the doctors and nurses ask so you'll get well soon? Then you can go see your new home in Nashville. Deal?"

"Deal!" Bobbie Sue said and gave Judith a high five.

A silver Lexus pulled up. "Miss Lee?" the driver asked.

"That's me. I'll be right with you."

"Janice, I'll be checking in with you about Bobbie Sue's progress, but please feel free to call me anytime. Okay?"

"I will. We're going to be just fine, thanks to the doctors here at St. Jude—and you. I'll be looking forward to your calls. Have a safe trip home. May God bless and keep you, Judith."

As the car pulled away, Judith took one last look out the window at Janice and Bobbie Sue as they waved an enthusiastic goodbye and Bobbie Sue blew her kisses.

On the short drive to the Peabody, Judith pulled out her cell phone and messaged Cara.

> Coming home.
> Please let Tiffany and Tony know.
> And tell Jerry to prep the Gulfstream.
> He can pick me up in Memphis tomorrow morning at 10.

Got it.
Will you be flying non-stop?

> Yes.

Pause

> On 2nd thought, let him know that we'll be making one stop.
> I want to drop in on a friend for a surprise visit.
> Might stay a day or two.

No problem.
One stop.
Where?

> Amarillo, Texas!

ACKNOWLEDGMENTS

The writing process was my way of working through my grief over losing my wife Sharee. From the day I met her on March 5, 1972, until the day she passed, May 11, 2019, Sharee was the center of my world. God blessed me. The memory of her smile, love, and laughter sustains me still. Sharee was bold in her battle with leukemia, never once asking "Why me?" or allowing herself the luxury of a pity party. She was a gentle warrior. During our marriage, Sharee showed me how to live and made me a better person. And in her last years, she showed me how to face the inevitable with strength and grace. Healing can be a slow process, and there were many days when I walked through dark valleys of sadness, but the key was that I kept on walking. The continued walk led out of the valley of dark sadness and back up into the light of God's beautiful world and the possibility of finding joy and happiness again. I continue to trust and follow Him.

Maybe you've heard the story about the farmer who found the turtle sitting on top of one of his fenceposts. He knew the turtle had help getting there. And, so it was with me and *Finding Grace*. There are so many people who have encouraged and helped me during my journey and it's impossible to remember them all, so please forgive any omissions.

First, Adele Booysen was my muse and an angel sitting on my shoulder. She, along with Mike Smuts, helped polish *Finding Grace* into what I hope the readers will find as an unexpected gem.

Thanks to my daughters, Sara Miller Cross and Rachel Miller Lance, and granddaughter, Daisy Cross, for their constant love and support. They are all amazing women, each in their own right. Your mom (Mimi to Daisy) would be so proud of you. My love for you is unmeasurable. Thousands of times you've heard me say, and I'll repeat, "Always keep a smile on your face and a song in your heart.".

Kathy Burns is my best friend and was my number one beta-reader during my writing/editing process. She has been my rock, offering her valuable, unbiased feedback and encouragement during every step of my process. Other beta-readers and supportive friends that I offer my sincere thanks to are my sister, Janice Miller Baker, brother, Ron Miller, Kylie Morgan, Sherman Smith, Judy Webster, Judy & Steve Raines, Jim Place, Barbara Harris, Amy & Bill Winchester, Karla King, Gina Bryan, Sandra King, David Wagner, Gary Samples, Steve Anderson, and Barry Courter.

Thank you to Brian Helgeland and Rose Locke, who opened doors for me, allowing me to experience adventures unimagined that I was able to share with Sharee and my girls.

Thank you to Ellen Levine and Anne Gallagher with Hearst Magazines for their support, introducing me to executives at St. Jude Children's Research Hospital.

Three months after Sharee's passing, in 2019, I spent the day at St. Jude touring the facility and learning as much as I could during the visit. Their people are awe-inspiring and, trust me, future cures for the various forms of leukemia will originate at St. Jude. They deserve our support. Thank you to Rick Shadyac, Steele Ford, Kevin Snyder, Mike Siegel, and Jason Potter.

Thank you to Sharee's primary care doctor, Steven Dowlen, oncologist at Vanderbilt University Medical Center, Dr. Michael Savona, her Chattanooga oncologist, Dr. Sumana Nagireddy, and her primary infusion-care nurse, Melanie "Mel" Savor. Their extraordinary kindness and compassion towards Sharee (and me) will forever be etched in my heart. It was because of their help that Sharee exited this life as graciously as she lived it. Blessings.

My appreciation of the staff at Morgan James' and their support and guidance during the publishing process is substantial. Thank you to

Founder David Hancock, Jim Howard, Emily Madison, Karen Anderson, Cortney Donelson, and Taylor Chaffer.

ABOUT THE AUTHOR

Prior to Gary Lee Miller beginning his writing career, he was a successful businessman and entrepreneur.

Miller's writing is rooted in life experiences and people who have crossed his path on his life journey. He draws on his ability to translate his observations into very relatable stories by readers.

Gary lives in Chattanooga, Tennessee—The Scenic City of the South—and has two adult daughters and one granddaughter who live close by. His favorite hobby is to occasionally act in movies and TV, and he is listed on IMDb.

Visit his website at "garyleemillerbooks.com".
To contact Gary, email gmiller@gmiller.biz.

A free ebook edition is available with the purchase of this book.

To claim your free ebook edition:

1. Visit MorganJamesBOGO.com
2. Sign your name CLEARLY in the space
3. Complete the form and submit a photo of the entire copyright page
4. You or your friend can download the ebook to your preferred device

Print & Digital Together Forever.

Snap a photo

Free ebook

Read anywhere